About the author

After an award-winning career in advertising, Jack Delaney thought it was time to start telling the truth.

WHAT MATTER WOUNDS?

Jack Delaney

WHAT MATTER WOUNDS?

Vanguard Press

VANGUARD PAPERBACK

© Copyright 2022
Jack Delaney

The right of **Jack Delaney** to be identified as author of
this work has been asserted by him in accordance with the
Copyright, Designs and Patents Act 1988.

A CIP catalogue record for this title is
available from the British Library.

ISBN 978 1 80016 279 2

*Vanguard Press is an imprint of
Pegasus Elliot MacKenzie Publishers Ltd.*
www.pegasuspublishers.com

First Published in 2022

**Vanguard Press
Sheraton House Castle Park
Cambridge England**

Printed & Bound in Great Britain

Dedication

Thank you, who suffered with me through the trauma, the heartbreak and the seventeen drafts and helped make this book better. And apologies to all of you who deserve one. You know who you are.

What is illness to the body of a knight-errant?
What matter wounds?
For each time he falls, he shall rise again, and woe
to the wicked.
Don Quixote

Chapter 1
I Don't Wanna Spoil the Party

It is a defining moment for anyone to turn sixty — or so I imagine. Still some way to go myself. But even at fifty-three, it's a defining moment to have a mate turn sixty. It was going to be a small family party and probably dull as fuck. So I did the only decent thing a child of the sixties who worked in advertising in the eighties could do: a big line of coke. Feeling slightly more excited about the party, I headed off to Pete's. He's a great bloke, but as I said, his party probably would be a fun-sponge. As a mate though, you have to make the best of it, don't you?

Now before you jump to judgment. I'm not a druggy. It's just that if you came into advertising when I did, it was a rite of passage to do a fair bit of Charlie. Especially if you were in the Creative Department like I was — although the suits weren't that shy either.

I gave up the marching powder when I saw really quite average minds being destroyed by an overpriced drug that made hangovers deathly. Added to that, my septum had already taken a lot of stick in the boxing ring and on the rugby pitch. But just as we play old records or reread favourite books, it's fun sometimes to go back and reminisce. Consequently, from time to time, I would have a little dabble.

So, there I was, late August in the affluent suburbs. Duded up, but not very, and coked up, but not very. The place and time made it sound like a Robert Ludlum book. But the plot was even more predictable. I saw a girl, I'd seen her before, and I'd liked what I'd seen. But this night was different, I saw a girl and I saw a chance. We were both on our own and even though we were both 'happily married', I thought, *Well... Why not?*

I walked over and said "Hi" to Kitty. (She hates being called Kitty; I will explain later.) Anyway, the first thing you notice about Kitty is frailty. Not weak, insipid wallflower frailty. No, while she is projecting all sophisticated, in-control wife of a successful man, you also see something ever so slightly off-kilter. She's pretty, slim, immaculately turned out, confident, open and clearly fun. Yet, yet, what is it? You, or at least I, get that feeling that there's something under the surface. It's a bit Audrey Hepburn, she had it. Julianne Moore has it too.

It was the little crack I made about her dress. She was really pulled together, even for a small party among friends. But I didn't want her to think I was trying too hard, so I said, "It's hard to know what to wear as a man, but a woman always has Coco Chanel."

"This isn't Chanel," she said with a condescending crinkle around the corner of her mouth.

"Yeh, it's certainly no classic little black number."

Her reaction wasn't anger, or "How dare you!" or even "Fuck you!" Just for a second it was as if she was thinking "Oh God, he might be right, am I fat? Do I look ridiculous? Were my dark angels right...? This dress is a disaster."

Then it was gone, and she laughingly did say, "Fuck you..." but it wasn't instantaneous — it was frail and ever so alluring.

I set the record straight. "No. it's not the dress. What I meant, was what Coco said: 'Dress shabbily and they remember the dress; dress impeccably and they remember the woman.' It's not a classic little black number, but it certainly does the same job."

That got a big smile. And she said, "Ah, a man who knows fashion."

"Not really, I used it in an ad, but it's true about you."

As an aside from this narrative, that is a line I have used before, and guys, feel free, it always works. I stole it from Coco, and in this instance, citing your source actually makes it less creepy and a lot more flattering. And when it is true, it is beguiling.

She's five foot seven, willowy, with a face cut just short of striking. With her big blue eyes and sexy mouth, it was all too simple. Nothing so pretty could possibly harm you, right? What's that Last Shadow Puppets' line? "Innocence and arrogance entwined — in the filthiest of minds." I so hoped that was true. It was only later that I came to see that she was also highly practiced at seduction.

Mostly she just let me feel in charge, guiding the conversation with unnoticed prompts. It was only minutes before I was jumping through hoops to please her. Her face, her body, and some clever wardrobe could get her anything and anyone. She knew that. I may have done too, but I was too distracted trying to get a look at her tits down the décolleté dress.

Women like her, too. She is pretty enough to be a friend, but not so pretty that the comparison would be really harsh. Except of course, with real munters and the ones who gave up years ago. They would just say she was "Too thin" or "Poor Kitty, so very particular about her looks." Or other faux compliments/concerns. Unlike many women, she nurtured her friendships and so was popular. She didn't really need to nurture boys — see above.

Anyway, the evening progressed, and as two married people can't talk to each other all night at a small party with just friends, or people will get exactly the right idea — we didn't. Even though all I wanted to do was be with her, she circulated, and I went to the bathroom more than was dictated by my bladder, to reload.

The evening progressed as such evenings do. I caught up with her later and we continued where we left off. It's that Jungian thing — connection. Sometimes you just connect with someone. It's effortless. You just riff off each other and it is delightful. I was loving it but then I thought, *Hang on a minute. She's not knockin' me back here… or am I kidding myself? Rob, you're acting like a teenager.*

And suddenly — "As your place is on the way to mine…" — we're sharing an Uber.

Here I have to make a confession. Despite having my nose mashed on the rugby pitch and in the boxing ring, I've got a thing for scent. Some people just smell right, and some don't. I had a girlfriend who once wore this stuff that smelled of roses, and it reminded me of old ladies, and it was a bigger passion killer for me than the thought of Bernard Manning in Lycra. (Kids, if you don't know who he is, then Google him, but you have been warned. There are things you just can't un-see. If you are of a sensitive disposition just believe me, the allusion is to something very, very unsexy.)

Anyway, on top of the Jungian connection and her looking great, she smelled fabulous — even through a coke-filled conk. Now, responsible grown-ups don't get drunk and coked up and try kissing, albeit beautiful, married women, especially ones they aren't married to. You can try and put any spin on it you like, but responsible grown-ups don't get drunk and coked up and do that. Yet as the cab wound through suburban streets, that is exactly what I did. And bloody hell, we were snogging. I even copped a cheap feel. Well, in for a penny and all that. And it was much more than a pennyworth. She was as keen as me. Was she drunk?

She didn't seem it. Crikey. "Well, I'm not stopping until she does" was my view.

The Uber driver was a bit surprised. He caught my eye in the rear-view mirror and gave a Gallic shrug. Which is a good trick for a man from South London whose parents were almost certainly Punjabi. Or maybe he just thought, "This Frenchman can really rock a turban."

After a couple of minutes of adolescent style snogging and me thinking, *God, she has fabulous tits...* I realised the cab had stopped at her place. "You know what?" she whispered, slightly out of breath. "You're about to be in a whole lot of trouble. We'd probably better stop." And she sent me on my way.

Like a sixteen-year-old, I was disappointed and also quite pleased. It felt like I'd missed out, but FFS, the upside potential and the downside risk made pretty scary reading. No sex, but no disgracing myself sexually while drunk and coked up. Then on the bigger picture stuff — a much better solution is a drunken snog we could both be faux-embarrassed about at the next family party. That could be a silly, fun memory. Two people, two partners, two kids each and a small nosey suburb made an affair a seriously dangerous option.

Now, anyone who knows about small, family-style parties also knows that you have to cover your tracks. So it was, "Driver, back to the party." Stick phone in a pocket that's easily accessible and ring the doorbell.

Only a couple of people left, and the hosts are cleaning up.

"Sorry, mate, but I've left my phone here." Everyone starts to look, and I surreptitiously put it on a chair.

"I will call it," says someone sober enough to think of that. And bingo, alibi and a cover story in place. "They left together but he was back fifteen minutes later because he'd left his phone here, the dick…" Into the bogs, another little line as a livener and back in the taxi and home.

Opening the front door, I cracked a can of beer and flattered myself that the sending away was given a slightly piquant flavour by the roughly five to eight percent of regret I think she felt at doing it.

Lying on the bed knowing I wasn't going to sleep for a while I pondered. Not a bad evening, really. Something to smile fondly about and remember the excitement that only that first kiss can engender. The frisson of really fancying someone and yes… the schoolboy thrill on copping a feel — don't judge me! It was delightful.

Could I leave it at that? Could I bollocks! I started drunk texting. The responses were between non-committal, to not totally discouraging. On sober reflection, there was a hint of "I'm flattered" and a large dose of "…calm down and go to sleep." Eventually, I did.

The next day you wake up with a strange feeling of being very hungover, yet with a smug grin — well, she didn't punch me — and a strange sense of foreboding too as I reached for my phone and saw I had a message… from the husband.

Fuck, fuck, fuck, fuck! While not exactly cordial, it was also strangely not pistols at dawn either. I didn't need to read the subtext to know he was clearly fucked off though.

> *Rob, we're both very lucky men. To say I am disappointed is an understatement. I would appreciate it if you leave Kitty alone and we will talk when my anger has subsided.*

Well, that's me told. And an over-riding confusion: *Why did she tell her husband? Blimey, is she a bunny-boiler? I need to think this through.* But first damage limitation.

> *Gordon, I want to apologise to you both, my behaviour was inexcusable regardless of drunkenness. I am ashamed and hope that Kitty is not too insulted. It will be excruciating, but when you're back, I would like to apologise to you both in person. Until then, it's so little in the circumstances, but my sincere apologies again.*

Totally insincere, of course. But while I have a small history of violence, no worries if it came to blows with him. Well, not many. I mean, you never know, maybe he's a right hard bastard, but I didn't think so. My reply was taken from the school of Mickey the Cornerman, "Strategy Rocky". Abject apology costs nothing and it leaves people with little room to manoeuvre. I've apologised. What more do you want? What more can I do?

None of which cleared my head or explained, what the fuck had happened. I didn't force myself on her. Did I? No, I did not. Yet post-coke paranoia knows no bounds. There's no solution to that, so I went for a run in the gym. Those five kilometres felt like fifty, but it did work. Then I took two litres of Evian into the sauna and blasted soothing music through my headphones.

Even after the Evian, I was still passing uric acid crystals. At the same time, I was some way toward feeling human again. I went home and downed several more pints of water. Then Knock me down with a feather — or frankly, the surprise level was more Fuck me with the rough end of a pineapple — she's walking up my drive!

Stay cool... stay cool.

It's a bit uncomfortable. She's a bit embarrassed and you're triangulating somewhere between confused, aroused and euphoric. She explains that her jealous spouse monitors her texts and mail and phone and FB and saw all my texts. Cringe, but you've got to love her. "Thank you for your note to Gord. He blamed it all on me flirting. I feel bad you are taking all the blame, but your note has calmed him down… a little.”

I shrugged and acted all coy and tried to be manly/boyish. Then strike me, amid the explanations and apologies and coy glances, we started kissing again and this time it’s sober and you really want her. I mean, really want her, not just the milk bottle in the pants sensation, but the soda water in the head sensation, the all senses working overtime sensation. But then, just as I’m about to try to move us from vertical to horizontal, it’s all over as she says, “We can’t do this…”

Bollocks, bollocks, bollocks! Not this time the relief of well, at least you didn’t shame yourself with thirty seconds of high passion and then an uncomfortable ‘Sorry…’ And her being really good about you being bad at it. No, this was totally unrequited passion. *God, I want her so bad…*

I was not just full of lust — this was what we read about in the books, this was the real deal, passion-wise. She was not just new — she was different. Walking down the drive, she looked back, and I swear there was a look that made me think she felt the same way. It didn’t stop her walking away though.

Well, there you go. That’s how these things start, or rather false-start and stutter to an emphysemic end. A wry smile thinking of what might have been. A closed-eyes look at the breasts you only felt and never saw. Lie in bed and write your own movie sex scene. And a lot of how do I manufacture the next meeting? *Stop, you mad fool, this isn't going to happen, besides you have yet to face the husband.* The only twist in the plot is that you've discovered the back-story and the paranoid-android checks all her calls and, emails and everything. So, she didn't throw you under the bus and you took all the blame — seemed like the right thing to do at the time and takes a bit of pressure off her.

All in all, a bit of a weird twenty-four hours. Write it off. Another leaf in my portfolio of misadventures and stupidity. My family came back. "So how was Pete's party?"

"Yeh, it was all right!" I left the explanations at that.

Life at my age is, as someone said, searching for islands of interest in a sea of ennui. It was a crazy, silly adolescent episode acted out by two people who really should have known better. Yes, I was confused.

Yet you can't imagine my surprise when a day later when karma jumped in with both feet. I got a Messenger text.

Don't reply to this. Come and see me at my house on Wednesday at 11. This is a one-time, never to be repeated thing. If you are coming, leave a note in my mailbox tomorrow morning.

Well, well, well? Well, she's not inviting you round to do macramé. But you know the smart move is to cut and run. You have a wife and business to run, and, and,

and… And you fancy her like mad and fear loses to lust every time with you. But at the same time, three days to think and overthink and overthink and aaaaaarrrrrgggghhh!

I wrote the note. Or rather wrote and rewrote the note. How could a man paid ludicrous amounts of money to write ads and commercials compelling enough to get people to buy something as vile as the Vienetta be struggling with this? "I'll be there." Too pithy and a bit threatening. "Can't wait, see you on Wednesday" — bit too keen. On about draft eighty-seven, I settled on. "Hi, how could I say no? I'm stupid, but not mad. See you then." Not exactly award-winning, but it covered the bases.

The note writing was nerve-wracking enough. Then I had to deliver the bastard. Walking up the post-box had me feeling nervous. How can a middle-aged man feel nervous about posting a letter? Well, you try walking up to someone else's house in broad daylight with your acceptance of a hopefully adulterous assignation to deliver — then you judge me. Anyway, with that out the way, I had to wait. It felt more like a condemned man waiting for the drop, than a lottery winner waiting to pick up the cheque. And that puzzled me too. Let's just say they were the longest days of my life so far. Half the time watching the clock not move fast enough, like some kid waiting for Christmas. The other half of the time feeling like the seventeen-year-old me waiting for my driving test. This could be the most important single episode in my life or the most embarrassing failure. Like, driving, there's no substitute for practice. But in this instance, practice was a difficult concept. The solo, 'one-winged angel trying to take off' variety is a bit demeaning at fifty-three. And rolling over to your wife to keep your hand in for a potential adulteress liaison is a bit shitty. No? But then in *There's Something About Mary* style, do you really want to risk going with a loaded gun and a hair-trigger? Really, at my age, how could a man of my age, education, and sophistication (or lack of?) have sunk so low as to ponder these things? Well, as I said, it was a long seventy-two hours.

Chapter 2
A Working-Class Hero is Something to Be

I had a funny upbringing. Not the barrel of laughs variety, more the funny old-world type. My mum and dad were solid blue-collar stock. She was the daughter of a docker (I believe they are now called port workers) and he was the son of a policeman. (They are still called coppers, but only in American films about England. No self-respecting British criminal would use such outdated slang.)

They both left school at fifteen and were married before they were twenty-one. Dad was a big, handsome lad and had done his National Service with the Irish Guards in Egypt. This meant he came back with a tan. That was a serious novelty in 1950s Liverpool. Mum at 5' 9" always insisted that meeting a man of 6'4" was great because it meant she could wear heels. I think the tan helped, too. Regardless of all that, the real truth is that they were hugely compatible. We, the kids, always came second to Dad with Mum, and Dad was on Team Mum, regardless of us ever having the facts, or right or anything else on our side. It was non-negotiable and we never tried negotiating. I was the third kid in five years. These days that seems fast but when you factor in they were Catholic and most likely virgins at the altar, it's no surprise that the first two were Irish twins born within a year of each other. The gap to me was longer though, just over two years. It was only revealed much later in adulthood that there was a late miscarriage in between me and Lottie — the number two. A psychotherapist told me about the concept of a replacement child and so much slotted into place. But growing up, I never understood why I was the different one. Slightly favoured by Mum and always slightly out of step with Dad.

As a replacement child, it seems obvious now, that for Dad I was a constant cruel reminder the loss of the much-loved child, the "angel," the perfect one that he had created in his head. But for Mum, after mourning and accepting the loss, I was a healing thing and an atonement for her guilt at not carrying to term. To be cherished all the more, as a second chance.

I know what they would both have said, if it had ever been discussed: "It's not all about you." And although we were English, left footers from Liverpool with a name like Delaney, it would be foolish to ignore the Irish element. I think Sigmund had a point when he said about the Irish. "This is one race of people for whom psychoanalysis is of no use whatsoever." Freud claimed that the Irish, when in psychic trouble, go to poetry, go to storytelling, or to escapism or drink. He believed the Irish have no interest in picking apart their own brains. Fuck you, Siggy, I'm doing my best! He also stated that the Irish are a mass of contradictions and impervious to the rational thought processes that might resolve them. Maybe he had a point. What is certain is that my lost sibling was never discussed and no issues were ever resolved.

Or maybe I was just odd. After all, the next two of us five all seemed to fit in perfectly well. Five kids! So, you've already guessed that we were not just a Catholic family, we were a practising Catholic family. Or rather Mum was. Dad never complained or said anything negative about religion, but he avoided church like a Scotsman dodging salad. Occasionally he had to fall into step, at First Communions and marriages and funerals, but truly, the only time he ever went to church willingly was the day we buried Mum. And that day church was no solace. One of the toughest blokes I've ever met wailed like a baby for six hours solid. Jesus clearly did not want him for a sunbeam.

Back to upbringing. Dad was a sales rep and Mum was a housewife. That wasn't unusual or pejorative then. Dad brought home the bacon and Mum took care of everything, and she firmly believed that a tight ship was a happy ship. And did she run a tight ship! Hard to believe these days when we live with what Bill Maher calls the "Fuck you, Ma!" generation. Swear at my mother? If I even dared turn my back on my mother when she was talking to me, I wouldn't be writing this today. The Fourth Commandment is "Honour your father and your mother" — in our house that translated into a zero-tolerance policy as regards behaviour, attitude, manners and obeying without question. Any failures on this score and we were physically educated. I'm not saying it was right — look at how I turned out. But I also can't believe these whiney, self-absorbed brats of today are much of an improvement. Parents trying to be their friends and 'negotiating' with their kids about every decision. "If we don't leave now, Simon, you will be late for the party and won't that be a shame?"

When I heard "Get in the car, Rob," I left skid marks on the ground for fear of the second reminder, which would be a smack around the head.

Religion played a big part in my early childhood. As practising Catholics, we practiced a lot. Prayers every night before bed, Catholic primary school, Mass every Sunday and Holy Day. Even Christmas was ruined by having to go to church for an excruciating two-hours-that-seemed-like-two-days Mass. Then there was Sunday School! It was brainwashing but Mao's *Little Red Book* was the Bible and Mao was Pope Paul the IV. Yet, it wasn't the rituals or the boredom that was most impressive, it was the stereotypical Catholic stuff. If we were enjoying anything, it was probably wrong. If we did anything wrong, it was either a venial sin that was very bad, or it was a mortal sin and if we died between committing it and our next confession we would go immediately to hell, forever.

Let's just say it wasn't a barrel of laughs. At the same time, we always had an air of elitism engendered into us. The idea that somehow, we were of the true faith and not just going to heaven but actually, somehow morally and socially superior to Protestants. Judaism wasn't really discussed, and other world religions were just fairy tales believed by stupid people. I mean, Mohammed was just a copycat with a very dim view of shoplifting!

I was happy at school, well, sort of. School was easy. I couldn't understand why people suffered. Reading was easy, sums were easy. Teachers liked me because I did my work well. Getting on with kids was okay, but many were wary of the clever kid. I think Dad meant well when he told me, "Keep your head down, son, nobody likes the cleverest kid in the class." That's what I did from there on in. Do enough to do well, but don't excel. It takes the crosshairs off you. In many ways, it was good advice, but it left a lot of free time in class while others strived, and so engendered many bad habits. Mainly, the need to show off in other ways to compensate. To be a smart-arse and put other kids down, to have a smart mouth. I can't help wondering what might have been if he'd said, "Always shine, be all you can be." I'd probably be a quiet, little intellectual with bad hair and heavy rock t-shirts in the wardrobe. Or maybe exactly where I am, but not such a smart-arse. We will never know. The lessons were easy. Coming to terms with what life was all about was not. Everything was taught from a religious perspective. Apparently, I was born "To know God and to love him." Whatever the fuck that means? On the other side of the coin was the reality. Life, death, sex… those we had to work those out for ourselves.

Thank God we grew up in time to miss the internet and social media, which has half the western population worrying about what everyone else thinks rather than what they think. Or maybe it's a quarter. The other quarter has absorbed so much porn that they find sex a bit of a disappointment.

In my teen years, all we had was an occasional well-thumbed *Penthouse* or *Mayfair* and I frankly found it all a bit disturbing more than exciting. The first time I saw a vagina in a magazine, I distinctly remember thinking, *Uuuurrrggghhh! That looks a bit sore!*

Anyway, I first became aware of sex at age six or seven. Or rather, I already knew about sex in its most basic mechanics from about the age of seven. It was explained by another seven-year-old who made a circle with his forefinger and thumb and then used his other forefinger to illustrate his point that "To make a baby, your dad puts his cock in a mummy's do-dah and pisses the baby into her and it grows until it comes out." This sounded a) untrue, b) disgusting and c) well, just not feasible. But I was reassured by my elder brother telling me that it was a) true, b) yes, disgusting and c) the mechanics of a do-dah made it possible, but "They do cry a lot when it happens."

This explained why Mum had wept in anticipation when she announced that another sibling was on the way. What I did know for sure was that sex was dirty and sinful. How? Because that's what everyone said. Mum would be shocked and disgusted by anything on TV that was in any way not pure. Married loving couples, big smile, any sort of sexual shenanigans, big scowl. Priests, it seems ironic now with all the scandals, but priests were not shy of it in their sermons. Kids in the church didn't understand much but we knew sex was fucking scary, mortally sinful stuff.

I first became aware of my sexual insecurity when I was ten. Still pre-pubescent, with not even a follicle in sight, never mind body hair, it was announced that the School Nurse would be coming.

The next day we were lined up for a health-check. This involved queuing in our underpants and vests in a corridor and going in alphabetically one after another. Just like every kid of my generation, I was victim to the cliché of one boy in the line-up whispering, "If your willy goes hard when she touches it, you get sent to the headmaster and caned for being dirty." I found this a) clearly true, b) scary and c) totally feasible that it would happen to me. My cock often got hard for no apparent reason and especially when I played with it, which was often. I was filled with dread.

These days, the oh-so-sensitive helicopter parents would, by seven, have told their wunderkind, "It's normal to get to know your own body. Don't feel embarrassed, you're not doing anything wrong or dirty." Then they'd probably put him in a cool bath and try to distract him and laugh gently, knowingly, among themselves. This idea was still decades away and so that was absolutely not my experience. An erection was a dirty thing of shame and embarrassment. Was I filled with dread in the line-up? Dread had been replaced by panic.

When it was my turn to go in, a nice mumsy lady told me to sit down and took my pulse and height and all the non-scary stuff. I thought maybe it was all a joke about the intimate examination. Then, just as I was relaxing, she told me to stand up and drop my underpants. I felt a warm, soft hand on my scrotum, and she told me to turn my head away to the side and "Cough." There was no sign of erection, even though it wasn't an unpleasant feeling, and I confidently coughed. Then she said, "And again." The hand stayed in place and there was a bit of fiddling, then "Cough again!"

I thought I was coughing wrong. So, I gave it my best shot and coughed like a man dying of consumption. She simply told me to sit back down and called the doctor. I sat down resentfully, wondering, how was I supposed to cough when I didn't even have a cough and she didn't say "Give me your best hawk a lugey cough" or "Just a polite cough like you're trying to interrupt adults"? I had no clear direction. This was unfair.

The doctor arrived and got me standing again, told me to drop my pants and he then cupped my scrotum. (Cold and calloused if you were wondering — definitely not erection inducing, so in that sense, quite relaxing.) He then had a fiddle and told me to cough then again. Still no direction on the type of cough they were after. Regardless of my window-shattering cough, he simply said to the nurse, "Undescended testicle. Give the mother a referral letter." I knew what a testicle was, and I knew I had erections and they were growing more frequent. Had this dirty sin of having a hard cock somehow caused problems with my balls?

I waited and the nurse came back with a letter for my mum and I was sent on my way with no further explanation. I smuggled it back to the changing room and evaded the questions from the waiting boys about "What took so long?" with a story about a broken blood pressure thingy they put 'round your arm. I actually knew it was called a sphygmomanometer, but why risk being called a twat?

Once home I passed the letter to Mum, fully expecting to be told that I was, "A dirty little boy who had broken his balls by fiddling with them too much..." or something similar. As it turned out, it was even worse. She read the letter and said, "I will make an appointment with the doctor and we will see what he has to say." This was KGB-level mind-games she was playing. Next, I supposed, it would be a leathering from dad when he got home for being a "dirty boy, who can't leave his privates alone." Dad duly arrived and still, nothing was said. At least not to me. Whoever said ignorance is bliss clearly never took an undescended testicle letter home to his parents. The next days passed with me not knowing what the hell to think. As a good Catholic boy, I'd made my first confession at seven. We had sin hammered into us. Thankfully this was mainly by nuns, so it was the only sin that they tried to hammer into us. The more hands-on approach to hammering things into us came later with the monks. That said, the slap of a nun on a bare thigh hurts a fuck-sight more than you might imagine.

Being so up-to-speed on sin — which incorporated pretty much everything from murder to not telling the absolute truth about absolutely everything, I pondered if this was something I should bring up with the priest on my next visit. Was fiddling with your balls a sin? Was it a sin to enjoy the feel of your little cock as you washed it in a warm bath? Was having a stiffy, as it was known, mortal or venial in the sinful charts? If I truly repented, would my testis descend? There was no confession that weekend. I remember being both happy and sad about the fact. Instead of suffering the embarrassment of telling a middle-aged man in a booth about my genital fetish, I went with Mum to the doctor in a state of perceived mortal sin, worrying that if I died on the way, I would go straight to hell and burn for being the dirty ball-sac-fiddler the devil had made me.

At the doctor's surgery, we played out the standard sitcom sketch. I sat, while Mum booked us in. Then, when we were called into the consulting room, she did all the talking. The doctor was a woman doctor, which made the whole thing even worse. I did actually need to be there, for a repeat of the ball manipulating (Warm and soft, sharp fingernails and frankly a bit brutal this one).

She then explained, "As a baby boy grows inside his mother's womb, his testicles form inside his abdomen and move down into the scrotum shortly before birth."

She said scrotum out loud! In my panic/hysteria state, I spluttered a laugh and got a hard stare from them both.

"But in some cases, that move doesn't happen, and the baby is born with one or both testicles undescended. Was Pat premature? This is common in premature babies."

"No, but he was a difficult birth. The umbilicus was around his neck and he came out blue. The midwife thought he was dead…"

This was seriously shocking news. Well, for me. I nearly didn't live at all. Cool! I was special and had stared death in the face — and death had backed down. I was a blue baby…fuckin' yeah!

This neonatal bombshell was shaken off as insignificant by the doctor.

"No, that's unrelated… Undescended testicles move down on their own in about half of these babies by the time they're six months old. If they don't, it's important to get treatment." Then looking at me, she said, "The testicles make and store sperm, and if they don't descend, they could become damaged. This could affect fertility later in life or lead to other medical problems."

I stared blankly because I had no idea what she meant, but as no one was talking about this being caused by dirty behaviour, I was also relieved.

"This is quite late to discover Pat's left testicle is undescended. It will mean surgery. It's a relatively simple procedure. We will cut into the groin and cut through the muscle and we'll pull it down…"

Fuck you! I thought. (I had learned all the dirty words by ten). *Yes, it's relatively simple when it's not your bollock!* Even at ten, I didn't know much about spermatogenesis, but I knew, viscerally, that my balls were important, to me if not to anyone else.

"It may already be atrophied…" Mum and I both looked blank.

"…withered!"

Even at ten, you know that nobody wants a withered bollock. Frankly, the doctor had not made me feel better. And while it had not been made clear that my sinful behaviour had caused this, it had not been ruled out conclusively. It was at least good to know that I was not the only one. There were other boys out there in the same position. Maybe they had brought it on themselves like me. I wouldn't be alone in hell as the sole sinner of my type. Why that was comforting, I don't know, yet it was. I never mentioned the subject again and it was never mentioned. I resolved to leave my genitals alone and see if this was penance enough for the big guy in the sky. That resolve lasted no longer than the trip home and the need for a bath.

I can't remember how soon afterward, but soon afterward, I was in the hospital.

It's great being a kid in hospital. You have absolutely no fear of anything going wrong or death and you don't have to say prayers. What's more, you got Lucozade, chocolate and everyone is nice to you and there's no school. I got into my pyjamas, got into bed got stuck into the sweets and chocolate and was bilious with Lucozade within minutes. Then another doctor came, and the screens came around and he took a look at my balls, or ball if anyone is counting? The nurse and Mum were also watching and really, I'd got used to it by then. I had no worries about an unruly erection and more women had seen my knackers than those of the town Lothario. After a preliminary feel (warm but soft, not manual labourer's hands), he got out a marker pen and drew a line down the left side of my groin and circled the bulge of the undescended ball. Then, as I pulled up my *Star Trek* PJs, he said to the nurse, "Nil by mouth from midnight." I had no idea what that meant.

Dinner arrived, and I was told that 'Nil by mouth' meant I would have no more to eat after dinner until the operation was finished. Sounded fair enough to me. I tucked in and while it was pretty shit, it was fine because Mum, God bless her, was an awful cook. I was the only kid at school who really liked school dinners. That's how bad my Mum's cooking was. Dinner followed by another small Lucozade digestif, and it was lights out at nine.

I was woken by the nurse and another doctor. I had my pyjama pants half down before he announced that he was the anaesthetist and so had no need to see the family jewels. He asked the nurse my weight and then asked me if I was allergic to anything? I had no clue. So, I said "No." He looked around for a parent. Dad had work and Mum had the other shit to sort out that clearly was more important than her child going into surgery. That's how we rolled in the 'seventies. These days a kid in the same situation would probably have an entourage and a priest and a counsellor and everyone looking out for PTSD. He accepted my "No" and said, "The nurse will give you some tablets and we will come and get you soon."

I wasn't scared. This was all just too good. If only they'd allow me another slug of Lucozade, it would be a top way to live. The nurse brought the pills and I had my first high. I didn't know at the time, but Valium is a really cool drug. I felt great. It felt like a lovely warm hug from your granny, and soon they did, indeed, come and get me. I was rolled down the corridors in the bed like a prince. It just kept getting better and better. Into the whatever they call that bit before the operating theatre and onto a new bed. Then the anaesthetist arrived and told me he was going to put a tube in my arm and without waiting for my princely nod of agreement, he stuck a needle in my arm. Full of Valium, I simply looked at him like, "Is that all you've got. This kid is tougher than that!" Then he pushed the plunger and asked me to count down from a hundred slowly. I got to ninety-seven. The next thing I knew I was back in bed and feeling like a horse had kicked me in the balls.

Mum was there and looking worried. Not worried about me, worried that this was taking too much of her time. She asked me how I was, and I knew that "I feel like a horse kicked me in the balls" would get me into trouble. So, I simply replied "A bit sore, but okay." I had my head rubbed and was told, "Dad will pick you up after work," and she was off. When I needed to pee, the nurse told me to walk carefully to the toilets but use a bottle that she gave me. It seemed odd, but okay, if that's what she wants.

If you are a man who's had a vasectomy (I had one of those much later), you will know the feeling. If not, then imagine yourself walking like John Wayne after a horse had, in fact, kicked you in the groin. Mission accomplished, I decided to never pee or leave the bed again. The surgeon came by, flirted with the nurses, and he ruffled my hair too. Dad arrived and ruffled my hair. After everyone wanting a handful of my balls, they all seemed to prefer the head now.

I was taken in a wheelchair to the car and home — to more Lucozade. That was that, really. A few days of soreness, a new, more dangly lefty. But the horrific realization that lefty was considerably smaller than righty. Withered, as the doctor had warned. It was the start and remained, a constant nagging doubt that I was under-balled compared to others.

The difference in size was not the biggest concern though. My elder brother let the cat out of the bag and so I got a knick-name at school. "Lackaknacker," which, looking back, is actually really quite clever and funny. So clearly it was not my big brother's invention. (Face it, David. It's true.) There was a splinter group that tried to introduce Tobermory. He was a character in the hit children's TV series *The Wombles*. Say Wombles out loud a few times and you'll get it.

Nickname notwithstanding, until at the age of fifty-four when a urologist felt my balls (Oriental, small, warm hands.) and told me that they both had "good volume," I had forty-four years of ball anxiety. This was suddenly expunged by a simple, offhand remark from a Thai urologist and poof! Gone. Fathering two children and no woman ever saying, "You know, one of your balls is so much smaller than the other," had never cured me of the insecurity. I needed a professional. Are you seeing a pattern developing?

Chapter 3
"Come in," she said. "I'll give you shelter from the storm."

It started, I suppose, that Wednesday. I thought this was going to be a quick fling and get it out of our systems. A lookback and smile job. I was on Garden Leave, I had a new job set up, and so it was easy to invent a meeting and be on my way, to be sure I wasn't late for my eleven o'clock appointment. Nothing to be proud of, but I'd had my fair share of girlfriends and shamefully, a few affairs along the way. Some just flings or pissed mistakes on trips and others that just seemed to happen and seemed to continue, then fizzle out. It sounds disgraceful to some people — the virtuous and the unimaginative. And about par for the course, to many others. Just to be clear on the depth of my depravity, I make no bones about also suffering from complete sanctimonious cognitive dissonance on this. My failings as a husband were because, as Proust put it, "No man can find everything he needs in the one woman he loves, so he finds the rest with women he does not love." If my Mrs tried to turn the tables and use that logic on me, I would not find it compelling. In fact, I'd have a shit fit.

But nonetheless, that's the truth about me. Go on, judge away.

There I was walking down a suburban street and I was nervous. I'd parked the car half a mile away. It seemed a good idea, until walking towards her house, I suddenly saw that for anyone who knew us both, there was only one place I was going. I'd be able to lie that off, but still, it added to the general level of nervousness. How was I going to play this? Just walk in and kiss her passionately. Sounds good, but what if she's outraged and treats you like some sex-pest as she explains she invited you around to explain about the other night. By the way, why is it that whenever a woman wants 'to explain,' it's never good? You never leave the conversation thinking, *Well, that all makes so much sense now. Thank goodness she took the time to explain*!

At last, I was at the gates. Shit! You have to use the Entryphone. "Hi, it's..." Of course she'd been expecting you, you knob! The electric gates opened and then I had to cross thirty yards of gravel. I wasn't sure if I was walking to the firing squad or a new nirvana.

She came out of the door and I was so glad I didn't bottle it. She looked good. She always looks good. This outfit I realise now was carefully selected: a blue sundress, fancy flip-flops, hair down and just a little bit wet as if to say, "Yes I had a shower and was getting ready for you."

Closer up, I saw she had a big smile on her face and she said, "I wasn't sure you'd come. I thought you might chicken out…"

I was too busy checking the surroundings for a *Candid Camera* crew or a husband with a machete. Just a beat too late, I managed to squawk out a non-committal, "Wouldn't have missed it."

We walked into her kitchen and it was an atmosphere that was tense and funny at the same time. She picked up her coffee and as she put it to her lips she asked, "Do you want one?"

I wanted to say, "No, absolutely not. I'm on pins here and frankly, I didn't come around here a for a coffee morning natter…" which came out as, "No, thanks, I'm good."

She put hers down and as she started to say, "Look we need to…" I did the only decent thing and moved in and put my hands on her hips. A committed move and pretty intimate, yet allowing the hip-owner to gently push them away and 'explain'. She didn't do that. She kissed me. It was like a first kiss all over again. I'm in my fifties and have kissed a lot of girls. I'm not going to make it out to be something that it wasn't. It was just perfect— Kitty's-soft lips, just the right level of insistent tongue and a slight tang of espresso. I did more than just not stop her. I kissed her back. A lot.

Do you sometimes get the feeling that modern life has become a movie where all the sex scenes are described in purely pornographic terms? Well, you're not getting that here, well, not totally. But after I had moved my hands all over her and could feel my cock hardening in my trousers, I moved a hand onto her thigh under the sundress. I think she took this as confirmation that I wasn't here just for the kissing and her hands went to my belt. Then time sped up and I was pulling up her dress and she was pulling on my belt and we were still glued together at the mouth. It's an awkward moment, especially when you're stone-cold sober. As I tried to do all of the above and push off a shoe, she pulled away from me and said, "Stop…"

Bollocks, bollocks, bollocks!

"…Come with me."

Yippee-ki-yay. Bruce Willis was shouting in my head.

And she pulled me out of the kitchen and into a bedroom, I couldn't help noticing it was a kid's room, not hers. Clearly, she had some decorum. Let's be clear, I would have fucked her just about anywhere at that moment. But a picture of her husband and kids looking on would have tested my mettle. In fact, I'd still fuck her just about anywhere at this moment, too. Let's move on.

In the bedroom, we kissed again, and she let me pull off her sundress. She was wearing a lacy bra and lacy thong. I was excited to an even higher level. She sat on the edge of the bed and I finally got to pull off, or half off, my trousers and underwear and was pleased to see my cock was as up for it as me. Then she did something incredibly sexy. She looked me square in the eye and then back down and I felt my cock slip into her mouth. No turning back now. We were game on. I struggled out of my shirt and pushed her away. It was a very hard decision, but necessary. No, I wasn't about to blow everything as it were. I needed to take off my trousers or fall over.

Cut back to me naked and priapic and she is looking fabulous on the bed. I took off her bra without fumbling and those breasts were no disappointment. And let me tell you, they had a lot to live up to after my earlier feel copping and even more because tits, after forty and after childbirth, can be disappointing. Hers were perfect. TV tits, as we called them in the ad agency world. She's slim, with a narrow back, but they were more prominent than clothes might suggest. You could see where the idea that the champagne coupe was based on the shape of Josephine's breasts. It's not true, that story. I mean, come on! "Empress, if I may take a mould of your breast, I will use it to shape a champagne glass. It will be a lasting testament to your tits. Think of how Napoleon will love the world knowing the exact dimensions of his bird's knockers every time they enjoy a bit of fizzy stuff."

You get the picture anyway. And the nipples were clearly defined, small and prominent, erect and firm at this point. Yes, it is an important detail.

I pushed her back on the bed and kissing continued while I felt her breasts and she held my cock. I slipped down and removed her slip and started to move my head lower. She pushed me away and reached to the nightstand and a condom appeared in her hand. "Sure," I said hoping that I could still do this. I hadn't used a 'Jonnie' in years and I could already feel my cock craning lower.

"I'm still, you know, fertile and …"

"Well, if that's your issue I had a vasectomy years ago…" She silently agreed with a nod of her head and condom was put down and the kissing recommenced. I started to move down again kissing her neck, tits, tummy…

"Just fuck me…" I loved this woman.

The first kiss is always hot and always memorable, but then so is the first time you slip yourself into someone else. It's always memorable (Or am I a fucking weirdo?). And every woman is the same, they all make a slightly different sound and movement. Kitty sighed. Not an, 'Is that it'? sigh, but a "Uuuuuhhhhhmmmm" sigh. And I groaned. And we were off to the races. It was really hot and yet there was something just off-kilter. I wasn't sure what. But before I could figure it out, she had her hands on my back and her legs clamped around me and said, "Fuck me… really hard."

So, I did. Yet there was still something off. I couldn't tell what. It was delightful and she was clearly happier like this and I wasn't going to complain. I tried to control the pace a little, but she just urged me on. After a few more minutes, the inevitable hove into view, for me at least. She was pushing back hard, and I grunted, "If we don't slow down, I'm gonna… gonna come."

She grunted back, "Just fuck me. I want to feel you come in me…" Well after that, there was no holding back and I went at it like some demented axe murderer, sucked her breasts like a starveling and true to my word and her instructions (and thankfully just after she showed all the signs of orgasming herself), I "emptied my river into her lake."

Both of us were breathless and naked. I stayed inside her as we flopped onto the bed. With what turned out to be a moment of inspiration I moved her hair out of the way and kissed her neck and shoulders and neck again. After a while, I leaned round to kiss her mouth. Eventually, we pulled apart and lay both on our back, side by side. With a big smile on my face, I said, "Well, that was all right then…"

She punched me on the shoulder and said, "Just all right…"

"No, it was amazing! Well, when I say amazing, the first time is always a bit fingers and thumbs isn't it, but it was great…" Oh god, I was walking on a razor blade, on eggshells in quicksand by a volcano.

Thankfully she saved me. She rolled on her front. "Men, you are so keen to impress. What's most impressive is when you don't try. Now kiss my neck again. That was really nice." So, I did, lying on top of her kissing her neck.

She murmured, "Uhhhmmm that's so nice. I wished you'd fucked me like this…" So that was it. She had wanted me from behind. Note to self.

It was about 1.45 by then. Fuck off! I'd arrived on the dot of eleven. If it was 11.45, I'd be impressed. She offered me coffee again as she set off to get a glass of water. She came back in a cashmere dressing gown that draped but didn't cover her. *Oh, Kitty, you know how to dress, even undressed.* I sat on the bed with a coffee and we chatted idly for a while, then she said. "Do you want a shower?" I didn't really, but maybe she was saying, "You're a bit whiffy" or maybe she wanted a shower or… anyway, I wasn't going to complain. "As long as we're coming back here," I replied pointing at the bed.

"Someone thinks a lot of himself!" was her response. And besides, soaping up a beautiful girl in the shower is never a chore, plus there seemed every likelihood that this would be the outcome Then she bit her lip as she smiled and continued, "Of course. Unless you want some lunch?" Kitty, society wife, and hostess to the end. Rather than answer her ridiculous question, I eased her towards the shower. Although I had no idea where it was.

Surely you can use your imagination for the shower scene. No? Well, tough luck! All I will say is that: One, It was all I had hoped for. Two, Never get a girl's hair wet in the shower. Three, Don't scrupulously clean your arse with soap when in the shower with a girl. Four, Always avoid soap down your Jap's eye. Girls, unaware of the sting of detergent in the 'urinary meatus' as the Japanese prefer it to be called, can be clumsy when soaping your dick. Because I already knew two and three, and Kitty knew four, or maybe we got lucky, it was a lovely experience and both draped in big bath sheets, we went back to the bed. Laying there all fresh and warm and clean and thinking "What's next?" It's great in summer when it's hot. In winter, it loses a lot of its sexual appeal. Ball-sack shrivelled and your junk looking like an obscene Nestle's Walnut Whip and girl shivering — not sexy. Thankfully, it was summer.

Back in bed, the kissing restarted. One thing led to another and this time I was not to be denied my march south. If I'm honest, there were several reasons to do this. One, apparently a lot of guys just don't, and a lot of women like it. Two, I like it and three, I was buying a bit of time. And no, you're not getting details, although a top tip from a book I read years ago, is to keep doing what gets a positive response and don't do what doesn't. But if you're running out of ideas, spell out the alphabet with your tongue. I don't know if it gets the best results, but it stops you from getting bored! This came into play as I was used to faster results, and so was heartened to hear, "I'm not an easy touch off... do you want to stop?" Ego-centric as I am, I was determined to establish my credentials in this department. I slid my finger around my tongue and vice versa and persisted until she, well, probably gave in, more than came.

Fair's fair, and as soon as she had her breath back, she was returning the compliment. Lying on a bed, sun streaming through the open windows and through the hair of your new lover as she sucks your cock and gently squeezes your balls is a pretty good way to spend a Wednesday lunchtime. But again, needing to establish my Don Juan credentials I pulled her off and pushed her over, but she jumped up and moved to the window. She looked out and held the frame as I slid into her again. "Is this what you want?"

The mind-reading minx said, "Yes, hard, really hard, until you come…"

So, I did.

Then the phone rang. I wasn't going to stop, and she let it go and so we completed chapter two much the same as chapter one. The next shower was perfunctory, as was the offer, and the turning down, of a quick lunch. She did say one thing I liked hearing. "You have a really nice body."

Now, I know you are saying, "Bullshit!" but I do, at least for a bloke in his fifties. I'm 6'3" and tip the beam at fourteen stone. I don't have a belly and I've kept my hair. I'm vain, so when I stopped playing rugby, I started running and going to the gym. All you middle-aged blokes out there who moan that their partner doesn't want to fuck their fat, bald flabby-ness might want to take note. The second thing is more divisive. I have hair everywhere you might expect, but my torso (excluding armpits if you want to get technical) is hairless. No woman has ever been so rude as to say they don't like it, but a few have mentioned how much they do. Oh, and I have urticaria. If I don't get sun on my skin, especially in winter, I get a rash. The answer is sunbeds, so I have a permanent light tan. This need for UV has been called into question in terms of veracity by my mates shouting, "You vain wanker," when they see it, but it is true. More importantly, no woman has ever said, "I wish you were paler!"

On hearing about my nice body, I did the only thing you can do in these circumstances. "Are you kidding? I can't believe how fantastic you look." That the truth will set you free has never been truer. She looked fantastic. So, getting dressed and feeling almost high, with all my past experiences, I wasn't surprised when it all went a bit tits-up. The phone rang. More accurately the iPhone signalled Facetime. She was still naked, and she looked scared, she picked it up and ran out of the room. Pointing to me to stay quiet and not move.

Through the doorway, I could hear.

"Oh, I was in the shower... Yes... No. Well, I didn't want to miss you twice..."

And so, it went on. It was clearly the other half. When she came back later, she was dressed and so was I. Heeled boots, by I believe Manolo Blahnik, jeans and a beautiful simple crisp white blouse. Her, not me.

"Sorry about that. Shit, look at the time. I need to get moving." I was good at being good at being ushered out. Another quick kiss and I couldn't resist.

"I don't want this to be 'a one-time-only never to be repeated thing…' "

"We'll see. I'll call you. Don't call me. He knows your mobile number. Look, I really need to go."

So not a yes, but not a no either. If only I had kept my mouth shut. I would have just those fond semi-pornographic memories to look back on. But I never was good at keeping my big gob shut. Back across the gravel, this time with a smug look on my 'physog' and a spring in my step and frankly feeling really so happy with myself you would want to punch me in the gob, and I wouldn't blame you. I looked back over my shoulder and she looked pretty pleased with herself too. All in all, it was only 1.45 and a great day already. For the more punctilious of you out there, it's not an oversight. Yes, she did have to be somewhere at 1.45. Kitty is always late. Or I will nuance, if she is ever on time, it is by mistake!

Chapter 4
And I don't want no one-minute man

Ernest Hemingway was a bit of a chauvinist tosser, I think we can all agree. Nonetheless, he wasn't a stupid tosser, and he was certainly right in this respect:

"The world breaks everyone and afterward many are strong at the broken places. But those that will not break it kills. It kills the very good and the very gentle and the very brave impartially. If you are none of these, you can be sure it will kill you too, but there will be no special hurry." It's from *A Farewell to Arms* if you want to check. It's a book worth reading. But only once.

I got broken in the weirdest way. For a man with a massive ego and a high libido, it was rather cruel. I'm not sure when, but I started suffering from anorgasmia. What's that? Well, let me, or rather the National Institute of Health tell you.

Delayed orgasm or anorgasmia is defined as the persistent or recurrent difficulty, delay in, or absence of attaining orgasm after sufficient sexual stimulation, which causes personal distress. Delayed orgasm and anorgasmia are associated with significant sexual dissatisfaction.

And because I know your next question, I looked that up, too.

The time threshold for distress is dependent on the partners involved. Some males will reach orgasm with one partner in fifteen minutes and have no distress, but with another partner, it may cause severe distress because the partner may complain of pain with prolonged intercourse. A population-based survey established that the median intravaginal ejaculatory latency time (IELT) was 5.4 minutes and two standard deviations above was approximately twenty-two minutes

So, the answer that so many men want: About five minutes is average and under twenty minutes is 99% of blokes. Over twenty minutes and you have a red-raw girlfriend, and potentially, a problem.

It's a weird one, delayed orgasm. It's not that you can't keep going, it's that when you start to think you won't orgasm, you start thinking just about that. Not the sex, and so the sex stops being great or even good, it's just see-sawing in and out of someone with your mind elsewhere. It can put a serious dent in your real life, never mind your sex life. The irony is that when you first start having a sex life, well, as a boy at least, it's the opposite problem. If you don't believe me, just ask any woman who had sex with a teenager. But then you grow into it and start to think, *Now I get what all that hearts and flowers stuff was all about because I can actually really enjoy this and get lost in the moment, not*

It all kind of crept up on me. When you've been
married for twenty-five years, you get lackadaisical
about sex. You shouldn't, but you do. Not just men,
women too. C'mon, admit it. Every now and again, a bit
pissed after a party or driven by petty jealousy or just
that the mood overtook you both, it can get really
seriously sexy. But for the most part, it becomes
ritualistic and more about pair-bonding than passion.
Me and Miranda were no different. That meant that if it
was taking a bit longer and a bit more effort was needed,
what was the problem? Ahhh, but then I started thinking
about it. And that's when the problems really started.

It's the final taboo really. Now we have Viagra,
Cialis and the other one whatever it's called. Blokes
don't need to worry, well not so much, about rising to
the occasion, but when you have risen, and there's, shall
we say, no end in sight, you have to fake it. And that is
somewhere between difficult to pull off and, in the case
of a blowjob, impossible.

Was this what drove me to Kitty? Was it, bollocks!
I know that because they taught us at school "Post hoc
ergo propter hoc" (after it therefore because of it) is a
fallacy. I don't know if it had started to be an issue
before that Wednesday at eleven, but it certainly
became one. After trying to fix it myself by closing my
eyes and thinking of something incredibly sexy or dirty
or both, and failing, I decided I needed professional

help. It was too embarrassing to make an appointment just for that, though. Imagine you get through to the doctor's surgery and the receptionist asks, "What would you like to see the doctor about?" and having to say out loud, down a phone, "I'm having trouble ejaculating!" to which she might then have a follow-up question. It was just unthinkable. I did have another reason to see the doctor as I had started having searing headaches. I never put the two together. Neither did the doctor, well, not until much later anyway.

Appointment made, I went to see the family doctor. He was a good bloke, not that I'd seen him that often. Just for sleeping pills when travelling and minor ailments. It was a bit disconcerting that he started the consultation by asking after my family. He was our family doctor, but it's difficult to jump from, "The wife's fine thanks" to "I'm having trouble coming!" We started with the searing headaches. We talked about this and then when that was thoroughly exhausted, I dropped in my other issue. He was a pro. He didn't snicker or look dismayed or freaked out. He raised an eyebrow and asked a few more probing questions. Since when? How bad? Et cetera. He couldn't see an obvious connection, apart from if you have a headache, you don't want sex. I was tempted to point out to him that I am not a woman. They may use a headache as a reason to not make love. Me, and I suspect many other men, want to fuck — because we have a headache. I explained that the issue was more nuanced. I had searing headaches and quite separately, was having trouble orgasming. He looked even more perplexed and sent me for an MRI for the headaches and to a urologist for my cock.

At the MRI appointment, I lay on the platform and the technician put a contraption around my head and shoulders to keep it all still and then put on a pair of earphones. "Please keep as still as you can. The procedure will take about twenty-five minutes. If you move, we will have to do it again." Then I was slid into the tunnel. I soon realised why headphones were necessary. It's really noisy having an MRI and it's also seriously claustrophobic. Then the machine thumps out repetitive bass beats and I swear for five minutes it sounded like it was shouting, "Die, Die, Die, Die, Die, Die, Die, Die, Die." It was at that moment that the thought struck me that maybe there was something seriously wrong with my head.

A few days later, the MRI results came back and there was nothing to report. Which was welcome news. The doctor then suggested we should do some blood tests as the headaches might be endocrinal in origin. He was an endocrinologist by training, so I guess he was biased.

As for my sexual issue, he sent me to a urologist. I'd never been to one before. The only preparation I received was that his receptionist told me that I should drink a litre of water before the appointment. With a full bladder on my part, we had a lovely chat about my general health. and then he asked me to go pee into a crazy machine that looked a lot like a big funnel with a spinning plate at the bottom. It was slightly surreal. Once I returned, he showed me a graph produced by the machine that showed I had a healthy flow with a bit of straining at the end. Perfectly normal for a man of my age. Then he ultra-sounded me like they do pregnant women. Thankfully I was not with child and my bladder was empty as it should be. Then he checked my prostate. Cue all the jokes. Nah, you've heard them all. It wasn't so bad, and he seemed quite pleased to tell me that there seemed to be no real issues with the plumbing. A slight enlargement of my prostate, but nothing unusual for a man of my age. Then he felt my balls and pronounced that they had "good volume," which if you remember my earlier hospital issues, gave me more pleasure than it would most men.

With all the preliminaries done and dusted, we went on to my delayed orgasm.

"How hard is your erection?" That's a bit of a strange one, no? I looked a little perplexed and he helped me out. "If one is just enough to achieve penetration and ten is so hard it's almost painful, then where would you place yours?"

I could see no point in lying. "If I've been drinking, then five to seven, and if very excited then nine, not often ten."

"Well, that's good." I was pleased I had passed another test. "The harder the penis, the easier it is for a man to orgasm. For your age you are fine." Then he smiled and added, "Men after thirty will rarely get a ten." So I assumed it was like the Olympics and they assume your high scores are from the East German judge… but still, it was good to know all was okay and I didn't have erection difficulties.

He then went on about *erection dissatisfaction.* Apparently, starting around age forty, erections change. In some men, the process is gradual, in others, it happens more quickly. Either way, older men lose the ability to raise erections solely from sexual fantasies. When erections do appear, they rise more slowly and do not become as firm as they were during men's thirties. And minor distractions may cause wilting. These changes alarm many men, who jump to the conclusion that they must have ED. He told me there is a definitive test: if you can still raise an erection during masturbation, you are fine. What you may have, is erection dissatisfaction for sex, which may have many causes. This guy was good. He was a mind reader. He said that there were no obvious anatomical issues, so maybe it was physiological or psychological. As he wasn't a psychologist, he would look further into the physical aspects and consult with colleagues. It seemed like he was a bit in the dark. He tap-danced for a while and promised to get back to me.

Chapter 5
Boys Don't Cry

In 1973, the Vietnam War ended, Britain joined the EEC, but the two major events of that year were that I discovered masturbation and went to big school. A clever boy at Catholic primary school, I was selected (more like singled-out) to continue my 'Spiritual Journey' at the Catholic College. This choice most often led to boys going to the Seminary to become priests or going to a psychiatrist for a significant portion of their adulthood. I did neither.

It was hard enough going through puberty going to school taught by religious maniacs. Yet that wasn't torment enough. We had to do it in a uniform that looked like something from the 1930s where the black and white picture has had the colour put back in. Purple blazer, grey shirt, gaudy purple, red and green tie and a pullover, black trousers and black, yes, no other colour allowed, black Oxford shoes. Running the gauntlet of other kids was difficult enough in trainers, but formal shoes?

My school day started like this: Up for breakfast at about 6.45 dressed in the above fancy-dress outfit. A cup of tea and cornflakes and a five-minute walk to the bus stop. Catch the bus at 7.10 to get to the local railway station Thirty-five minutes later, the train dropped us at Reading Station. Walk to the bus stop and then catch the bus to the school.

There were two issues here. The buses didn't allow for this horde of schoolkids, so it was a bunfight to get on the bus or you would get into trouble for being late. The other issue was other kids from normal schools. Let's just say there were few insults about us, and what we did to each other, or what the monks did to us that came as any sort of a shock after the first few weeks. The bus stop outside the school was a zoo and everyone was far keener to get home than they were to get in each morning. The solution was a twenty-five minutes' walk to the station. This gave the added incentive of keeping your bus-fare and spending it on sweets. On the downside, it meant you were out on the street and fair game, especially as the journey necessitated passing the shopping centre. It was a magnet for the local youth with nothing better to do. Nothing better than taunting the weird, purple-blazered Catholic schoolboys who were passing. We had to take the short-cut through a churchyard. Strangely, outside the church among the tombstones was their favourite hunting ground. So, we moved in small packs like gazelles avoiding hyaenas. And I do mean like gazelles. If we saw an attack coming, it was 'run like fuck' and just be sure you could run faster than someone else.

Only once did I really suffer. Cornered by three or four comprehensive boys (comprehensive schools took all kids regardless of academic or any other standard. Consequently, the over-developed aggression/underdeveloped brains brigade always went there). The normal insults and jostling took place and into the mix was thrown, "You think you're so much better than us…"

It was out before I could stop myself. "Yes, because I am!" More out of defiance than really meaning it. The problem was, this was their real grudge and I would have been better suggesting that their mum and dad had only met once, and money had changed hands. They went mental and punches and kicks rained down on me like a storm. Thankfully, this was the early seventies and people didn't carry knives and passers-by didn't look the other way and walk on. So, a man dived in and shouted, "Break it up!" and pulled them off me. They left with another barrage of insults and the warning that if they ever saw me again, I was "dead". Again, this was the seventies. It wasn't literal as it might be now. My good Samaritan wasn't hanging around either and just sent me on my way. One hundred yards around the corner, my mates waited. I felt a bit let down. At the same time, I don't know if I'd have gone back to help one of them. I like to think so, but if you're never challenged, you never know. Later in life, I did go back to help a mate in similar circumstances. The result is you just both get beaten up. But we are still close friends and so I guess it has some merit as a bonding experience.

As I said, at "big school, we were taught by monks. They were said to have a teaching vocation. Looking back, this vocation consisted of joining other psychos who had transferred their libidos into emotionally and physically beating young boys. Of course, to be allowed to do that, they had to do some teaching, but it was very much a side-line to religion and sadism. At least once a week, we had Mass in Latin. They weren't so bad, just boring. It has left me with the party trick of reciting all the prayers in Latin. Heh, it's not magic tricks but you can do a really good exorcist impression. Not Max von Sidow standard, but it can get a few laughs (see later). The lessons were diligently given, and any infraction of the disciplinary code was dealt with by being hit — hit hard! If they didn't think that was enough, you would be sent to the Brother Superior (the headmaster) who caned you. Not on the hand. That would be not demeaning enough. No, you leaned over the back of the chair and held the front legs. Then you were caned on the backside. I deeply suspect that under his cassock he had a raging hard-on, but that's just how it was. Once, when the Brother Superior was away on retreat, his stand-in, Brother Fergus, took things further. He drew a line on the offender's arse with chalk, to give himself a better target. And between each stroke made you stand up and stretch, then bend down again. This was really painful. Maybe just standard caning of boys didn't get him off. Ironically, we saw caning as fair enough punishment; it was the norm. But Brother Fergus and his 'chalk and stretch technique' was agreed by all in the schoolyard to be, "A complete cunt's trick."

The school day was rigorous. Thirty-six to a class (Read it and weep, the class-size whiners. We were rammed in; they may have ruined our lives with their religious bullshit, but they kept academic standards ultra-high). We did the normal core curriculum, plus Latin.

What is the point of learning Latin? For us, it was the liturgical language. That argument falls down as we knew all of the Mass in Latin and English and all the prayers, so why else? It's said that studying Latin is fantastic preparation for learning and becoming fluent in one or more of the Romance languages. Bollocks or should I say, testis? Latin prepares students for several important professions that are steeped in Latin or English words derived from Latin. These include law, medicine, science, music, theology, philosophy, art, and literature. Nonsense — you don't have to study Latin to understand Habeas Corpus. Some argue Latin enables students to more fully understand and appreciate the Roman Empire. No, it doesn't! You don't have to know Kanji to understand Pearl Harbour. No, the real value of learning Latin is that a little bit of pretentious knowledge that really impresses Americans. Don't ask me why, but throw in a bit of Latin and they think you were Einstein's mate or something of the like.

More important even than Latin, was that every day we had at least ninety minutes of 'Religious Education'. More than any other subject! We did more R.E. than Mathematics and Science put together. The only upside I can see from this is that I do know my Bible and I do know a fair bit of Christian dogma, belief, and practice. Which is more than you can say for most Christians. That's something I still find remarkable. Sports fans know more about their team than most Christians do about their imaginary friend, his history story and how you are going to gain immortal life.

Weird, isn't it? It's supposed to be the most important thing. The reason we're even here — but I'm not going to read the books or learn any whys or wherefores. Men of my generation can still name the '66 World Cup winning team. (Gordon Banks, George Cohen, Bobby Moore, Jack Charlton, Ray Wilson, Nobby Stiles, Alan Ball, Martin Peters, Bobby Charlton, Geoff Hurst, Roger Hunt.) Ask your average Christian to name the twelve apostles. They will get stuck at around four or five. While interestingly, always remembering Judas! (Peter, James, John, Andrew, Bartholomew or Nathanael, James the Lesser or Younger, Judas, Jude or Thaddeus, Matthew or Levi, Philip, Simon the Zealot, Thomas. If anyone is interested.) They don't even know the basic rules. You can win money with this. Ask people to run off the Ten Commandments. I'm yet to meet anyone who isn't a pro who can do it. They always get coveting and adultery and thou shalt not kill, but then they start to struggle. Stealing, shagging, and killing — beyond our basic motivations they get lost looking for a moral code. At least I know what I don't believe, while they believe what they don't actually know.

Anyway, while that and much other religious esoterica was hammered into us and may have led to spiritual salvation for some, I can't help thinking a bit more science and arts would have been more enlightening.

One disciplinary/pedagogic episode sticks firmly in my mind. My handwriting was appalling. Even by the standards of young teen boys. This was due to two things. One, I have appalling handwriting and two, I had learned to write in three different primary schools. This was due to Dad being relocated for his job. It wasn't a big deal. Or it didn't seem like it at the time. You just rocked up to the new school and got shoved into a class and got on with it. The issue was that one school taught cursive, the other italic and the third something else, I don't remember what. Net result: my handwriting was a hybrid of the three, with the penmanship of "A drunken spider walking through ink!" said Brother Athanasius in a Latin class. Looking back, penmanship must have been his thing — alongside beating the living shit out of schoolboys. A strange combination, but then Stalin liked purges and Westerns, Hitler loved dogs and Holocausts… people are strange combinations. So, one day, my scrawl was just too much for him. His frustration manifested itself by him writing an alphabet in perfect cursive on the blackboard and having me copy it out. While I was doing it, he continued teaching the rest of the lads about the third declension. Once I had done an alphabet, he looked, sneered, rubbed it out and told me to do it again. The rate of improvement was not to his liking and after about forty-five minutes, he went red in the face and pointed to a letter and howled "What is that? What is that?"

I swear I wasn't being flippant. I just answered his question. "It's an e." The next thing I knew, I was on the deck seeing stars. I never saw it coming. He had given me a right-cross that hit me square on the left cheek. He was about sixteen stone of furious Irishman, I was twelve years old, nine stone wet through. As I staggered back up, I could see my classmates transfixed, mouths open, just staring. Then I saw Brother Athanasius. I didn't understand then, but he was really scared. He knew he'd gone too far, but I didn't. We were inured to violent monks.

As I wobbled on my feet, he looked at me and said, "Back to your seat, boy." And like a boxer in the 'Land of Shadows' as Ali called it, I shambled drunkenly back to my desk and flopped in the seat. He wiped the board and just carried on with the lesson as though nothing had happened, or hoping, I suppose, that that would be the end of it.

As we filed out of the class, I already had a livid duck egg on my face. Wary of him, to say the least, I kept my head down and as I passed by, he ruffled my hair and said, "Aaargh, you're not such a bad lad." It was then I realized he knew what he'd done was wrong and I felt sorry for him. My handwriting was shit and he thought I was taking the piss. So, I forgave him, good Catholic boy that I was.

A psychologist later told me this is a classic example of 'Reconciling the Aggressor'. The idea is that we look to make the person less responsible for their actions because we are complicit in it. "Well, I brought it on myself..." At its most extreme, say, a girl is raped. She says, "Well I was drunk and wearing sexy clothes..." but rape is an act of violence and hatred. It would be as bad if she was sober and dressed demurely. The rapist is the aggressor. The girl somehow reconciling him is a way to make it less hateful and somehow less of an offence. Good people try and find less vicious explanations for the bad things, aggressors do. But it is a mistake. People must be responsible for their actions. We are responsible for ours. Back to the girl. It may be foolish and dangerous to be drunk and sexily dressed, but that is not in any way a justification for the attack. They are two different things.

According to my psychologist, reconciling the aggressor is a self-harming mechanism. But as psychologists were in short supply at the time, I carried on like it was nothing.

In the schoolyard, everyone was talking about it. I just brushed it off. "He lost his temper and it's okay."

By the time we were on the train home, my bruised face was more of a running joke than an outrageous assault by a teacher on a schoolboy. When I got home my mum saw it immediately and asked, "What have you done now?"

"I fell," I told her. Which was true. Of course, the complete truth was, "Brother Athanasius king-hit me, and I fell like a sack of shit," but swearing was totally forbidden at home, so she got the edited version.

Later, when Dad got back from work, he saw it and wanted to know, "Were you fighting?" I knew how to handle this.

"Yeh…" As ever his face darkened, and he wanted details.

"Did you win?"

I told him the acceptable truth. "The other guy only got one punch in. He was sorry he started it." He beamed like Mickey when Rocky won, then ruffled my hair and said, "Good lad. Never back down." This is really bad advice, by the way, but again, bad advice is generally the only advice I take. So, the psychotic Latin Master got away with it. Maybe he was sorry, maybe not. I had a cheek like a baboon's arse for a week and that was that. I can't, however, finish this without mentioning that my Latin grades seemed inflated beyond their worth in the following tests, and he never picked on me again. Seemed fair enough at the time. Just FYI: After the hospital and these events, to this day, I fucking hate people ruffling my hair (but not splitting infinitives).

Chapter 6
Parrot Fashion Love

Kitty called. I was ecstatic and arranged to meet as soon as possible. Not back at 'Chez Elle,' I was disappointed to be told. Instead, it was a quiet coffee shop. I can still see her walking in now in my mind's eye. You can build people up in your imagination and then get disappointed. I was concerned that seeing her again would be a bit like that. It wasn't. Maybe the sundress and sandals (different sundress, different sandals) brought back memories of Wednesday at eleven, or maybe she really was that hot. One thing is for sure: I wasn't disappointed. I stood as she approached and, not sure of the etiquette in this situation, as we were in public and on show, I went to kiss her cheek. She grabbed my face and gave me a big kiss and then pulled back and said, "You're funny. We've been naked together. Don't kiss me like your sister"

She ordered an espresso. Never milk in Kitty's coffee. Not because she didn't like it — because of the calories. As it arrived, she looked at her watch and told me, "I'm sorry I can't be long…"

"Really? Then why were you ten minutes late?" I didn't say that. What I did say said was, "All right then, ·

I will be quick. I want to see you again. When can you be free for a morning or an afternoon? We could have lunch or something…"

"Hhhmmmm or something? What could you mean?"

Enough of the 'he said she said.' She teased me a bit and I suggested that I could get a hotel room and she could meet me there.

She agreed, but said, "I will only have a couple of hours…"

I wasn't going to split hairs. All faux manly and in control, I said, "Leave it to me." The following Tuesday morning at about nine-thirty to lunchtime was agreed.

That's when she hit me with the zinger. "Rob, what do you really like sexually?"

You would think that by adulthood we would be comfortable with questions about sex. But we're not. Well, I'm not. There's so much about sex that is learned and it's that Somerset Maugham line that always springs to my mind. "My own belief is that there is hardly anyone whose sexual life, if it were broadcast, would not fill the world at large with surprise and horror." And I didn't want her recoiling in horror. But I didn't want her thinking I was a boring, in-a-rut old man either.

We all think we aren't in a sexual rut. We're wrong — everyone is after a while. Try this out on your parents, and if you have kids, on yourself too. The human gestation period isn't nine months. It's forty weeks. Most birthdays coincide with a significant date forty weeks previously. Now most people hate the thought of their parents having sex and if they do have to think about it, they imagine in the dark, missionary position, slow-mo but over quickly stuff. Certainly not anything that would involve anything raunchy or in any way sexy. And looking at the forty-week rule you would be heartened. Trace your birthday back forty weeks. Mine is, give a day or two, forty weeks after Dad's birthday. My elder brother and younger sister share the same birthday. And would you believe it? Forty weeks after Christmas. Lottie came into the world forty weeks after their anniversary and Jonnie, well, Jonnie makes no sense at all to us. Maybe he was a one-off or maybe some date at the end of March had a special significance. But it's a difficult subject to bring up with your parents. My point is this: it meant that they weren't hit or miss every night in the sexual shenanigans department. I find that rather reassuring.

Oh, and just as a point of interest, the 'give or take a few days' has a relevance. Conception takes its own sweet time. It can take up to forty-eight hours for the lucky sperm to hit the jackpot. Rather sobering to think that the act of love may have been on a special day for your loving parents, but you may have actually been conceived in the bakery at the supermarket or on the bus or even while your mum was having tea with her friends a couple of days later.

We don't apply this filter to our own sex life, but still, I know my kids and most others feel the same way about me as I do about my folks. It's the one constant of sex across the generations. I'm not in a rut but everyone else is. Except you're wrong by one.

On the flip side of that, I remember a stupid incident when we kids were all grown up. Sitting in my parent's kitchen was me, Lottie, my younger sister Caroline and Mum. I can't remember why we were all there, but it was at the time that Hugh Grant had just been caught with Divine Brown. I just checked — the summer of 1995. The full gory details were all over the press and it was the lead story even on BBC Radio four. Mum seemed to be treating it like a car-crash — repulsed yet at the same time compelled to watch. As the news report of the oro-genital exposé ended, she looked over and said, "What kind of a man would want a woman to do that?" None of the three of us wanted to field that question.

Lottie leaned into me and whispered, "Poor Daddy!" I laughed and Mum just ignored us and carried on blithely. At the same time, while I was disappointed by proxy that this seemed to confirm that Dad had never enjoyed such ministrations, it was strangely gratifying to know Mum was not some demon sword swallower.

We get so much from our parents, except for sex. They tell us nothing and we don't like to think about parental sex. Our sex life doesn't mimic our growth in understanding or openness about what we like or don't. It doesn't grow that much from experience. Admittedly we learn a bit along the way, and we pick up a few tips and few kinks, but the horrible truth is that to a huge extent, sex follows porn.

Philip Roth's Portnoy was obsessed with blowjobs. They were an essential naughty extra in porn in the seventies. Now they are seen as a basic building block of a normal, sexual relationship. In my youth, all we ever saw were porn mags and the girls were seriously hairy. Then they started grooming and even depilating and now, what's unusual is an untrimmed pubis on a woman. Even the boys are at it. I will add that in this respect, most women in my straw poll were not fans of men shaving down. The last turkey in the shop may look grander for the trimming but doesn't seem to score aesthetically with the dames. Factor in maintenance and if stubble comes into play, well, let's just say, I overheard one saying, "Yuk, it's like being fucked by a badger brush." During the eighties and nineties, anal sex was the big thing. Now it's maybe still taboo, but it's not shock and horror stuff. I'm now a low-interest porn consumer, but I think group sex and other distractions seem to be the order of the day. Not my thing, well, apart from the odd WWM threesome, but generally, I am a child of my time, shall we say.

So, "What do you like sexually?" How to answer that. I tried to be coy. "I like everything, I like sexy, I like losing myself in the moment and I like to know we're both liking it."

She wasn't having it. She made a facial gesture that was somewhere between 'You scaredy-cat, cop-out wanker' and 'Oh God, are you really that dull?'

Finally, I gathered my wits enough to navigate a course that meant I would not repulse her but would not miss an opportunity either. She smiled coyly as I told her and said, "I bet that's not even the half of it. I will see what I can do."

Chapter 7
Truth and Honesty

With the Brothers, Sex Education was not on the curriculum. Or rather anything and everything to do with sex were simply sinful. Just to make that lack of understanding worse — check out this little wrinkle that I bet few of you had to go through. The monks were bad enough with their "Even impure thoughts are a sin." They also had a resident priest. He performed the Masses and wandered around the grounds and then to help us spiritually, he offered face-to-face confession. Offered? Of course, it was just a nice way of saying 'obligatory'. Imagine you are a healthy, normal just-teen boy, i.e., in danger of a Repetitive Stress Injury to the wrist. Then you sit face to face with a middle-aged man. No confessional booth, no screen, just face-to-fucking-face. If you wanted absolution for any sin, you had to confess all fully and frankly. Now that is truly a test of faith. I tried to do the politicians' trick and hope he didn't see the big issue in among all the garbage, as I looked him straight in the eye and speed-spoke.

"Bless me, Father, for I have sinned. Since my last confession, I have been untruthful, I was disrespectful to my mother, I masturbated and I took the Lord's name

in vain, I was envious of my brother's new bike..."
(Actually, the full truth would have been, I have cranked one out about three times a day. Every day since my last confession. But if he didn't ask, I wasn't going to volunteer)

Now, in that list, they are all sins, some mortal, some venial. Honour thy father and thy mother is the fourth Commandment. It is a mortal sin and if I died without absolution, I would be damned to eternal hellfire. Nowhere in the Bible does it mention that adolescent boys should not 'crank one out'. Guess which one he homed in on? It's why I never truly confessed after that. When a priest has looked you in the eyes and asked you, "And what do you think about when you masturbate?" you don't go back for more.

I told the priest something lame like, "A girl's breasts," and he bought it. But not until I had been grilled on: Why did I like breasts? And did I look at breasts? And had I seen my sister's? And did I understand that it was disrespectful of women to think about their breasts before you were married? And that I should think of all girls as like my sister, or my best friend's sister. Then he let it drop. This was difficult advice to take though, because I often thought about my best friend's sister's breasts! But heh! He was a professional and maybe this was the loophole in the rules I was looking for? What I did know for certain was that I hadn't told him the truth, and if God did know exactly what was going through my mind at the time he would have blushed. No, I'm not going to tell you! So, I was left in a permanent state of sin. He hadn't definitively stated it was mortal. I hoped for venial, as then I would only be bound for a long stint in purgatory for my wanking.

By the way, it's a really good way to make just about anyone feel immensely uncomfortable. Try it at your next dinner party. "Jeff, that's really interesting about your re-mortgaging mezzanine finance. Can I ask you: what do you think about when you're masturbating?" And FYI, if your partner asks you the same question, the answer is "You!" They won't believe you, but any other answer is going to lead you into a world of pain. And for God's sake, absolutely never tell them the truth.

That was the limit of sex education at school, professionally delivered anyway. There was schoolyard stuff but that was either not-credible or scary or homophobic. In the classrooms, we had two lines of moral mentoring. One was the recurring motto: Virtutem Petamus. The Latin scholars have a bit of trouble with it. You could argue that it means 'seek virtue' or that 'virtue makes us'. The really clever ones would tell you that idiomatically it means 'Be a man'. A man, that is, as defined by a bunch of psychotic men in black cassocks.

As far as women were concerned, this meant being passionately mentally and physically celibate and vigorously anti-abortion. Yep, that's right, the whole student body from eleven to eighteen was taken to rallies, carrying banners that these days you only see carried by nutters at anti-abortion rallies. I distinctly remember thinking that if they were right that life began when a sperm fertilized an egg, then I guess I was okay. But then sometime later than my first masturbatory confession, we actually covered the sin of Onan in RE. It isn't necessarily the wanking; it was that he orgasmed and "Spilled his seed on barren ground." Incidentally, all you Catholics who try the withdrawal method: yes, it is a sin like Onan's. And while we're on it, here's a good Catholic joke: What do you call a woman practicing the rhythm method? Pregnant! Not very funny, just true. My point? Being celibate and not even thinking about sex was what we should be aiming for. Anything else was a sin. No wonder I turned out I did.

The second strand of sex education came from our Latin Classes. We had to study Pliny and Caecilius and Catullus. (No, not the big black bloke from *Pulp Fiction*. That's Marcellus). Catullus was a tortured adolescent around the time of Julius Caesar. He was always moaning about his lover Lesbia. The name was enough to get us interested. Looking back, Catullus was a sort of Roman Morrisey. Among his poetry, there were dirty bits. The best, i.e., the dirtiest bits, were censored and not in our books, I later learned, but there was enough to get us sex-starved adolescents interested.

We had:

> Cum suis vivat valeatque moechis,
> quos simul complexa tenet trecentos,
> nullum amans vere,
> sed identidem omnium ilia rumpens.

Each boy could attempt a line and you put your hand up
and were called upon for a translation:

> Let her live, and good luck to her,
> as she holds three thousand lovers
> to her breast, loving none truly,
> but again and again
> bursting their balls.

Hands shot up for 'sed identidem omnium ilia
rumpens.' On that one, the Latin master jumped in and
insisted that the last line was "But again and again
breaking their hearts."

Ha! We all had English-Latin Dictionaries. "But
Brother, in the dictionary…"

"Be quiet, boy!"

His most famous poem is "Odi et Amo." It's one I
had to learn off by heart. I can't remember my sibling's
birthdays, but I still remember "Odi et Amo." Weird
huh? I wasn't to learn its lesson until much later though.

> "Sed mulier cupido quod dicit amanti, in vento et
> rapida scribere oportet aqua.

"But what a woman says to her passionate lover, ought to be written on the wind and swift-flowing water."

Maybe those monks were onto something after all? I learned to hate Latin and certainly hated the truth of Catullus, far too late. They all write it on wind and water. Men do, too. I knew it, but you keep thinking no, this time it's real. But it isn't.

Chapter 8
In the Clearing Stands a Boxer

I suspect, in a vain attempt to get out minds off sex, we had hours of Gym and sports and also we had to box. Nowadays this would seem brutal. It wasn't. It was brilliant. All that pent-up, repressed adolescent anger and sexual frustration. It was the best outlet I could imagine. Well, second best, but the best outlet came at a cost to a Catholic conscience. For many people, it is repulsive. For them, by watching boxing closely, and seriously, they risk moments of almost animal panic— a sense not only that something very ugly is happening but that, by watching it, they're an accomplice to a vicious beating. Not me, it's like ballet, it's like the knights of old. Joyce Carol Oats hit the nail on the head. "Boxing is a celebration of the lost art of masculinity all the more trenchant for being lost." Another myth is that it hurts. It does, but only the day afterward. In the ring, the old trainer's adage is true: you only feel the first six punches. Again, a bit like heartbreak, really. You are insensate at first, numb, disbelieving. Then it comes down on you like a ton of bricks. More of that later.

My only issue with boxing is that I really wanted to be good at it. Unfortunately, heart and courage are not nearly enough. You need coordination, a way to control anger and most importantly, the ability to avoid being hit. This is what most people don't understand. Hitting comes second to avoiding being hit. Are you seeing a pattern between my love life and the noble art? I did, but only much later. I had heart and I loved it. Yet my limited career was defined by my head rocking back as another jab got through, more than standing nobly over a fallen adversary.

I have a clear memory of my first competitive bout. I was only thirteen and scrawny, but then so was everyone. I was tall and long-armed. My cornerman and trainer was also a monk and he gave me very clear, comprehensive instructions. "Jab and move. Be first!" That was it. The bell rang and out into the middle, I moved. Overconfident and foolish, I walked directly toward the other kid and threw my left arm out and hit nothing but air. I didn't see it, only felt his right hand hit me in the chops. I hadn't been expecting that. So, I started again. Same result. This continued for ninety seconds. We were only thirteen, and ninety seconds was easily long enough for a round. If you don't believe me, set an egg timer and start punching something. By sixty seconds you will feel like your arms are falling off, by ninety, you will just be weeping. For me, at that time ninety seconds seemed like ninety minutes and after the first sixty, my jab was so lazy, I think my granny could have walked around it. The kid opposite me clearly could, so I did the only noble thing. I took one on the chin and held on for dear life. That ate up another ten seconds. I moved around for another ten and then he moved in and spent the final ten seconds punching me more. The plangent sound of a bell will never sound so good. I went to my corner and it dawned on me that my cornerman was a true optimist. "He's tiring!" Was that my only hope? That he would just get tired of hitting me? Rather than boring you with the details, he didn't. They don't.

Regardless of my failings, boxing teaches you to be physically confident. Even when you've taken a pasting, you feel better for having gone down swinging than tamely walking away. It also takes away a lot of the need to swagger and strut. Real confidence comes out via osmosis, not gesturing. Go to a live boxing event. A more friendly crowd you will not find. Totally the opposite of football. What you also see is that anyone who has boxed (look for scar tissue around the eyes and busted noses) would still rather be in there than watching. They move with the fighters like bad passengers in a car who brake and steer and look around even though they are in the passenger seat. For me, the ring mirrors our romantic life. Falling in love is exhilarating like getting into the ring — the bell rings and you are totally in the moment. The problem is when you're not evenly matched. Then the blows just keep on raining in until you fall down and can't get up again.

Falling out of love is more painful than any beating you
will ever take. And yes, I know, I am not a well-adjusted
man.

Chapter 9
Sisters are doing it for themselves

The religion, the discipline, and the uniform were far from the worst of it. My sister Lottie is two years older than me. She is the only woman who totally gets me. She is empathic and kind and generous. We are about as close as two people can be, in a platonic, non-hierarchical, loving relationship. So, it may come as a surprise to hear that when I hit my teens, my sister was a total cunt.

Why? Well, I will tell you. Running the gauntlet of Lottie was far worse than running the gauntlet of yobs or the gauntlet of religious zealots with psycho-sexual issues. It was something that would make or break a man. What did it do to me? You decide.

My sister went to the local comprehensive and she learned the life skills necessary to survive. This involved not learning about the Bible or much else besides how to act tough, be sexually aware and to keep her friends close. With no big school bus and train journey, she would be home well before me and would sit in the kitchen with her friends (Yes, Rita, I remember you more than any of the others). I would be around thirteen, they were around fifteen/sixteen.

Consequently, they were like goddesses that fuelled my burgeoning sexual fantasies. They were also older, worldly-wiser and seemed so much more confident. Each school day I would have to walk past them to get into the house. Every day it was a fresh way to make me go bright-red. I can't blame them. I was dressed up like a pouf' and the uniform and the 'special' nature of the school just painted a huge cross-hairs on me. Then factor in that we carried books and stuff not in a rucksack or a sports bag but a briefcase! The uniform specifier at that school was a sadist and a sadist who specialised in really painful details.

As I walked around the side of the house, they would spot me from the kitchen window. Cue huge amounts of witchy cackling. I would already feel my gut drop and the fear would start. As I walked in, they would then ask me nicely, "How was your day, Rob?" or "Would you like to join us for a cup of tea?" Did they, bollocks! The feeding frenzy started as soon as I was through the door "Oi! Prof! Do you know what a clitoris is?" "Look he's blushing!" "Want to see my clitoris?" and as I waded on past, it would continue. A regular favourite was, "Bahahaha. He's off for a wank, aren't you?"

Ironically, that would have been a fair bet. I may have been traumatized by three or four teenage girls, but I was still a boiling sea of testosterone, too. I was never sure if they knew that, despite all the cruelty, they did indeed feature heavily in my, shall we say, more introspective private moments. In my imagining, I was never nasty back or did anything painful or weird to them. No, the fantasy was that they were just nice to me. Well, nice and gave me blowjobs or hand jobs or got naked. At that stage of my wanking career, the thought of fucking one of them was a performance-anxiety-inducing, thought that was either too scary or meant it was game over really fast.

Once or twice, I tried to fight back. When cornered and asked if I'd ever felt a pair of tits, I said "No."

This time Rita wouldn't let it go and moved her hands over her body and said, "C'mon. Do you wanna see mine? Show us your cock and I will show you mine."

Now what I should have done was either laugh it off, or pull out my pubescent dick, or just keep on walking. But just as in the shopping centre, big mouth struck again. She kept on going, "Show us your cock and I will show you mine."

I replied, "I didn't know you had a cock, Rita!" I thought the girls would cackle and laugh at my clever repartee. But the silence was deafening. They all just looked at me like I was a monster.

Then it was a tirade of "You wanker!" "You… How could you be so fucking rude?" "Fuck off and go play with yourself!" et cetera, et cetera. So, I went to the bathroom, checked the door was safely locked and did just that. I kept Rita from my mind's eye. The thought of her with a cock would not have a place in my masturbatory thought palace, or it might make me think I was gay. I guess that was the day I discovered I was very heterosexual. Or so far in the very back of the closet that there was no way of it ever getting out.

All to say, I hit adolescence with some seriously mixed-up shit about girls and sex. That is not in the least unusual, I know. The life lesson, I suppose, is that girls can give it, but they rarely take it. And they really don't like being accused of having a penis. Not worth the price I paid to get it. But that is solid gold advice that you would be a fool to ignore.

Chapter 10
You can check in any time you like

It's really hard to not stay in a hotel. By that I mean, when you book a hotel, you have to check in, and do you need any help with your bags? Then there's a turn-down service and then do you want breakfast and when will you be checking out? All of this seems simple and perfunctory when you are travelling on business. When you are planning a tryst with your new lover, it's all a bit daunting. You really want to say, "I won't be staying the night but will meet my new lover here in the morning and we want a late check-out to maximise the erotic potential and then after we have finished that we will leave." Is it my age, or the social conventions or do 'respectable hotels' have a policy that precludes this? I don't know. And I wasn't going to find out. I booked a local hotel by phone, (Four-star, you don't want a grubby flophouse for a super-sexy tryst, but five-star seems a bit over the top). I said I would arrive in the afternoon. I then did so, and that's when the first hurdle I hadn't seen coming, came. "…and your address, sir?" Why would anyone book into a hotel in their hometown for a night unless it was for illicit sex? Trying to be cool, I gave them my home address and the lady didn't bat an eye. Why? Because there are thousands of reasons someone might book a hotel in their hometown. People staying with you and not enough beds, a romantic night with your partner, a big row at home and you just need space. None of these occurred to my guilty conscience. Anyway, I checked in and then went up to the room. Anyone looking for tips here, this is actually not a waste of time. A good recce saves a heap of trouble later. In my bag that I had smuggled out of the house was a bottle of champagne — non-vintage — and two flutes. The recce is essential as it takes about twenty minutes to figure out how to get a standard-sized champagne bottle into a standard-sized minibar. It's a feat of engineering I can tell you. Water by the bed, wash bag in the bathroom — assuming you are going to shower before you go home, and you want to smell the same as when you left, and you certainly don't want to smell of perfume and sex. Unless you want a flaming row.

Then leave, after ensuring you have a late check-out. With standard check out being eleven am and her only arriving at nine-thirty, that would be cutting things fine, well, for round two anyway. Added to that if I'm honest, which we know is rare, I'm thrifty. Not mean, thrifty. I grew up with no money for a long time. I can be, in fact, I am, generous. But wasting money is anathema to me. Mum would be proud of that bit. About the rest of my hotel economy, not so much. (And while we are at it, the monks would be pleased about the excellent use of the word anathema.) Back to thrift.

£200 quid for ninety minutes? Actually, it would be absolutely worth it. So, three hours for the same amount was just double-bubble.

I went home and did some work, some pottering about and generally tried to relax. Not easy when you're fifteen hours away from a tryst and if you are honest, you're not sure she was even going to turn up. Every scenario from alien abduction to walking into a friend in the hotel reception plays on your mind. Well, on mine. Cut to me the next morning, freshly washed and shaved, special attention paid to the membrum virile — washing, not shaving, that is. I got there at eight-thirty and sat on the bed. That lasted for about three minutes until I paced the room for a few more. Checking champagne temperature used up another twenty seconds and it was then I wrote a mental note to self: getting to 'tryst hotels' early is not a great idea. I tried reading a book and the local paper and frankly, I was on edge. After forty-five minutes that seemed to take a couple of days, I presented myself in the lobby. Feeling a bit James Bond, I positioned myself in a chair that overlooked the door and had a newspaper ready to hide my face if I saw anyone I knew. I waited. And waited. And then waited a bit more. Should I call? I could use my mobile, the number would be logged. Going out to find a phone box could mean I would miss her. Do they still have House Phones in hotels any more? Then, if himself checked that number he'd see it was a hotel. It's hard to be cool when you're sat in a hotel lobby and checking the entrance every ten seconds. A waiter came over and asked me if I'd like a coffee. Flustered, I said yes and with the luck that has followed me everywhere, just as he brought it over, in she walked. Scalding coffee swallowed in one go — why didn't I just leave it? I went to find her. I went to kiss her. This time, she dodged my full-on the mouth attempt and offered up a cheek. By way of explanation, she looked carefully around the room.

"I came by bus, and I ran into Julian. He asked what I was up to. I bet I blushed. There was part of me that really wanted to say 'I'm off to fuck Pat Delaney. Just so I could see his face.'

Blimey! Well, one of my fears was already dealt with. She was coming here with a clear goal in mind. I looked her up and down and she said, "Anyway, I will show you later what may have caused the blushing."

Key card in hand, I led her to the lift. As she looked around and took in the airport art and floral arrangements,

"This is all right, isn't it?" not in any impressed way. She'd stayed in the best hotels in the world. No, it was clear she meant, "This is all right, well done, you have chosen well. Not shabby and not flashy."

Frankly, I was too busy looking at her, in her big full-length grey woollen overcoat that was tight to the body and flared out to the ankle. As she walked, I could see the coat flare open and suede boots were on display. She also had a big bag with her. I wasn't sure if this was for hotel purposes or maybe she had to go shopping later. Either way, she looked fine. Not fine as in "fine" but fine as in fine dining or fine wine. As soon as the lift doors shut, I kissed her. FFS, she was twenty minutes late. The lift doors opened far too soon, but the room was only ten paces away. I opened it up and she walked in.

I moved to kiss her again, but got a hand to the chest and was told, "Help me off with these boots." I wasn't going to object. It's perhaps not very sexy — except it was. It did cross my mind as why the boots before the coat, but I let it go. I faced away, pulled her left leg through mine and pulled. Then the right. Then as I was turning, I saw her reach for her bag and pull out a pair of very shiny Louboutin (red soles, always a giveaway) stiletto-heeled shoes. Standing up, she put them on.

"This is half the reason I flushed on the tram. I wasn't sure that Julian could see…"

As I started to answer, "I'm lost, what are you…" she unbuttoned the coat. And halleh-fucking-lujah, it was a schoolboy dream come true. The matching bra and panties were skimpy but not whorehouse, the hold-up stockings were silk, and they went all the way down to the stiletto heels.

My mate Webster often used the expression, "It was like standing on a rake" (keep up, like in the cartoons, when someone stands on a rake and the pole springs up in a flash). I can confirm this doesn't just happen in cartoons.

"Well, you said it's what you liked…"

Mute, erect and massively aroused, I did the only thing possible. I kissed her and held her, then pulled back and looked her up and down. Step and repeat, two or three times. She started unbuttoning my shirt and I felt her cold hand on my torso. But I didn't care, it could have been iced, I was feeling everything and at the same time and not feeling a thing. It was a sensory overload. She smelled great, she looked great, she had a great figure and she was in *GQ* quality lingerie This was dreamland. Now I won't say I ruined the moment. But this never happens to James Bond. I proceeded to break the moment by scrambling about trying to take my shoes off while still in the clinch and tripping up over my trousers. Then hopping around like a baboon. And a baboon in a high state of arousal is not a pretty sight.

If you're now expecting the blow-by-blow, (well, actually there was a bit of that, and it was delightful) tough luck. We're not doing that again. But I will say that once I was disrobed and we moved to the bed, she made to push off the shoes.

"Oh no! you got that wrong. The shoes stay on!" I insisted. And they did. They must have been a good fit, because I dived on her like a pirate on plunder and did everything in my power to shake the Louboutins off.

Sometime later, we were sipping champagne and I can confirm that a woman you really fancy like mad, moving around a bedroom in the middle of the day wearing only hold-up stockings, and stilettos, holding a flute of champagne, is something that really should be on your bucket list. Even more so, when you've just spent time having sex. No, that's under-selling it. When you get to middle-age, you have tried most things, experienced some big highs and had your fair share of failures. This wasn't sex. This was worth missing the football for, worth missing your brother's wedding for sex. And unless she was RADA trained, she had found it pretty rocking too. And if you wonder why I mention it, it's yes, a bit to show off, but also because I was starting to realise that I/we had another gear. Then I thought it was just a physical compatibility thing. Looking back, I was already falling out of lust and falling into something much, much more dangerous.

We sat up and talked for a bit. And a bit more of her story became clear

"Do you remember when we first met? Before Pete's..." she asked. Thankfully, I did, and I told her about that drinks party and the blue and burned gold dress and how we had talked about nothing in particular... I was just yammering on.

"I really fancied you then. I thought after so many corporate events and middle-aged guys, that I had no expectations. Then I saw you and thought, 'Hello. He will do'. Tall, slim, broad shoulders, funny, full of himself, but not too much... It's a bit Freudian, but you reminded me a bit of my dad"

"Fuck, if only I'd realised, we could have been here six months ago." Wrong answer.

"You really are very full of yourself, aren't you?" Desperate to make up the lost ground, I explained that I was so taken with her that I never imagined it could come to anything (lie), never thought about her like 'that' (even bigger lie) and just thought we really connected, and I liked her (complete truth).

"Being so not-posh, I've always been attracted to posh birds like you. Some people like ice-queens, some blokes like jolly, some like sporty. You know what I mean. I have this thing about posh. All that good breeding and good manners that translates into absolute dynamite in the 'heave and grunt' department."

She laughed, thank God! Even to the point of spilling a bit of champagne that I lasciviously licked off her. I was pushed off though and she continued.

"Well, I suppose that's a compliment. One big mistake. I'm not posh. Well, maybe half-posh."

Enough of the she-said-I said. It's annoying me, so you must be way beyond that.

She told me about her life history. Her dad was an East-End-of-London boy made good. Not the 'Cor-blimey, guvnor' type, but a grammar schoolboy with a few rough edges. He was very smart but didn't go to university and had a chip on his shoulder about it. Her mum was posh. Rich parents, public schools (that's private school to all you foreigners) and even a Swiss finishing school. Neither family approved of the match and even though it produced her and her little brother, it was not a happy union. Dad fucked about a lot and it was not a happy or a rich household. The grandparents (maternal) paid for the kids to go to posh schools. This sounded case-closed to me until I was enlightened.

"Being the poor kid at an expensive school is hard. During the term, it was okay, as we were all in the same boat. In the holidays though we couldn't afford to 'Come to Mauritius, it will be a hoot' or anything like that. And I would have died if friends had come to my parents' perfectly respectable, but humble country cottage. Then during the holidays, we didn't know any of the local kids and if we did, they thought we were stuck up and posh. Schooldays weren't easy."

I looked into her eyes and could see for the first time, what was behind that vulnerability. There was much more I'd discover along the way, but it was the first time I saw it. I knew not to make a joke. I knew not to bring it back to me. For the first time, I just held her out of real affection, not lust or passion. It felt great. The hug turned into a kiss and a kiss turned into more and just as I thought I'd played a blinder, she pulled her head off my growing cock and asked me again. "What else do you really like sexually?"

There were many things I could have said, and a few would have been true, but I was still unsure, so I simply pinned her to the bed and said, "Tell me what you like." A cop-out, I know. But I am glad I did.

Kitty pointed at the mirror on the wardrobe door. "I want to watch you fuck me in the mirror." I was game, so we choreographed it. Me lying on her as she looked in the mirror, but she slithered out and got the stool from the desk and bounced in my lap looking over my shoulder into the mirror. But that didn't fully work for her. So, we changed again. Standing, my hands on her hips, her hands on the mirror. Only one thing was wrong. I was pleased to be able to keep going for a good while as we changed positions. It's the changing positions as much as the positions themselves that is sexy. No? All right, please yourself. Then I got the feeling that I wasn't going to come. That started a downward spiral in my head. *But god bless you, Kitty. Were you a mind reader or could you feel my cock deflating or were you just as sexy as I dreamed?*

She reached a hand back to her beautiful rump. Arched it slightly in the air, gently pulled her butt apart and said, "Now fuck me really hard and don't stop. I want to look you in the eyes as you come inside me." I could see her in the mirror, I could look down and see my cock sliding into her and that level of raunchy talk and our eyes locked in the looking glass, it kick-started my libido, remedied my concerns and I did exactly what she requested.

Soon after it was the same story: "I'm sorry I need to get moving. I have so much to do…"

I didn't mind. We kissed some more, and I explained I had to check out and if it would be embarrassing or risky if we were seen leaving together. She could go, and I would follow later. That was agreed and more kissing led to me being rebuffed. I mock-complained but really was pleased because I was seriously writing a cheque that couldn't be cashed. We agreed that she would call me from a phone box, and we would see each other soon.

Smug McSmugface (that was me) sat naked on the bed, poured the last of the champers and smiled to myself. *If it doesn't get better than this, then what do I care? Because this is fucking brilliant.*

I thought about the mirror. It was really exciting, but why? There was a sense of voyeurism. You get the angles you don't normally get — fantasy and reality are fused. "What do you like sexually?" Kitty wanted to be objectified. I would later see that it was also a weird self-love, intimately tied to self-stimulation, that for her is a lifelong romance. Maybe her only one. What wasn't in doubt was that it was really hot and that wouldn't be the last time we reflected. Later, I got to thinking. Dad, tall, smart but academically falling short, rough around the edges, but smoothed out, serial adulterer, full of himself. What could she see in me?

The delayed orgasm was a bit concerning though. But the urologist had got back to me. It was a few days later that he called me and said he had found some compelling research that suggested Tofranil had been seen to work wonders in similar cases to mine. So, with a spring in my step and a song in my heart, I went to the pharmacy and got myself some Tofranil. It was going to work wonders. The wonders, it turned out, were not of the sort I had imagined.

Chapter 11
This is the modern world

I hated the seminary school, the monks, the beatings, the religion. There was no way out. It was awful. But then one day out of the blue, I realised there was a God. Dad came home and announced we were leaving and moving to Norfolk, where he had been offered a new job. Simple as that. No discussion, no explanation, and no waiting until the end of the school year or any of that nonsense. I was ecstatic! Six weeks later and the monks were just a bad memory. Thank you, God.

After leaving the mad monks, I ended up in a 'normal' school. The Paston School, it sounds grand, but it wasn't. It was a grammar school in Norfolk. I still had to wear a uniform. This one, though, was really cool. A black blazer, a white shirt, a black tie, and black or grey trousers. We looked sharp, not ridiculous.

I was a clever lad, and I was a big lad. The school hard-nut felt the need to establish his credentials early on. After I had put up enough resistance to mean I was too much trouble, but not a threat, he left me alone and concentrated on lower-hanging fruit. What was really fabulous was the complete lack of monks. There was still a kind of Christian vibe. But it was just like the

Church of England, more about fitting in, singing a few hymns and harvest festival bullshit. Nonetheless, after so much Catholicism, especially with the black-cassocked lads of church's militant wing. I was quite a shy boy. There were two ways to escape. Music and girls.

I was fourteen in that summer. 1976, the summer of punk. It was also the summer we had to get some O-levels out of the way, and it was a scorcher. While Johnny Rotten was outraging parents and Virginia Wade was winning Wimbledon, I was sweating through Maths and English exams and discovering music. Every generation of teenagers takes music as their own and realises all their parents' music is shit. This was easy in my case, as my dad loved Country and Western and with few minor exceptions, it is actually shit.

The reason behind discovering music is apparently, that there is a connection between how the brain develops during adolescence and how young people hear music. Overrun by emotions and a prefrontal cortex demanding instant gratification, we seek advice from peers, not parents. I just know that music became incredibly emotionally charged, a way to fit in and stand out, and that has stayed with me ever since.

You had to have strong views. Pop was shit. That was a given. Then you could go the esoteric route. My mate Jezz insisted that Jazz-Rock was 'real' music and we had to listen to all manner of awful Chick Corea and Herbie Hancock albums around his house. This, of course, didn't prevent him and others from idolizing Pat Travers and/or Rory Gallagher (We all did). Pink Floyd was acceptable, even Tamla Motown at a push. The 10CC albums I'd arrived with had to be destroyed before anyone found out and I became a social pariah.

Looking back, I have a clear memory of The Jam talking to my soul. They were good, but what I really liked was the snarling attitude of Paul Weller, the only man I have ever seen who can look cool in a Burton's suit, chewing gum, smoking and singing at the same time while simultaneously educating me about The Modern World (and yes, if you want to get picky, Modern World wasn't released until '77. Like I said, the level of detail and esoterica we indulged in never leaves you).

Bands came and went into and out of fashion, but the music was the bedrock of so many discussions that weren't about sex or sport. This came to a head every Wednesday when the NME came out. In my peer group, the enabler was Smyth. His dad ran a news agents' so we could get it before anyone else. *The New Musical Express* was our Bible. There was also *Melody Maker* and *Sounds* as organs of the music business. Many will say they were very similar, but it was very *Life of Brian* at school.

Melody Maker was the JPF to the *NME's* PFJ.

"Are you the Judean People's Front?

"Fuck off!"

"What?"

"We're the People's Front of Judea!"

"Judean People's Front? Cunts."

The most important thing in the *NME*, way beyond their reviews of bands and albums, and way more important than the gig guide, was the crossword. Huddled around a desk at break, we would try and show off by solving clues or totally not getting a clue that showed the wrong sort of knowledge.

I distinctly remember a narrow escape when the clue was "Four across. "They gave us the sweetest girl. Three, seven." After some pondering, I shouted out "The Archies! Sugar Sugar. Gotta be." Let's be clear, the Archies were not cool in any way. Before the ridicule could start, I ad-libbed, "My little sister plays it all the time. It's shit. But it's right and will help us get us eight down." It was a narrow escape. I nearly became known as an Archies fan. That would have made me at least a pouf, and a pouf with no musical cred. The lowest of the low. Music was everything. Everything apart, of course, from girls.

As for girls, I was also far shyer than the lads who had just the normal deeply seated, teenage hang-ups about girls and sex. That wasn't really a problem at fourteen, you could just be shy and leave it to the more advanced boys. At fifteen you really had to show an interest or else you were, in those less politically correct days, in danger of being branded, yes, you've got it, 'a pouf'.

You have two choices, either learn early that girls of fifteen, are just like boys of fifteen. Well, actually, they're not at all like boys of fifteen, they are more like boys of eighteen. That's why they always wanted older boyfriends. But they were similar to boys of fifteen in that they were just as nervous, shy and desperate to impress their peers as us. Once you realized that, you knew you simply had to be normal, kind and just talk to them like you would talk to anyone else. Talk to them just as you would talk to a friend. At least how you would talk to a friend who wasn't obsessed with music, sport, wanking, Monty Python sketches, fart jokes, homosexuality and absurdly fantasist stories of sex. I have seen no research to confirm this, but I believe I can accurately put the figure at about 1% as the number of boys who went this route. They were also in the 1% who were branded as poufs.

So, along with the other 99%, I went for foolish bravado and 'peacocking'. This would be primarily noted by anthropologists at the bus stop. The boy's school and the girl's school were about one hundred yards apart. We were taught and fed separately, but we mostly bussed into school together. Small morning pods of peacocks at each stop, building to a full aviary by the time the bus got to the school. The reverse was true in the evenings when everyone congregated around the same stop and different buses took people away on different routes.

Just as peacocks flaunt themselves and their decorative plumage whenever a female peacock is around their immediate vicinity, we went for all manner of flashy behaviour whenever there were girls in the area. We firmly believed it was the way to increase our chances of attracting a mate. We couldn't flaunt our looks by dressing up in a trendy way, because we had a school uniform. Showing off gym-sculpted muscles was about twenty years in the future and if you were that forward-thinking it would immediately have branded you as a pouf.

Showing off wealth was an option, but no one had a car and it's difficult to look rich in a school uniform at a bus stop. So that really only left the option of dominating the conversation with wit or just talking bollocks. The latter was far more prevalent than the former. To make matters worse, the level of peacocking is directly proportional to observing a female's level of attractiveness. The key was to hold the two in balance. Showing off and being sensitive enough for girls, but not being in any way a pouf. This could be difficult as any sign of sensitivity was de facto — gay. This covered everything from wearing a colourful shirt — "Did the guy in the shop suck your dick when you bought it?" To not liking the right music — "Bony M is exclusively for poufs." To liking salad — "Do you love that cucumber up your arse? To liking pets — "Do you get the dog to lick your cock with 'Good Boy' chocs?" It was relentless. I would feel sorry for the 8% of boys whom statistics worldwide will confirm were gay. Well, I would be, if they hadn't joined in just as vigorously. There again on reflection, they had to, or those poufs would have been correctly identified, albeit for the wrong reasons — as well, poufs.

While it may sound superficial to show off whenever a girl is around, it works — not well, but it offers a level of success for men. And that is one reason why this behaviour is deep-rooted in the system. Yes, I really am saying girls — it's your fault! If all showing-off was ignored, then we'd stop doing it.

There was another vital component to this that I only understood much later in life. If you think of it as a sexual marketplace, then nature has biologically built-in a disadvantage for men. We, especially when we are younger, have a huge desire for sex. If you are heterosexual, that makes you dependent on women. Just like when two parties are negotiating a possible sale or deal, the one who is more eager to make the deal is in a weaker position than the one who is willing to walk away without the deal. Women certainly desire sex too — but as long as most women desire it less than most men, women have a collective advantage, and social roles and interactions will follow scripts that give women greater power than men. As a result, at least in the late seventies, girls sustained their advantage over us boys by putting pressure on each other to restrict the supply of sex available. As with any monopoly or cartel, restricting the supply leads to a higher price. Girls who put out too quickly carried around the slut tag, not just from boys but even more so from girls.

It's an old joke, but it illustrates male thinking of the time. What's the difference between a slut and a bitch? A slut is a girl who will have sex with just about anyone. A bitch is a slut who won't have sex with you!

Chapter 12
Yes, sir, I can boogie

Then next step in the ritual involved discos. There were youth club discos and village hall discos and the daddy of them all — school discos. They always followed the same pattern. Shit music of the moment, boys in pods at the edges and girls dancing in groups. Then the more adventurous boys would ask a girl to dance. This was dangerous territory. You might get knocked back and make the humiliating walk back to your pod to be jeered at. You might be accepted and then you had to dance. Being too good at dancing was a clear sign you were a pouf, but being a rubbish dancer could lead to the girl not being impressed by this particular peacock. Things warmed up as the evening drew to a close and the DJ started the slow songs. Then the boys were like a pack of starving wolves. You grabbed a girl and all you had to do was hold on and gyrate. Hopefully, the overpowering scent of Brut would have her swooning and really you didn't have to say much. "I really like your hair/dress/shoes/" was a bit gay, yet acceptable. "How did you get here?" showed interest beyond her looks and was tactically astute, as you would find out if her dad had dropped her off, he was also probably going to be picking her up. If you were feeling that the vibe wasn't quite right, and she wasn't into you, then the only reasonable thing to say was "I really fancy your mate…" and let her tell you either had no chance or that she would pass on the message.

We were so stupid and believed whatever our mates told us. Doug, who was clearly a man of the world, because he needed to shave at twelve, reliably informed us that when slow dancing it was vitally important to ensure that you not only had an erection but pressed it hard into a girl's thigh, lest she "Thinks you're a pouf.". For me, at least, this added an extra level of pressure as slow dancing didn't always have the desired effect on my cock.

Either way, if things went off well with the slow dance, the next step was to suggest, "Maybe we could go outside for a bit?" We thought this was a cunning plan that girls were naïvely unaware of our true intent. God, we were the naïve ones. If she was agreeable, this led to standing outside the disco and you could go straight for the snog, or talk for a bit, then go for the snog. The talking for a bit was far more man-of-the-worldish, although this ran the risk of her actually wanting to talk and then leaning in mid-sentence to kiss her was awkward and the tension just mounted as each minute of potential snogging time went past. The nightmare scenario was when she said something like, "Nice talking to you but need to go back in now." If you avoided that, then the snogging could commence.

Generally, it was feverish rather than tender or passionate. Again, subtlety was for poufs. What was generally considered the best approach was to try and get your tongue into her lung. If she didn't find this revolting (bless you, girls, you deserved so much better), then the feeling-up could start. There was a strict code of bragging rights as to how advanced you got. At the time we never realized girls had cracked the code millennia before.

Our value system was not the American four bases. We had upstairs outside: feeling breasts through clothes; downstairs outside: intimate touching through cloth. Then upstairs inside: touching breasts in the flesh. Then the big winner, downstairs inside. No joke, this was the Holy Grail. We never thought that a girl would reciprocate at this early stage. You needed to get them into a state of total arousal by pawing them and fingering them up against a wall outside a disco. Ah! The romance of it all. Then the disco would wind down to a scene of all lights on and people shuffling off home. If it had gone well, you could — in fact, part of the social contract was, that you had to — ask the girl out. No one had mobile phones then so plans had to be made. Cinema was the best bet, although you would spend all week wondering if you had to pay for both tickets. The other option was a truly shitty hamburger. Real burgers hadn't been invented yet, but the rubberized Wimpey Burger started many a torrid affair After either date, upstairs inside was a reasonable expectation. Less than that and she was a "bit of a prick tease." The much-vaunted hand-job was a pipe dream, but we could dream. She might give you a bit of reciprocal downstairs outside. Downstairs inside was only for couples. As a couple after a few weeks, you could realistically expect to be tossed off. Oral and vaginal sex was beyond realistic expectations at fifteen.

If all went well at the cinema/Wimpy Bar, you could be accorded the status of going out. Then as long as you played your cards right, you would enjoy a lot of snogging and abortive attempts at the four stages, and freedom from the tyranny of not having a girlfriend.

Having a girlfriend who got the same bus was a balancing act. Spending all your time with her increased chance of carnal knowledge but it was a high price to pay, as it would inevitably lead to you being branded a, you've guessed it, a pouf. I had a few girlfriends and the truth is I was happy kissing and pawing and also quite relieved when they restricted the pawing and made it clear there would be no sex. Why? Because if they didn't, I would actually have to do it! I really wanted to do it but was scared I might actually have to. Fifteen was the emotional cliff edge. The water looked so inviting, I wanted to jump, but it seemed a hell of a long way down and if I belly-flopped — it would really hurt.

That was life at fifteen to sixteen. The next hurdle was the Age of Consent. In the UK it was sixteen and to remain a virgin for much beyond being sixteen meant you were a… FFS, you get it by now or you never will.

As we grew older but no wiser, this was accelerated by parties. These were informal social gatherings held when people's parents were away. This meant the snogging, fondling and other nefarious deeds could be consummated indoors, or at least in a garden.

Before I tell you my next step, Sophie, wherever you are, please accept my heartfelt and really sincere apologies. I cringe and so wish I could make it right. We met, Sophie and me, at such a party. She was a bit timid and shy, which worked for me. The confident, worldly-wise girls were intimidating. They knew more about 'it' than me, so the chance of humiliating myself was high. With these girls, unless they made the running, I was out of the running. Sophie was also the friend of Sally Fox, a goddess who had 'done it' with apparently more than one bloke and one of her boyfriends was like nineteen and had a car! Nonetheless, she had a shy timid friend and I followed the pattern above and we ended in the garden. I pushed her against a tree, and after feverish kissing and much feeling up and 'downstairs inside' accomplished, she had her hand on my cock. I took things a step further and unzipped my pants and pulled out my cock. A hand-job might be on the cards here. She grabbed hold of it and inexpertly started tugging. Before this led to its hasty and natural conclusion, I upped the stakes. Being the classy dude, I was at sixteen and a couple of months (still in heterosexual territory, but the clock was ticking), I pulled out a condom, she saw it and she nodded and whispered "Okay". Fuck,

fuck, fuck! This is really going to happen. Seven years before Morrissey penned it.

> "I thought oh God, my chance has come at last
> but then a strange fear gripped me and I
> Just couldn't ask."

Unfurling the condom onto my cock was already having a small but significant flaccor-inducing effect. She remedied this with her hand returning to my hard-on which returned to its duty. The whole situation was compounded by my inexperience (read: total lack of experience) and my ignorance of the simple fact that sex face-to-face, standing up, against a tree, is for the advanced class only. So, with trousers around ankles and her legs around my waist, I attempted to break my duck. But it wouldn't go in. It's hard to see now how the romance and passion of the situation hadn't elevated her to the throes of sexual need and had her wetter than a fish's wet bits. But it hadn't. Added to that, I had no idea, A. Where I was pushing, and B. What to do now? The excitement of the moment, her rummaging to line me up, the insistent physical pressure and the libido of a sixteen-year-old and… and, yes, I came in the condom and it was all over. I look back now and cringe. I'm so sorry, Sophie. I pretended that I hadn't self-destructed and told her she was "Just too tight and not ready" and pulled off the condom and got us both dressed and walked back into the party. She wanted to kiss, but —

oh God, please forgive me — after a perfunctory little kiss, I said, "I'll catch you later, I need to see my mates." She looked upset and went in the other direction. I saw her looking over at me and talking to Sally Fox. Humiliation was just around the corner. I was sweating like a gypsy with a mortgage.

Bless you, Sophie. Either you were so totally confused you didn't know what to think, or, more likely you were a lovely, generous, forgiving sixteen-year-old girl, who thought she was about to lose her virginity too, and didn't. Maybe you were glad, maybe you were disappointed, I will never know. I never spoke to you again. I was too embarrassed. Yes, say it. Say it because it is true. I was a complete and utter cunt.

Chapter 13
Uh, Jesus, ha, I've never had this problem before

Kitty and I had been meeting whenever we could. Coffee, shopping and cheap hotels, and occasionally at her house, if the coast was absolutely clear, i.e., Gordon was out of the country and the kids would definitely not be coming home unexpectedly. The news from the MRI was that there was nothing to be seen. I suppose I was happy but as the headaches still seemed to be getting worse, I went back to the doctor and he talked me through why we should try a raft of blood tests. He scheduled that and I awaited the results.

I also excitedly started taking the Tofranil. Soon I'd be coming at will like a seventeen-year-old, but with the control of a middle-aged man. Nirvana. Even after a couple of hours, it had a profound effect. I was woozy and, head spinning, I took the next dose and it was almost trippy. The third dose was in the morning. I was feeling really weird but stuck with it as the upside was so promising. Kitty said she was free for a quick walk by the river and I found an excuse to be out. We met, she looked smashing in her walking gear, Lycra leggings and a Lycra top with a top layer that was loose so it didn't look slutty. Full of Tofranil and high hopes, we found a secluded spot and started kissing. One thing led to another and it was then I realized, one thing was not leading to another. My cock was not responding at all! She was so beautiful and sexy and as she reached into my pants, I could see the mild surprise on her face too. But ever the people-pleaser she pulled my cock out and started sucking gently. Still nothing! I panicked. Pulled her up and before I could speak, she said, "It's okay. Don't! Don't go into your own head. It's fine, it's not you…" I was deaf to all she said, yet the kindness and the empathy without ever being patronizing or anything but just wonderful made me love her all the more. She handled it brilliantly. I didn't. For me, this was it — the end of life as we know it. We walked a bit and talked of anything but what had just happened. I just couldn't wait to get away and ring the doctor about this emergency.

Only a man who has suffered this can know the feeling. Brewer's droop through drink has happened to most couples I should think. Pill dick from ecstasy and coke is not rare. But stone-cold sober, with a beautiful sexy woman and nothing. Not even the semblance of a chubby! My dick was numb. So, I called the urologist in a panic. He told me to stop taking them immediately and that the half-life of the drug was eighteen hours so all should be well within thirty-six hours. I went home and waited. It's a funny thing, erections and reflexes. As he told me, things did get back to normal after thirty-six hours. I flew a solo mission to confirm all systems were working. But that day I went from having all manner of sexual hang-ups but always knowing that I would always get hard, to always have that nagging doubt that it might happen again.

As soon as possible, I fixed another rendezvous with Kitty. Without being told, she knew what it was all about. I went to her house and she was playing it cool. Sensibly not wanting to force the issue. I wasn't. I dragged her to a bed and thank god my cock responded. It was the best/worst fuck of the affair. I just needed confirmation that I wasn't broken. Totally selfishly, I just used her to prove it. No subtlety, no reciprocity, just fucked her purely for my own ends. Ironically, she rather got off on that. "Sometimes it's really sexy for me to feel just used by you, it's no stress and makes me feel wanton…" So, a win-win really. As a novelty yes. As a standard MO — dangerous, I'd say.

The longer-term effect, though, was that I'd lost confidence in my dick. If it didn't respond immediately, I would get worried and it became self-fulfilling. I'd lose my erection. What was the point of a lover who couldn't provide the most basic instrument of physical loving? There were a few could-go-either-way moments, but again she was wonderful about it.

Apart from once. She had been shopping and presented me with a bag of sweets. I looked confused. Then saw the name — they were soft candy snakes called Floppies. I flinched. She laughed and just said,

"Too soon?" Actually, she was always brilliant about it. And we had loads of excellent fully turgid sex. This, on top of my delayed orgasm. Life was just falling apart. The urologist asked me to come back in for more consultations. But he was another dick I'd lost confidence in.

Chapter 14
Workin' on our night moves

At sixteen, my chance at redemption, or at least my next chance of a sexual encounter, came at another party. Now petrified that I would jump the gun if ever I got the chance at a shootout, I set my sights on a girl called Jane. Not stunningly pretty, but nice enough and definitely in my league. We were talking and getting along like a house on fire. Jane had come to the party with her friend Mandy Corbett. La Corbett was gorgeous and way out of my league. Not just pretty, she had to our certain knowledge, older boyfriends. One even had a moustache! I can see now that my behaviour could have been seen as a cunning ploy, but it really wasn't. I talked exclusively to Jane and ignored her beautiful friend. The effect it had on La Corbett was amplified by the fact that I wasn't ignoring her for affect. I was ignoring her, because I never dreamed I had a chance. I know, I know you can see it coming and you're right. Ms Corbett was a good friend of Jane, but she was not having that. She joined our conversation and even though she laughed coyly at my jokes and 'Tits and Teethed' me, I was still oblivious of what was going on.

Quick sidebar: They teach beauty queens and ice skaters — well, the girls anyway — to shove out their chests and turn a little to the side, bring the head back and give a big beaming smile. It's supposedly a way to get men and lesbians on your side. AKA, 'Tits and Teeth.'

Even the hair flick and holding my gaze tactics went over my head. Little did I know I was playing an absolute blinder. When Jane went for another drink, she pounced on the idiot-child in front of her, and I was whisked off to a bedroom and within seconds we were kissing. I'm sorry, Jane, but what else was I to do? There was a stack of coats on the bed and soon we were crumpling and creasing them. I started chancing my arm and felt her tits. Large without being comedy, and warm to the touch when I got to upstairs inside. I thought that would be the limit of my exploration when her hand moved between us. *Here we go*, I thought. The arm of the groping law. But now that hand went onto my cock which was by now harder than quantum thermodynamics (A real urologist's ten. I could have punched holes in cheap doors with it!). Totally inexperienced in this kind of forward behaviour, I was slightly concerned about coming in the pants. Emboldened and as a distraction, I put a hand up her skirt. I had no idea then what I was doing, but the serious moisture I encountered seemed to coincide with the information gleaned at the bus stop that this signalled she was turned on, so my fingers found their way into a girl for the second time. Of course, now, we, or rather I, know to be gentle, but firm — to tease and to caress. Back then it seemed to be the received wisdom that vigorous finger-banging was the way to induce sexual ecstasy. Despite, rather than because of my clumsy efforts, I then felt my flies being undone. This was fantastic but the aforementioned scenario was now a real possibility. Done, I might add, without ever stopping the frenzied kissing. God, the nostalgia of it. I think I'm getting a chubby as I sit here.

So, her hand on cock and my fingers in her, I tried to mentally picture my granny in a bikini and reached for a Jonny. We never called them condoms. This was going to be it. I was going to break my duck and fuck me, with a really beautiful girl. Story of my life: it wasn't to be. The bedroom doors were suddenly thrown open and in poured Jane and a friend, who "needed their coats." It was a clear espionage job. Well, you couldn't blame her.

Much laughing and bellowing followed from outside as we hastily reassembled our dishevelled clothing. My erection was blindingly obvious, and we had to wait a bit to re-join the party. At the same time, I was a little bit relieved, as I might have given her my virginity, but all the signs were that it would have been a very short-lived gift.

Once we were, 'shevelled', I thought we would just get back to the party. But God love her, Mandy, not me, suggested we take 'this' outside. Passing the first niches and spaces that were already filled with snoggers, we got a bit of privacy. It was freezing and with my experience with Sophie still fresh in my mind, I was happy to just kiss and grope. That, however, was not on Mandy's to-do list. She very quickly got my cock out and after a vigorous thirty seconds of tugging, I could now brag about my first hand-job.

Eventually, we went back in and we agreed to meet after school on Monday as she went to the girls' school opposite my boys' school. That worked for me. The party broke up and she got into a car driven by her dad and Jane got in with her. I bet that was an interesting conversation, hopefully once Dad was out of earshot.

I was interrogated by my mates but gave them no information. This, I realised from their questioning, was a brilliant ploy. So much better than bragging. The more I refused to give them any details, the more convinced they became that things had gone far further than they had. I met it all with evasion after misdirection and it worked miraculously. By the time we got home, they thought I had gone the distance. To this day, it is a wise strategy. Girls think you are discreet and guys over-estimate your success. By the time I got home, my fingerfucking finger was still all pruney like I'd subjected it to an individual hot bath all on its own. Which I suppose, in a way, I did.

Monday came around and Mandy was as lovely as I remembered. Snogging opportunities were limited as she went a totally different route home. However, we talked and arranged to 'go out' on Friday. My hopes were built up, only to come crashing down on Tuesday. "I can't meet up on Friday, we have relatives coming over." Was I being given the heave-ho? Did I do something wrong in the hand-job department? Are you supposed to write a thank you letter or something? Before I could be devastated and walk away with my tail between my legs… "But if you come over on Saturday lunchtime you can have lunch with my mum and dad?"

"Great."

"And if you want to stay over, we can babysit my little brother together."

"That would be brilliant," is what I said and frenzied kissing resumed. On my way home, the enormity of this all started to sink in. I was going to have to sit with her parents and talk to them. That was a bit daunting. What's a million miles beyond daunting? Whatever it is, that's what I was facing. Saturday night I was definitely going to have sex. The fear vs. desire index was high on both counts. Is it like that for everyone, or just me? Forty years later I still don't know the answer.

By Saturday I was a wreck. I swear to you, I couldn't eat, I obsessed, I was surely close to a panic attack. Anyway, armed with flowers for her mother, we set off. (Bless you, Mum, you didn't know at the time, but you greased the skids of my lost innocence. I was sixteen, I would never have thought of flowers.) I say we, because the Corbetts lived miles away and there was no bus. Dad kindly said he would drop me. It was kindly, but I was made even more nervous by the thought that they might ask him in. My dad was pretty cool back then. At the time I thought he was a complete embarrassment and dreaded him meeting them. I didn't have the balls of kids these days. So, I didn't ask him to drop me around the corner. But God bless you Dad, you diamond geezer, as soon as I was out of the car, he said, "Apologise to her parents, will you, I have to rush off." I didn't apologise. What sixteen-year-old would? But Mrs C. loved the flowers. And Mr C. approved of Mrs C.'s approval. So, I was off to a good start

The next hurdle to get over was lunch. It was a pork chop with herb crust (we didn't get that at home). I made appreciative noises even though it was like ashes in my mouth. Mr C. asked probing questions about my family, what my dad did, et cetera. Mrs C told him to "Leave the boy alone, Don!" I balked, but not visibly, at the 'boy' tag and also at Mr C. not offering me a glass of the Liebfraumilch he had carefully selected from the off-licence. Bizarre really, when you think about it. Surely, he knew that if not fucking, then at the very least, serious petting was going to rain down on his daughter as soon as their car left the drive. Yet both protagonists were too young to have a glass of shitty German wine. I didn't want any of the vile stuff. But I was fucked off at the snub.

After lunch, it was decided we would go for a walk along the beach. Yes, Sherlock, they lived on the coast. I wasn't sure of the etiquette. Should I walk with her, her dad, her mum or befriend her little brother? I tried a bit of them all. It seemed to be the right thing to do. As we walked back to the house, Mandy took my hand in hers. We were clearly going out with each other and it did help me relax a little. For about thirty seconds. Because after thirty seconds of blissfully innocent hand-holding, she nuzzled into my ear and said, "I can't wait for them to go out tonight and we get my little brother to sleep." It was so clearly game on. There was no escape. Half-euphoric and half-petrified, we walked back in.

I was then shown to where I was sleeping. A bed in the attic up a flimsy ladder. As far away from Mandy's bedroom as you could get in that house. Her dad was clearly not as stupid as I thought. Again, it was the seventies, so I dropped my sports bag which only contained a clean shirt, undies, and a toothbrush. (The condoms I had bought with a bright red face in Boot's the chemist, were cunningly hidden in my wallet.)

We then sat in front of the TV for hours. No chance to canoodle as little brother was always around whenever her parents weren't. Eventually, they left.

Once the older generation was gone, we needed to get rid of the younger one. Having a younger brother and sister, I knew how this game was played. Push for them going to bed too early and they wouldn't. So, I engaged him in boys' stuff. And after several intense games of Sports Car Top Trumps, he was ready for his big sister to send him off to bed. "Mum said eight-thirty and it's already a quarter to nine!"

In one respect I was sad to see him go. But that was trumped by the glint in her eye and the bulge in my trousers it elicited. We kissed for a good ten minutes and then she broke away, "To check he's asleep." What a smart girl. Confirming that he was asleep, she shut the door to the front room, and it was game on.

Now, imagine that you play a bit of tennis, you may even think you are actually quite good. Then imagine you walk onto the court for your first competitive match and you're playing Roger Federer. Well, that is what it was like for me. Or I suppose in this case the metaphor would need a very pretty and not-lesbian Martina Navratilova on the other side of the net. Mandy Corbett was either a sexual savant or a quick learner with very experienced ex-boyfriends.

Of course, it's only looking back now that I realise this. At the time, I had no frame of reference. We went from passionate kissing to fumbling and she, bless her, said, "Shall we do it?" I blurted out a far too loud and fast "Yes!" and reached for my wallet.

She looked a little quizzically at me but then in a moment of understanding, said, "It's okay. I'm on the pill." Blimey! Thank you, God, thank you! We undressed each other. Why lie, Rob? She basically took charge and we undressed and were naked on the sheepskin rug in front of the fire. Honestly, it's true. The effect may diminish in your eyes when I point out it was a wood-burning stove, still for my first time at bat it was still pretty stellar. I want to tell you that instinct kicked in and we just went with the feeling and it was fantastic. I want to tell you that. The reality is that she rolled onto her back, I got in the saddle and she very kindly and gently positioned my now aching cock against her most intimate parts. I was so keen by this stage, my cock was like the victory at Iwo Jima. So, she saved herself from severe bruising without realising. Or maybe she did. Then with sweat beading on my forehead, I advanced. I was in! This was it. Anybody with an ounce of sense would then have surrendered to the moment and enjoyed the ride. Not me, my fear of ridicule and need to impress had me hanging on for dear life to just not come. It was not easy. It became a lot harder when she started to push back and up with her hips and wiggling. I had no experience of wiggling and it took things swiftly to the point of no return. And so, with her hips wiggling and mine see-sawing like sewing machine, I became a man of the world. I reckon, all in all, it was two minutes. But it certainly wasn't three and it could easily have been less than ninety seconds. She made appreciate noises and we cuddled while my cock deflated.

The great thing about being sixteen, though, is the deflation lasted about ten minutes before 'flation, and we started again. This time I'm reasonably sure I beat my previous record, yet I doubt that we hit double figures. I had discovered that fucking was fucking fabulous. The only downside was that the sheepskin rug shifted and left me with the weight going through my knees onto a parquet floor. A wiser man would have stopped and moved the rug or moved us to the sofa or anything other than what I did, which was just kept going and rubbed my knees red-raw. Would I do the same again? Dead right, I would.

By now there was every danger of her parents coming home. So, we got dressed and actually watched the TV. I am sure I must have looked so self-satisfied you would never tire of punching my face in. (This smug look is becoming a pattern, I know.) I should have told her she was beautiful and marvellous and sexy and so hot and… but I was an idiot and tried to be really cool. What a dick! I think we may, between kissing sessions, have talked about shit like how pop music was ridiculous, and that prog-rock was serious music or some pseudo-intellectual for a sixteen-year-old idiocy. We may even have discussed the guest on the chat show we were not really watching. It still makes me cringe to think about it. Why didn't I tell her how beautiful she was at that moment? She really was. Why not talk about how wonderful the last hour had been? What freshly fucked girl wants to hear your opinions on the sophisticated chord progressions that made Tangerine Dream unique. Especially when they don't. Tangerine

Dream were, are, and always will be, pretentious German synthesizer shit.

Anyway, we heard the car come up the drive so we separated and smoothed our clothes down. Looking two pictures of innocence, we looked up as they came in and while her mum put the kettle on her dad suggested, "We're turning in, don't be up too late…"

They went their merry way and I thought that would be that. We would kiss a bit more and it would be off to bed. And indeed, there was more kissing. Pretty soon my cock announced that it was game and my hand in her pants confirmed that I had produced a lot of my own fluids. I was scared that her parents were only feet away, but my cock had its own plan. I can still see her face now. It is one of my fondest memories. She looked me straight in the eye and put a finger to her lips to say "Be quiet," then she undid my trousers, pulled out my cock, and slid down my chest and I felt it go in her mouth.

The reason I think that guys obsess about blowjobs is that there is no performance pressure. That was certainly a subconscious factor, I am sure. But the amazing sensations that I was feeling also put this experience right up in the higher percentiles. Again, it's only with hindsight I can see that she was really, I mean really, good at it. Soon enough things were reaching their natural conclusion. I had read enough porn and heard enough bragging to know that I should warn her. But she had gestured to make not a sound. In a moment of inspiration, I tried to gently pull her off my cock. In what to this day, is still one of the most erotically charged moments of my life, she didn't let me, and instead took me even deeper in her mouth and swirled her tongue and I erupted like Krakatoa. She didn't flinch and just swallowed and gently removed herself. She looked me in the eye and smiled. I was smiling too. She leaned in for a kiss…

God, I was a moron. I was repelled by the idea of having my own cum in my mouth. Okay in hers, but mine? Eeeuuuughh! She had swallowed, I had seen that and I leaned in. But she saw that half a flinch before I kissed her. Still to this day wonder if that was the cause. You'll see. You decide.

I went off to bed and so did she. I was in the loft and it was up a pull-down stairway. I didn't care. I'd have slept on a clothesline after the night I'd had. Lying there, smiling up at the ceiling, I fell into a hugely contented sleep. Now, you won't believe it, but honestly, it's true. In the middle of the night, I was woken by someone coming up the ladder into the loft. Of course, it was Mandy. Fuck me! This was dangerous territory, but I was too young, stupid, horny, or all three, to care. She climbed into the bed in her nightie and grabbed my cock. I was sixteen and it had had plenty of time to recover. I responded instantly. She then straddled me and rubbed it against what I know now, but didn't then, to be her clitoris. This continued for a few minutes and she dropped her tits into my face. As I sucked on them, the rubbing had the desired effect for her and I was a party to being absolutely sure a woman had an orgasm (with me, that is, not for the first time ever). Then she slid me into herself and with a series of what I now know to be Kegels and that hip wiggling, I came for the fourth time. Laughing ever so quietly with joy, we snuggled for five minutes and she left. Halfway down the ladder, she slipped and there was a crash. Lights went on and muttering was heard.

Then she said, "I just needed to go to the bathroom." More whispering and that was that.

Apart from the tumble at the end, can you imagine a better ignition night? I couldn't. I can't. The next morning, I had breakfast and Mandy walked me to the bus stop. She showed me the bruise on her shin where she had fallen, and we snorted with laughter. "Last night was brilliant, you were brilliant." I said, and she just smiled, and we kissed until the bus came. See you tomorrow said as she waved. I was euphoric. No longer a virgin, proud recipient of a blowjob. I had a super-smart bird and there was the prospect of much more sex to come.

We met after school on Monday. And she dumped me.

To this day I still don't know why. And it still troubles me. Seriously, it troubles me. Then, all it did was rob me of all sexual confidence. Had I done something wrong? Now, I can speculate that maybe it was because she was embarrassed about all we had done, or her parents knew what the tumble was really about and forbade her to see me, or she didn't like boys who didn't kiss immediately after a BJ or whatever. But back in 1978, all I knew is that I went up to heaven and then came down with a massive thud. What made it worse was gym class on Tuesday. My mates knew I was staying over at Mandy's. They didn't know about the Monday dumping. But in the gym, my grazed knees were noted and mocked. But rather than a red badge of valour, they too seemed to mock me. Fucked and chucked all within forty-eight hours. It was a hard time.

Then, to add to my woes, my dad had a heart attack. Or rather he didn't. Showing all the symptoms of a heart attack, my forty-four-year-old dad was rushed to the hospital. A man in a highly stressed job who took no exercise and smoked sixty a day. Who could have seen it coming? They ran tests and then discovered it wasn't a heart attack at all. It was a panic attack. Of course, I was happy he wasn't going to die. But there's no romance in that. It was just sad and embarrassing. Fuck you for judging me. I was sixteen, heartbroken, confidence shattered, and it should have been all about me.

Dad came home from the hospital and stayed in bed. He stayed in bed for three months. Then it was described as a nervous breakdown. Now I suppose we would call it acute depression. Now, this may surprise you. There was no wallowing from me, I stepped up, and was pretty much the perfect son through the next six months. I was responsible, thoughtful. I got on with schoolwork and played nice with my siblings. Apart from one appallingly stupid Friday night.

Word reached me that La Corbett now had a new boyfriend. He was a year older than me and his name was Woodrow. The worst thing about this was that he was a really good bloke. I liked him. This is, for a lad of my age, a huge dilemma. If you get upset, then the girl has gotten under your skin and you can't laugh it off and be cool. I could pick a fight with Woody but that would confirm that I was chucked and upset, also he wouldn't necessarily go down easily and, fair's fair, he had done nothing wrong. It was awful.

At sixteen or so we were just about able to get served in some pubs, so I very maturely went out on that Friday with my mates and got hog-whimpering, fucked-up beyond all recognition drunk. The night isn't even a hazy memory. I only know what happened because I woke up the next morning and had a stinking hangover and cuts across my face and my mate Jezz sleeping on the floor next to me. I got up feeling my face, knowing something was wrong and once I was in front of the bathroom mirror, I could see just how wrong. Two parallel lines of minor cuts, and one deep incision on the bridge of my nose. What the fuck happened? I went to the kitchen and made myself a cup of tea and Jezz a coffee (pretentious cunt even then, "I don't drink tea").

He woke up and didn't laugh at me. Fuck, this was going to be bad. I dreaded the answer yet knew I had to ask. "What happened?"

"You were drinking like a madman and having a whale of a time. Then you got really drunk and the barman told us to get you out of the pub. Then you started shouting, 'Why Woodrow? Why Woodrow?' and being a cunt! We thought it was quite funny until you decided it was all too much and ran off. We chased after you, but we didn't need to. You suddenly stopped dead in your tracks. For fuck's sake, Paddy, you ran into a barbed-wire fence. You are really lucky you didn't fuck your eyes up. I brought you home and Lottie cleaned you up."

Maybe it's because he's a truly great friend or maybe it's because he loved my mum and didn't want to make anything worse or maybe he is just kind and discreet. Jezz never said a word to anyone at school. So, I wasn't ridiculed by everyone. And the cuts were explained away easily "these five skinheads started giving me shit so I said c'mon then wankers and it all kicked off, so the first one came at me and..."

"Fuck off, you fell off your bike or something."

It was the first, but not the last time I would handle rejection in a totally self-destructive, pathetic and disproportionate way. If I had truer self-confidence, I would have shaken it off and understood that Mandy Corbett had her own issues. That teenagers are fickle. That it's not important. But being a wanker, I turned her into the first love of my life instead of what she was. The first fuck of my life. Rather than feeling so lucky that I'd been shown the way by a beautiful and frankly (scary when you think about how she could be) so very adept woman, I was resentful about the dumping and decided I was a victim and that all women were just ball-busters. That was a cool word back then. 'Ball-buster', fresh from America. Now it sounds rather silly, like hunky-dory. Let's not get side-tracked. I was now a non-virgin, bitter, self-obsessed wanker. All the hurt and anger didn't stop me knocking one out that night at the memory of that fateful Saturday. Heh! We all have our coping mechanisms. That's mine.

Chapter 15
She's a Femme Fatale

More weeks passed and after meeting Kitty for coffee or walks in the woods and in hotels, I got a text message. "Let's meet for a beer and clear the air. How's Wednesday at six-thirty?" Fuuuuck! It was from Gordon. I couldn't say no. So, I said, "Sure. At the Three Crowns?" By this stage, we had graduated to me having a second phone (a ho' phone as my American colleagues called them) and I called Kitty. A brief chat established that this was not about the current state of affairs, but just clearing up about the 'party incident'. That at least was a relief. I wished I could share her confidence that this was just about a drunken snog, not about a serious breaking of marriage vows.

I got there on time and he walked in soon after. He was smiling. That was unnerving. Was he simple or really good at mind games? Before I could say anything, he took control.

"Look, I was really angry at the time, but I know you're a good guy. Your apology showed that. Let's just let it go and move on. Yeh?" Fuck me! That was unexpected. I started to apologise again but he cut me off and asked, "So what are you drinking?" and got the beer in and we sat down and talked. God knows what about. It certainly wasn't women or sex. He was playing a blinder. I was wracked with guilt. What a good guy. I was getting off scot-free. Then he blindsided me. "I reacted so badly because Kitty and I are just trying to get past a big issue that nearly ruined our marriage." I looked dutifully interested without being too concerned, what I hoped was the look of a man trying to be a friend, not someone who was desperate to know with a "Really? What?" look on his face.

"Yes, we've had our troubles and she had a stupid affair. It's over now and we're rebuilding."

WTF! Is he playing mind games?

Thankfully, he continued. "It was with a teacher at the kids' school, stupid, meaningless, but it was hard to take."

WTF x2! I nodded. She hadn't mentioned this. Was it still going on? Was I part of a male harem? "I overreacted when I saw your messages. You've explained and so has she, so let's leave it at that." I was in shock. If I was a cuckold, I'd do everything in my power to keep it a secret not tell people. I needed time to process this bombshell.

Then before I had time to even start the bombshell-processing, he dropped another bomb. "I thought it would be good if Kitty joined us and we can put this all to bed." Then looking to the door, he said, "Here she is."

I was not expecting this. *Do I kiss her? Do I shake hands, do I apologise? Do I shout, "And who else are you fucking?"*

Again, he took it out of my hands. "Darling, it's all sorted, there's no need to be uncomfortable, we are all squared away."

Then she took over and kissed my cheek and sat down. I went to get the drinks and tried to get back some equilibrium. What the hell was going on? The conversation was a bit stilted, to say the least. He probably thought I was a bit shamefaced, what she thought I had no idea. Can you be cheated on by the woman you're cheating on your wife with? I tried to not catch her eye too much or make any signs that would lead him to believe that me and his Missus were having unbelievable sex, or for her to detect my mystification mixed with a bit of jealousy and anger. At some point, Gordon looked at his phone to check messages then announced, "I'm just off to the gents." Here was my chance to talk to Kitty and understand what was going on.

Just before I blurted out "You look fantastic…" or something even more incriminating, I saw that his phone was set to 'record'. All was not as it seemed. He was smart, and not as naïve as I had thought.

I gestured to the phone and said, "Kitty, I really am so very sorry for how I behaved…"

She looked puzzled so I gestured again to the phone. Then she got it and replied, "Let's just put it all behind us. Gordon is prepared to and so am I." Innocent small talk ensued until he returned and small talk got even smaller until they had to leave. As they walked away, he took her hand. It was very proprietorial, as was the kiss he gave her. He wanted to believe that was that. But Gordon was no mug. That much was clear.

Consequently, we were much more careful about meeting. The next time was in a coffee shop by her manicurist. She always had to have an alibi. I challenged her about her affair. "Yes, it's true, I was at a low, and it just sort of happened. Gordon found out and sorted him out. It was over before it even got going" So he did have a violent side. Or not. "He said he'd have him sacked by the school if he didn't cut it off immediately. He ran scared. Gordon told me we could rebuild, but any repeats and it would be all over."

I was a dick. It was bigger than me. I couldn't stop myself. "So, is it over?" No concern for her or her marriage, just jealousy.

"You're a bit jealous, that is actually rather cute. Big tough Pat all green-eyed-monstery." My charmless lack of a smile in return was met with a fuller explanation. She confirmed it was all over, and that it was nothing like 'you and me' and how I was a completely different story. Maybe it was to convince me, or maybe the whole thing had got her feeling frisky, I will never know. But we ended up in the coffee shop toilet, where I fucked the jealousy out of my system. It was a quickie and heaven or possessive obsessives know why, Delayed Orgasm wasn't an issue. Then we arranged to meet for more than a quickie and I went home sexually sated and more than a little confused.

All said, I always craved quality time with Kitty. Now I was like a kid before Christmas. When could we get dates in the diary? Soon, please soon. She had to balance the kids, her husband and school and finding a reason to be in Paris. I just said I had a new business meeting there. So, for me it was easy. Eventually, we got a date. She booked the hotel because she needed to have cover at home. I offered to buy the plane tickets. Again, she needed cover. Even dinner was out of bounds until I suggested she could, "Just have a club sandwich in the bar..." which we could leave, then I could take her for dinner.

There were several intervening meetings with Kitty. It wasn't always about sex. We had coffee or lunch or walked and talked. The more I got to know her, the more I got to like her. We liked many of the same things. I could bore you rigid if you want. I suspect you don't. It was simple really. I was in big trouble. The amazing physical attraction wasn't added to by the fact I really liked her — no, it was multiplied out of all recognition. And I didn't just really like her, I fucking adored her.

Chapter 16
Steady as she goes

After three months, Dad got out of bed. And announced we were moving back to his roots. Apparently, while lying in bed, he'd quit his job and started applying for others. He didn't have one yet, but we were moving 'Up North'. My elder brother and sister decided they were happy where they were, 'Thank you very much,' and found a flat to rent and that left me the eldest. School was finished and so 'up north' we moved. Dad found a job and a house, and I found myself in the Northwest of England, the eldest child and starting school all over again.

New house, a new area, and a new school. You might think this was intimidating, especially as everyone sounded like an extra from *Billy Elliot*, except me who sounded like a kid from a London satellite town. I suppose in that sense it was. But it was also a chance to totally reinvent myself. Literally no one knew me. I was a big lad of 6'3" and decided there were only two options — hide in the shadows or be as bold as brass. So, I went for option two. The chosen seat of learning was Leigh College. It sounds rather smart. But it wasn't, it was an educational experiment — the tertiary college. All the academic kids sixteen to eighteen went to the same place as the girls on secretarial courses. Yes, there were only girls on secretarial courses in 1978. Lads doing apprenticeships came in once or twice a week to do the theory bits of their course and so it was a real mash-up. No uniforms, no real classes as such, every subject was a mix of different kinds. Some people knew each other from former schools but there were no real cliques to avoid or break into. Having moved school so often before, it was easier for me than just about anyone.

Lads took the piss, saying I sounded 'gay' but the lasses (we were up north now so lasses, not girls) thought I sounded 'dead sophisticated' and apparently, I was also 'dead fit'. I hadn't realised physical fitness was so valued or noticeable. Added to that I wasn't that fit, just a bit skinny. Thankfully, before I could make a tit of myself, someone told me 'dead fit' meant 'quite attractive'.

It was a whole new experience: no uniforms, girls and boys together. Teachers who were used to teaching adults didn't treat everyone like a twelve-year-old. Their attitude was much more "If you want to fuck around then fuck off!". There was a canteen, not a dining hall. Whoever said it was grim up north? Well, actually they were right. Closing mines and closed-down mills. This satellite town between Liverpool and Manchester was truly grim. Bizarrely, like all these places, it was fiercely protective of its identity and uniqueness. This, despite every single fucking town being a clone. "A homogeneous conurbation of despair," my seventeen-year-old self wrote pretentiously in his diary. That of course became a journal only years later when diaries were for Samuel Pepys and the like. The new-age man keeps a 'Journal'.

The first few days were, like at any school or university, all about finding your feet, finding the lavatories and finding your friends. I'd moved school enough to know that the best strategy was to play the long game. Any swift moves could backfire. Feel your way in and spy out the ground. Who's a dick, who's cool, who's got the drugs…?

This place was also a hotbed of rugby. Football was popular but only as secondary to rugby. I had never played but was told I should give it a go. When I demurred, it was like a beauty queen saying she didn't fancy modelling, or Ollie Reed turning down a drink. It was simply unthinkable someone my size wouldn't play, and so I went along. I'd seen it on TV and had a very rough idea, so why not? Well, the why not became very clear in the first training session when naïve me, not knowing instinctively what to do, was knocked down like a bowling pin — repeatedly. But I was a fast learner and soon realised run forward or pass back is essentially all you need to know. The rest they teach you as you go along.

Unless you are an effeminate male model when you will be expected to kick the ball, not get dirty, shy away from tackling and drop the ball at critical moments. They're called 'backs', but they are more easily identified by never having a dirty shirt or a broken nose. A cheap gag but every forward reading this has a knowing smile on his face and is wondering whether or not I am also going to reel out the classic that backs also sit down to urinate. Do you really think I'd miss that opportunity?

After being knocked down a lot, I discovered that when the shoe was on the other foot, it is delightful to smash other people into the ground. I had found the vocation that the monks went on and on about. Smashing into people defensively or offensively is just so much fun. The added bonus, no matter how bad you are at any and every other facet of the game, fellow players, coaches, and anyone watching always loves someone who tackles. I was an instinctive tackler.

The other truism about rugby, at least then, is that is incredibly friendly and sociable and fun. You also get really dirty. So, while it may sound like a story from prison, I made my first friends washing my bollocks with twenty-five other blokes. The two who I bonded with first were Greg and Jimmy. They were kind enough to say that for someone who had never played before that I "really wasn't that shit". They also played for a club and insisted I should come training with them. The club, Tyldesley, was like something out of an Allan Sillitoe novel (if you haven't read one, imagine somewhere bleak and seemingly always in black-and-white, despite the pitches being grass-green and the clubhouse painted sky-blue.) The setting was grim, but the reception was warm and again friendly. This, even though there were men there, not schoolboys. It was the old cliché, doctor, accountant, lawyer and miner, plumber, builder, all bonded together at first sight of me, by their unquenchable desire to "Toughen up the soft lad". Apparently, they could see I was "a big lad, but soft!". Skills training didn't come into it. If I had the ball, they would smash me and if they had the ball, they would run into.

Within a few weeks of weekly school training and twice-weekly club training, I was more bruise than pale white skin with a good grasp of the game. I had new mates, a hobby and a feeling of excitement mixed with fear. I was going to make my debut on Wednesday afternoon. The emotions took me back to memories of la Corbett. Would I shine in my own eyes and then be suddenly dropped? As it turned out, I didn't shine, neither did I make a dick of myself and neither was I dropped. I could make something up about the match if you like. But honestly, I don't remember a thing about it, other than I loved it. Oh, and rugby's communal baths are splendid. It is a travesty that they have gone out of fashion. Eighty minutes running around clobbering and getting clobbered, especially in the cold, is beautifully remedied by slipping into a boiling hot bath up to your neck and having a laugh and a joke with the other men. If you think it sounds homoerotic, well I can tell you that the word had not been invented back then and you think beefy, athletic boys all haring around naked and falling over each other in hot baths, with soapy water to cover any arousal is somehow homoerotic, you need to take a good hard look at yourself. I've just done that, and you're right — it is really quite gay, isn't it?

Nonetheless, it was innocent in my eyes at the time and soothing as anything. I loved rugby. I got off the bus with Greg and Jimmy who again reassured me I "wasn't totally shit..." and I went home for "me tea" (That means my dinner. I was getting the hang of the lingo) with a smile on my face and a bag full of kit that was more muck than material). Tea duly eaten, schoolwork duly done, telly duly watched, I went off to bed. Slept like a baby. Then I woke up feeling like I'd been in a road accident. Nothing prepares you for your first game of rugby. I can honestly say I ached, literally (No, fuck you! Not figuratively, or metaphorically). I ached literally everywhere. Even the soles of my feet were sore, and the shower hurt as it hit my head. Why do I mention this? I'm not entirely sure.

Oh, I remember now, why I mentioned that it's such a tough old game. That's because once you get fired up in such a physical game, you don't feel the hits. Until the next day, that is! I learned to play rugby. What it also taught me so much better than boxing was how to front up, how to fight and that the truthful cliché should be, "the bigger they come, the harder they fucking hit you". Or if you prefer concision — a big fucker fucks a little fucker, every time.

Today, rugby players are fitter and stronger than we were, and they are better refereed. In fact, fighting has been refereed out of the game. It may make it more of a spectacle and safer and more acceptable to the mums of precious little boys. The downside is that being in a brawl on a rugby pitch is excellent fun and excellent life training. How? Well, as a team, we are all in this together and you back up your mates and they back you up. Otherwise, you are simply ostracised. At the same time, in a brawl, it's every man for himself. And of course, when it comes to punching, as with gifts — it is truly better to give than to receive.

You also learn that toughness is all about attitude. In every team, there were many types of fighters. Keen ones who looked for it, quiet ones like me who would be reactive, the ones who quietly relished it and the ones who never needed to pretend, because they were really, naturally, effortlessly tough. Learning to spot these different types I swear is a life skill if you have managed it. If not, look out, because another adage is very true: it's the size of the fight in the dog, not the size of the dog in the fight that matters. Except when it's a very big dog with an enormous amount of fight in it — then you really should forget all your pride and run away. Or as I learned, get them in a bear hug, your head closely beside theirs and roll on the ground until the cavalry, in the shape of your mates, arrives. Failing that, I don't know, fake a heart attack, but he'll probably still give you a kicking, just to make sure you're not faking.

Yes, rugby toughens you up to live in the world of men. You start to believe it toughens you up for everything. I thought I was hard (or hardish!). The world had better get out of my way. I was seeping confidence from every pore. It wasn't long before I realised it does nothing to toughen the heart or the soul.

Jimmy was also my pimp. He simply wouldn't let me not have a girl. With him, I met Eloise in some class or another. Sorry, darlin', I don't remember it. Do you? Anyway, she was slim, all the girls were slim in 1979. Unless they were fat. There was no halfway house. When did that start? I'm just rambling, but it is worth remembering. This chubbiness is a new phenomenon. And I will say it here and stand by it in the hail of feminista bollocks that will rain down on me: there is no redeeming feature in fat. Not on blokes, and for me, a heterosexual male, absolutely none in women. Yes, yes, I've heard all the arguments and I know that it's the person inside, that matters. Well, try telling that to my libido. Don't waste your time, it's not listening.

Anyway, Eloise was slim, and brunette and pretty. Now you might think that with a name like Eloise, she was posh. Well, she wasn't. Everyone pronounced it 'ello-iss' not 'elloeeees' as the French might. It was her mum's attempt at 'little finger raised while drinking tea' class. Nonetheless, she was lovely. We chatted a bit and flirted a lot and eventually 'copped off' at a dance.

There was lots of snogging and I walked her home and more of the same and so now I had a girlfriend, I supposed. It was a Friday and I suggested we meet on Saturday night, but she demurred. Well, she said that she '…couldn't make it as I have plans…"

I was good about that, and frankly, it meant I could go out with the lads and get drunk and well, that suited me. Added to that, if a lass knocked you back, you had to be cool. The ball was very firmly in her court and she played a beautiful forehand pass. "We could meet on Sunday afternoon and go for a walk or something."

You are fucking joking, aren't you, walking around a north-western shithole for a few hours freezing my bollocks off with no chance whatsoever of any form of sex! was what I was thinking. What came out was, "Great, where shall we meet?"

Time and place fixed, I took my unrequited, demi-erection home and wondered WTF that was all about. Saturday morning, in the clubhouse before rugby, Jimmy took me aside and started taking the piss — "So, did you shag her?" et cetera. Learning from earlier days, I played a straight bat, and this got the usual results. He was convinced I had been on the receiving end of the Holy Grail — the first night fuck. But then followed it up with, "Better watch yourself, she's got a boyfriend, a right headcase called Clive!" Even then Clive was not anywhere near a cool name. In fact, since the battle of Plassey it hasn't been a cool name (look it up! Clive of India and all that. Not important, but anyway). Clive was a physical threat. I wasn't that bothered though, I was getting hard and I had hard mates. What a delusional wanker I was.

We played rugby, I have no idea against who or what the result was. But post-bath, beer, home, shower, tea and night on the ale with lads, I climbed into bed, a bit pissed, but sanguine enough and slept. On waking, I set about my breakfast and my schoolwork. Yes, I was a right inky-swot and I was, oh joy, going for a walk later, so I needed to get it out of the way.

Don't laugh, oh go on if you must, but my chosen outfit was a leather blouson jacket over a cheque shirt, and a pair of tight jeans. All good so far. But foolishly, on forty years of hindsight, it was rounded off with a dashing pair of cowboy boots with big Cuban heels. I felt like a million dollars. On reflection, I almost certainly looked a right dildo. Note to all male readers, unless you are Clint Eastwood, cowboy boots, with Cuban heels or not, are never a good look on someone of 6'3". In my defence, I can assure you the jeans were boot-cut and stayed outside the boots. Only a cunt or the bloke in Spandau Ballet would tuck his jeans into his boots. Actually, there is redundancy there.

Moving on, we met at the gates of the local park at two. I was early. It has been my virtue, that all of my life I have been punctual. I'm yet to find a girl who doesn't see it as a complete pain in the arse. "Look, everyone will be late, we don't want to be the first to arrive when they say eight, they mean eight-thirty," et cetera. Of course, the exception is when they are kept waiting when apparently, "It so rude, to be late…"

Eloise arrived at five-past. She understood, as they all do, just how the game is played. Had she been there waiting for me, the moral advantage would lie with me. This would show she was dead keen. If she arrived at a quarter past, I could be gone, or justifiably pissed-off. Again, advantage Bob. But just late enough to not be left waiting by herself and just late enough to be not too keen and to be acceptable. Her timing was perfect. "Sorry, I'm a bit late…" I smiled knowingly.

As we walked around a shitty park, she explained that she couldn't see me last night as she was in the midst of a break-up with a lad called Clive. *Ah fuck me, I have to walk around a park in the freezing fucking cold to hear a sob-story about your love life and gently be sent on my way!* was what I thought. What I said was something like, "Oh, that must be hard." Or substitute in any old clichés you like. We've all been there: semi-listening while plotting an escape, that, while not really plausible, would at least not be downright rude.

On she twaddled with the 'He said, and I said' stuff. On I plodded making the necessary noises. We stopped at a bandstand and she said something deeply profound.

"We've split up. He was horrible about it. Really nasty…" She had tears in her eyes, so I did the only decent thing and gave her a hug. The hug continued and I moved in for a kiss. That's when the Cuban heels betrayed me. They slid on the smooth concrete of the bandstand and my Trevor Howard/Celia Johnson moment was ruined as I slid away from the wall in a comedy moment. I narrowly avoided bringing her down with me and landed on my arse. I looked up to see her laughing uncontrollably. She had a fantastic laugh — probably still does. She helped me up, to add insult to injury and, failing to stop laughing, she kissed me. I fell in serious like at that moment. After a long and really rather splendid bit of necking (bit of touching up, but only really a hint of upstairs outside and a bit of bum grabbing), I walked her back to her house where I was offered a cup of tea and the chance to meet her mum and dad. Yes, mum and dad. Only posh folk had 'parents'.

If you've ever seen *Coronation Street*, no further description needed. If you haven't, google *Coronation Street*. It will save you a few hundred words of description which add nothing to the story. We walked into the front room and she opened the door to the kitchen where her mum and dad sat at a table. I was introduced and the biggest issue was not laughing at her dad. Why? Because he was sporting the most obvious wig I have ever seen on a man. A piece of carpet would have worked better, a top hat would have looked less obvious. I tried, I'm not sure if I succeeded, to not stare with my mouth hanging open. Her mum was small and quiet and said hello and nothing more. The kettle was boiled, and tea made, and the fire lit in the front room. I assumed this meant we would all adjourn to the said front room for an incredibly awkward afternoon tea. I was surprised when the teapot and two cups were taken by Eloise and put on the table then she closed the adjoining door and we sat on the sofa. Tea was poured and more chatting ensued. Then her mum and dad came through and announced they were "Off out!" and wouldn't be back until later.

Eloise explained they were going to the British Legion Club and wouldn't be back for hours. More details of how Clive was so very nasty and more of me making what must have been the right noises because we were soon kissing. "Don't worry, they won't come back."

Blimey, she had left enough time to ensure they hadn't left keys or a wallet behind. *She was planning something,* was actually what I thought. Kissing resumed, and my hands wandered and the Eloise let her hand wander to my cock which, despite all caution and residual fears of my times with Mandy, was like a milk bottle in my jeans (all right, one of those half-pint bottles they don't make any more). Encouraged, I made for her tits and they felt lovely. Her wandering hand was now grabbing, not rubbing. This could only be considered a big result for the second date.

Growing more adventurous, I flipped a couple of buttons on her blouse and reached in. Upstairs inside, this was a slam dunk win, not just a result. All my suspicions were confirmed. Her breasts really felt smashing and mid-nuzzle I made sure I had a really good look at them. They looked as smashing as they felt.

But as all good things must come to an end, she let go of my dick and pulled away. Or so I thought. She then undid my belt and pulled out my cock. I was speechless. Not a normal state for me. She then knelt in front of the fire and her mouth slid over my cock. Double blimey. Head bobbing commenced and in a state of shock, I was beautifully fellated. I murmured, as a gentleman always should that "I'm coming…" but undeterred Eloise stuck to her task and so I duly came. Looking up, she smiled closed-mouth, and, in a gesture, I will never forget, she demurely pulled a hanky from her sleeve and spat my cum into it. The hanky went up her sleeve and she rejoined me on the sofa. This was Mandy Corbett's style all over again. Did all girls do this? Why had I never been told? As I, and we all get to learn, no, not all girls do this. But I would say the world would be a much happier place if they did.

As I got my jeans buttoned up, she picked up her teacup and said quietly, "Was that good?"

"Brilliant," was my reply (At that age all blowjobs were brilliant. But to be fair this one really was. Later you realise, some are just awful).

She then explained that Clive had given her schooling in exactly what he liked, but she hadn't done it just to get back at him. She really liked me, and she "…hoped I didn't think she was a slag…"

I made all the right noises when really, I was thinking, *Thank you, Clive, I wish now you'd been even nastier to her*. More kissing and a seemly amount of time later, I told her I had to go.

At the front door, she asked me, "Does this mean we are going out?"

"Yes," I said without hesitation. Walking home, it dawned on me, I had a girlfriend. All previous experience led me to have a nervous Sunday night. Would this all be still on, on Monday? Would I be summarily dumped for some unknown violation of a code nobody had schooled me in? Walking into Leigh College that morning, she saw me and confirmed definitively that it was definitely still on. No, not like that, you animal. She confirmed it by taking my hand and we walked into the canteen. This simple act confirmed to all the world that we were indeed going out.

Chapter 17
You can tell me anything

Soon after the drinks with Gord, in another hotel room, we had another sex-fest. When we had time, I was always so attracted to her, that, while the delayed orgasm might be present, it was not that limiting. Not for round one at least. Stolen moments, having to be quick was problematic, but when we had time, I was more relaxed because I knew I'd get there in the end. We were getting more comfortable with each other and it wasn't just sex: we talked, we laughed, we just lay there comfortable in each other's post-coital arms. It was at that moment she asked me again.

"I don't believe you're being totally honest, just tell me. What do you like sexually? Don't be shy, I know there's something… tell me, come on, just tell me." I knew, and she knew. Or at least, I think she knew. With much humming and aaaghing and beating around the bush, she had the nerve to say what was obvious. "You'd like to fuck my arse, wouldn't you?"

I had to admit the answer was an emphatic "Yes."

I waited for Kitty to look at me and tell me that I was a pig or that she wasn't that type of girl or that it was just too much to ask. She just looked me in the eye and said, "Well, you'll have to wear your wellies." Perplexed I looked back at her. Was this some kind of role play? Did I have to be a farmer to her milkmaid? She put me out of my misery. "You wally, I mean you will have to wear a condom."

We didn't have a condom and we didn't have any lube. I knew that was also an essential part of things too, even if she didn't. After a decent pause and more mundane conversation, we set to again. Things were always hot with Kitty, but my delayed orgasm was getting worse and I wondered if I was going to finish or have to fake it. That's when she whispered in my ear "Next time, you will be doing this up my arse." It precipitated a more than healthy response and in fact, she was a little surprised at my promptness and said, "God, you really do want to get in there, don't you?"

Out of breath and drained, I still had the strength to say, "God, yes."

"Come to Paris with me and we will do it. It's not something I'm totally au fait with…"

I loved that. "Au fait." She was such a lady. For me, it translated as "yes, I have done it, but not often, maybe not at all." My stupid ego hoped but didn't believe. At the same time, I wasn't going to object. To live out a fantasy with a woman I was seriously falling for, and found incredibly sexy, for the price of a plane ticket and a hotel. That was a bargain. She had an amazing bum and I had seen the target of my affections, and if a sphincter can be beautiful, which I believe they can, hers really was. It was round and pink and when fucking from behind it seemed to wink up at me, challenging me to ask her. But she beat me to the punch, not for the first time in my boxing or romantic career. This time, however, it put a smile on my face rather than wiping one off.

I was not a complete novice in this department. The anal sex department, I mean, not going to Paris. I had wanted to try this with other girls, but it was always drunken, at least on the girl's part, and always begrudgingly rather than willingly given. Most often it was abortive "It hurts, stop it" or the more diplomatic way to make you feel better about the rejection "You're just too big…" Other times, if we were both drunk, then it was just clumsy. But very occasionally the stars aligned, and it was seriously sexy. Now here was a beautiful woman suggesting it. Why was it such a Holy Grail?

Here's what I think. Judge away…

Some men are boob men. For others it's legs. But all men of my generation are bum men. Some claim to be not interested, but this normally means they are too chicken to ask their partner.

Only, why do we? And why don't so many women? I know plenty of women who've tried anal play, but up until Kitty, I'd never encountered one who initiated it. At its most basic, I think men crave novelty more than women. The anus and anal sex are more taboo than vaginal sex; it's perceived as dirty. If a woman is open to it, it implies that your sex life is dirtier, too." And dirty is a label that I and other not-well-adjusted guys crave. Maybe for some men, a sense of power and domination comes with that. But not me, I like intimacy, I like shared experiences. I don't like pain — either giving or receiving.

What's more, ask a sex therapist, as I did, and they will tell us men are secretly fascinated by their own bums. For guys, their anus can be the source of enormous pleasure, with the prostate located up there. Many men have not experimented with that, but in their psyche, they know that part of the body is capable of giving great pleasure. We will come on to this later when I asked the question of Kitty, "But what do you like sexually?"

Or you can jump ahead but I'm not telling you where to go, you'll just have to be patient. Finally, because of lingering homophobia in our culture — even though homosexuality is normalized, good and healthy — there's still this internalized idea, "If I enjoy having something up my arse that means I'm gay, and I am not gay." So, we men displace our own desires to experience pleasure in that part of the body and put them onto women. Or that's what Freud would have said.

I can't resist it, it's an appalling pun, but at its most basic, we have a posterior motive! Boom, boom! Tip your waitresses, I'm here all week.

Chapter 18
Dedicated to the one I love

What followed the cup of park/tea/fellatio afternoon with Eloise was a really nice time in my life. She was really rather lovely and for God knows what reason, she really liked me. We soon moved from blowjob to sex and that was nice, yes, nice is the word. We were both a bit fingers and thumbs to start with but soon got the hang of each other. She was no La Corbett. I found this reassuring and it was nice to learn together how it all worked for each of us. Finding the right venue was the problem. We both had parents at home, and I had younger siblings too. So, the chance of a bed and peace and quiet to get loud and rowdy was rare. But we jumped at any opportunity whenever it presented itself. And besides, her front room and a BJ in front of the fire was far from a bad way to spend the evening. In fact, it was a fantastic way to spend the evening.

All sex aside, we were a good couple. We had fun, we went out, we watched the telly, and it was all going well. Yep, you can see it coming a mile off, can't you? Well, you're wrong. It wasn't me who bolloxed it all up. I had a smart bird who was as keen on me as I was on her. But slowly, almost by osmosis, things started to emerge that were troubling and then plain fucking weird. It was never mentioned that my family was Roman Catholics and she didn't say much about hers. But she often used phrases like "Bless them" at the end of sentences. "The neighbours saw our front door open and closed it and left a note — bless them!"

Once, when we were out, I did my trick at a party of pretending to be *The Exorcist* and on hearing the Latin prayers and me saying "The power of Christ compels you!" she didn't reply, "Your mother sucks cocks in hell!" But she did look at me like Damien's sister. I just thought that she thought my Max von Sydow impression was shit. That wasn't it, though.

Eloise never said where she went on Wednesday nights and on Saturday mornings. I never really asked, almost certainly because, I really didn't care. One day at school, when we had a free period, she announced she had the keys to a house and that we could go there "For a bit..."

I bounded out like a rutting elk, so excited that I almost forgot to bring her with me. It was fifteen minutes away, but I had high expectations of a bed and real, naked, uninterrupted sex. Trying to be cool, I just held her hand and pulled her along the streets at a slow jog.

We arrived at a simple, terraced house, not unlike her parents', and she unlocked the door. It was her big sister Linda's place. As she was closing the front door, I had my trousers half-off and lurched towards her. She caught me and stood me back up. She looked me in the eye and said, "You know what we are going to do is a sin?"

Frankly, I was taken aback. This had never come up before and I was the religious one. Or so I thought. I silenced her with a kiss, and she responded. We went upstairs and pulled off clothes. Things got frantic, as they always do when you're seventeen. Languid, slo-mo, Hollywood-style sex is for grown-ups. I knew little of foreplay, only what Mandy Corbett had taught me. This put me well ahead of my contemporary competition, but still way behind Warren Beatty. Just as my limited foray into foreplay was about to move on to the main event, she took hold of my hard cock and held it against herself. "Will you try tracting with me?" I had no idea what this meant. Was it a sex act that I was unaware of? It sounded a bit weird but why not?

"Yes, let's do it."

She relaxed her grip. Or rather one grip was replaced by another and I thought, *If this is tracting, I'm a tractor*. For this coupling, the marks for effort rather than style or content would be my high score, I suspect. She made the right nice noises and I tried a new technique. A friend had suggested that reciting the names heights and weights of the England rugby team could be a useful distraction to avoid being "A bit quick on the trigger." I'm not sure, but I think I got no further than Wade Dooley, 6'7", eighteen stone six, before I was ready to kick for the extra points. (For those not familiar, Wade played Number Five).

I wasn't squeamish about oral sex, but in my desperation, I hadn't warmed her up and I was squeamish about encountering my own emissions. So, I gently brought her to orgasm with my hand. It was really quite lovely, and as a seventeen-year-old, I knew that, given fifteen minutes, I could play the second-half before we had to head back to school. Lying sated in my arms, she looked up at me and rather than saying something romantically appropriate like "Thank you Conan!" she said, "So can we go tomorrow night with Linda?" I was a little perplexed and it must have shown because her look darkened and she then said, "You promised. Tracting!"

I said something like, "Well, yes. But what the fuck is tracting?"

Oh God! Why did I ask? I learned that 'tracting' is fun for everyone. Any person can do it. That's because while we can't all preach or conduct meetings, we can all select useful tracts and then hand them out to others. It is a line of work in which every man, woman, and child can engage. She was a Christian Congregationalist. A fucking Presbyterian looney-tune. She had kept this quiet because to Congregationalists, Catholics like me were forbidden fruit. I suppose that was part of the attraction. For her family to know her boyfriend was a 'Pape' would be like some white trash family in Louisiana finding their daughter was dating a black guy. At the same time, if she could bring me around and convert me, I would be a huge feather in her cap. She read from a leaflet that she had thoughtfully brought along in her pocket: "For the conversion of the unsaved. A tract will often succeed in winning a man to Christ where a sermon or a personal conversation has failed. There are a great many people who, if you try to talk with them, will put you off, but if you put a tract in their hands and ask God to bless it, after they go away and are alone, they will read the tract and God will carry it home to their hearts by the power of the Holy Ghost."

Fucking hell! She really was a religious nut! I was going to have to stand on street corners and hand out tracts if I wanted to sin with her any more. The weird thing was that as she was explaining this, she had started playing with my cock, which started making it very clear that it felt tracting was a small sacrifice for the rest of my body to make. As if reading my cock and my mind simultaneously, she showed that while she 'could not speak with the tongue of angels', she could put her mouth to other saintly uses, and I became very quickly 'the noisy gong or a clanging cymbal'. (You don't get it. Look it up 1 Corinthians 13:1. If you're still struggling, I meant she sucked me off. It's not often blowjobs and Corinthians come together, but they did for me.)

Back we duly went to school. She was so happy. A few days later I discovered why she was never free on a Wednesday evening "It will be great you can meet the

congregation and we can decide on which tract and…"
My heart was full of dread. But sex is a powerful
motivator and I was so not above acting in bad faith.
The congregationalist meeting for 'tracting' purposes
was everything you can imagine, but worse. A stern-
looking middle-aged man tried to be friendly, but you
knew it was an effort. His default position was
somewhere between Ian Paisley and someone in a UVF
execution squad. There were some teenage girls, badly
dressed and geeky and Eloise who was clearly the best
looking and me looking very uncomfortable. I sat
quietly and pretended to be interested. What I really
wanted was to be anywhere but there. She kept beaming
smiles at me. Half-proud that she had a boyfriend and
half in the expectation of how happy the Reverend
Grumpyfuck would be when she had led me to
denounce Rome and all of the Anti-Christ's evil ways.
There were endless discussions of strange doctrinal
nuances. And an even longer one about the tract for this
week. The Rev said he would make copies for us all to
hand out. This was well before photocopiers. He had a
Roneo! It used a thick stencil that was typed on and then
fed through rollers to put the ink on the paper. The
results were smudged, blue type on a paper that
dissolved when wet. Insult added to injury, I was going
to stand with loonies in the market square handing out
shitty bits of Bible preaching to people who had to get
to Tesco's to get food. I was going to look (and feel)
such a complete dick. Eventually, it ended, and we left

together. It should have dawned on me earlier — Eloise was a true believer. I had a lot of experience in this area, how could I have been so blind. I was an idiot. This had to end now, or it would only end badly.

My mind was turning so fast the rev counter was very much in the red. I didn't really hear what she was saying until we got home, and she said to come in. When you're seventeen and torn between escaping a cult and sexual favours in front of the fire, there's only one winner. Even as her tongue swirled around my membrum, I was still in two minds though. Then she turned the screw. "Mum and Dad are out tonight. We can have sex…" (Oh the romance) "and I want to try it from behind. Have you ever done that?"

What I will say, while swearing on a pile of Bibles, is that watching yourself slide into a woman from behind while you look at the Violon d'Ingres nature of her back, is a small price to pay for looking like a cunt on Bolton market.

Chapter 19
She's in Parties

It wasn't all sex. Not for lack of trying on Kitty's part as well as mine. It's simply impossible for two married people to have sex every time they meet. What's more, we moved in the same circles, or rather, our two circles overlapped. At dinner with friends, it was very hard to not stare at her and give the game away. Hard to not overcompensate and pointedly ignore each other. Striking a balance was hard especially with spouses watching. And me knowing that Gordon was especially jealous and on guard for any sign of shenanigans. We did a pretty good job, I think. It wasn't always easy though.

At one dinner for eight, we were sat opposite each other and while I was trying not to stare at her as she went to the bathroom, I felt my phone vibrate. I ignored it. I hate the people who check their phone while we're supposed to be having dinner. It's just rude. Then from the doorway, Kitty signalled by waving her phone. So as soon as I could I surreptitiously, looked at the message: "I really want you. Do you want me? I'm wearing a Basque, pull-ups and no panties. Dare you look?" She came back to the table and smiled knowing that, while it was childish and tawdry, I was also more than a little excited. After a respectable interval, I 'accidently' dropped my fork and reached down to pick it up. As I did, I saw two things: Kitty gently opening her legs a little. It was so dark I didn't get a *Basic Instinct* shot, but I did see Gordon tying his shoelace and checking we weren't playing footsie. It was just a glance, but it reminded me we had to be very careful.

Once we we're home my phone vibrated again and I got photographic proof that she wasn't lying. She was stood in front of a full-length mirror in her full outfit just without her shirt and skirt. "Told you. now I have to get all this off before Gord sees it." She could read my mind. I stared at the photo with my mouth hanging open while cleaning my teeth and a definite 'chubby' was definitely developing. Getting into bed, the aforementioned chubby was duly noted and claiming I wasn't turned on would be demonstrably untrue. One thing led to another and it was awful/wonderful at the same time. Sex with one woman while thinking of another is hardly unique. I would bet most men have done it and most women have put out the bedside lamp and imagined their partner is somehow George Clooney or the like. For me, though, it was awful. I was somehow managing to be unfaithful to two women simultaneously.

Bigger gatherings were easier because with more people around, there were distractions and more importantly, we could talk without being overheard. She always looked fantastic. Not just my biased opinion, Kitty always dresses well, but when she knew we'd meet she pulled out all the stops. I didn't complain. It was still necessary to be discreet. We really should have pretty much ignored each other. The temptation, though, was too much. So we skirted and flirted and flew ever closer to the sun.

At one big party, when Gordon was away, she whispered, "Follow me to the toilets in two minutes." She walked away. I stared at my watch willing one hundred and twenty seconds to pass. I tried the bathroom door and it was locked. Then the lock turned and she pulled me in. Frantic snogging ensued and she grabbed my cock. I tried to pull up her dress, she said, "No, we can't! Well, not that, anyway. I want to taste you" Then she pulled out my cock and sat on the toilet. It was odd and grubby and yet so silly, naughty and sexy. It was wonderful, and then I realised that I wasn't going to come. By this stage I just knew, and it was self-fulfilling. That was bad enough, then someone rattled the door.

We both panicked. I reacted first. "Sorry, won't be long. But I'd give it few minutes…" Kitty stifled a laugh and we heard someone walking away. Then I whispered. "Just in case there's someone else out there…" I rubbed some soap into my eye. It stung like hell but with a big wadge of wet tissue it would be our cover story. I had something in my eye that was killing me and she had come to help. Not much of an alibi, but something. "Walk out bold as brass. Don't stop and I will follow in a minute if there is no one there." There wasn't and I had a big bloodshot eye for no reason.

Re-joining the party, I suddenly realised I wanted her more than anything. Not for silly high-risk sex, but to be with her in every other way, too. Maybe I didn't even mind if we got caught because maybe it would make us make a go of it together. Was she subconsciously thinking the same way with all the risk-taking? Did we think that love conquers all, or it would in our case?

It can't, it doesn't, it didn't.

Chapter 20
Lust for life

I never made it to Bolton Market, to look a cunt or otherwise. Yes, I was that much of a vain, selfish bastard. Talk to my penis if you have a problem with that. It was not my fault. Lamely, I claimed an 'away game' of rugby and used my money running out in the phone box to silence her. "But Rob. You promised…" I said I'd see her on Saturday night and in my heart, I was already steeling myself to break it off. She shouted back, "Don't bother!" and hung up.

So instead of getting the dressing-down I merited from the super-sexy God-botherer, I went out with Jimmy and Greg. Neither was religious nor super sexy to my eye, so it was a welcome relief all round. We ended up at a bit drunk at some party or other. I was a bit bewildered and frankly shit-scared. I would have to face her sometime and would have to turn down sex or make a twat of myself every weekend and pretend to be finding salvation. Then it dawned on me that they had meetings on Sunday too! This was simply not going to work. How do you break up with a girl and deal with all the inevitable weeping? I drank beer and parked that thought as Jimmy pulled, yes, literally pulled, a girl over and said, "Ann. Rob. Rob. Ann" and hared off after a girl who had caught his eye.

"Hi, Jimmy thinks he's very cool on the matchmaking front," I blurted un-cooly trying not to be uncool as I took in the girl in front of me.

She was cool, and simply replied, "You think this is matchmaking? I think I get to decide that."

Ann was about five foot seven (probably still is), willowy and a face cut just short of striking. How's your memory? Remind you of anyone? Anyway, she caught my eye in a good way and we started talking. I'm pretty sure I was still trying to be cool. As I have pointed out to my kids, if you have to try to be cool, then you are by definition not cool. At that age, I was still too stupid to appreciate that, and absolutely not cool enough to rely on the advice of my mum. "Just be yourself and people will like you."

More importantly, Ann was cool when she wasn't trying. Cool the way that all the girls are in those teen shows, but none are in reality. And she was taking no shit. Before we'd discussed much, she hit me with a jab and right cross combination. "Should you be talking like this? You're going out with Eloise, aren't you?"

I knew the relationship was in the death throes, but not in any way over. So, I lied emphatically. "No. That's all over."

She looked sceptical and made a moue (*Moue Noun. a pouting expression used to convey annoyance, disbelief or distaste*). Women don't moue so much any more. But back then it spoke volumes. Or at least it said, "I am not entirely convinced. I will give you the benefit of the doubt, but if this turns out to be a lie, this face will be right up in yours, because we have a girl code and my reputation is on the line and I will not be taking the fall for your lies. If you have not split up with her, I will drop you like yesterday's lunch and you will never have another chance to discover the wonder that is me."

So let's agree it was a moue that spoke a clear and concise, strangely sexy, threatening paragraph.

I held my nerve and we kept talking. She kept accusing me of putting on the softy southern accent. I acted all worldly-wise and a bit hard. She mentioned that "All that male macho shit is just shit..." so I dropped the rugby talk. Until she mentioned her dad had been a semi-pro rugby player and she liked it. So back to self-deprecating tales of scraps on the pitch until she said, "All seems a bit pointless if you just fight..."

So, we moved onto music to show my more sensitive side. I mentioned I liked Echo and the Bunnymen, she dropped in that while Rescue had its merits, they were a bit derivative. I back-pedalled and said "Well, sure... they are a bit pretentious but..." I could play this game. Talking bollocks about music is easy for me.

She immediately came back with "That Ian McCullough is really fit, and I really fancy him." This was not how it was supposed to go. She was keeping me tap dancing. Whatever I said was challenged, but in a teasing way that I lapped up like a man in the desert who just found chilled Perrier.

Then a man of 5'1" came to my 6'3" rescue. The DJ played "Lust for Life" and I said, "It's non-negotiable. You have to dance with me to this." Bingo! "I absolutely adore Iggy Pop!" she said. And before anyone says anything, or brings up *Trainspotting*, this was 1980. Ewan McGregor was still in primary school. Sixteen years were to pass before our anthemic song became a staple for everyone trying to be cool. So, it's our song. Mine and Ann's. Fuck off you can't have it back.

Dancing seemed to do the trick. Maybe because I am such a shit dancer. I could sidestep on the pitch and move like a disabled butterfly in the ring, but on a dance floor, I never made the grade. Ann felt it was worth pointing out that my real ability was "…to be off the beat at every point during the song." I can still hear her laughing. It was musical and at the time at least, more important because it was the precursor to our first kiss. Even that was funny. My freshly broken nose was bent to the left and she moved in from her right. She didn't have a big conk. But big enough for this memorable moment to be forever the moment she got 'nose-butted' by me. We both laughed and tried on the other side. I'm happy to say that it was the start of something beautiful.

Much snogging later, I walked her home. No invite in, no jiggery-pokery in front of the fire. But what did I care? I was smitten. The big problem, though, now I had to definitively end it with Eloise.

There were no cell phones in 1979 and that was a blessing and a problem. No way to keep it going with Ann with cheeky texts and no way to break it off over the phone with Eloise. Why? Because there was only one phone in our house and it was connected to the house, in the hallway by the front door. Everyone sitting in the front room could hear every word. The immediate decision on how to proceed was taken out of my hands by my mum. She shouted "Robby. It's for you." And as I came out of my bedroom, she held the phone up and said "It's Eloise, love… she sounds upset."

It was a long walk down the stairs, my heart racing and I was truly scared. Scared of a 5'2" girl who had Jesus as her personal saviour? "Hello, sorry about …"

She cut me off. "We need to talk. Can you meet me by the bandstand in Palmer Park in half an hour?" I agreed. Not because I wanted to, but because my family was all within feet and the embarrassment of having that conversation with an audience overrode any and all other fears. When I got there, she was waiting. For this sort of meeting, she had to be early to ensure I knew the serious nature of this. It was cold and she was wrapped up in a big sweater and coat and a scarf and, I suspect deliberately, she looked fucking adorable. "I've decided to forgive you…" Shit! This was not the expected line of conversation. Then she leaned in and kissed me. Still shocked, I didn't do anything but kiss her back as her tongue slipped into my mouth. Panic set in as I thought of Ann's moue and my cock responding to her kissing. Was this the horn of a dilemma? Thankfully, she took the lead. "I know it's not easy to embrace Jesus as one's own personal saviour" (One's? Why do people get all formal when religion is the subject?). "Especially when, like you, you have been brought up in a corruption of the true faith. But I am going to help you find your path." Fuck me, she really was a religious nut!

"I'm not sure that that is what I want…" was all I could get out.

Then she was off again. "Our love-making has been sinful, but if sin leads to salvation, it can be expunged…" She was playing her Ace card: come to Jesus or you won't be coming in me any more. It was a seriously difficult decision, but steeled with the promise of Ann and the escape from handing out fucking loony religious leaflets, I trumped her Ace.

"Then I suppose I will not be forgiven or saved."

She was not expecting this, and I swear if I had punched her in the guts, it wouldn't have been such a body blow to her. "But I love you. I gave myself to you. I have damned myself to hell for you…"

"I'm sorry" was all I could manage. She started to cry. Then wail, then whatever is the next up from wailing. I stood mutely looking at her and then the ground.

"Say something!" she shouted, no screamed!

"It's over, Eloise. I don't love you or Jesus." She went mental. Hit me on the chest and then suddenly turned on her heel and walked away. "Eloise…" I called after her, but she kept on walking. Actually, I was glad. I didn't have anything else to say. I walked home in a strange mood. I was quite jolly. I thought, *Well that wasn't that bad*, and conjured thoughts of dates with Ann, all Iggy Pop, and clever repartee. No more Bible-bashing loonies. Back home, I got back to schoolwork and looked forward to my tea. Yes, at seventeen I was a sociopath.

But at seven o'clock the doorbell rang. I didn't take any notice. I was just annoyed by the distraction. Physics needed concentration. Then it was like a horror movie was on the TV and someone had turned up the volume really loud. I went to the head of the stairs and at the bottom, Eloise was weeping like a demented banshee in my mother's arms. "But I love him, we must be together, tell him, you're a religious woman. I sinned with him…"

My mum looked up at me. She wasn't angry — she was incredibly disappointed. Then Eloise looked up, and the volume went up too. This was painfully embarrassing and shaming all at the same time. I started coming down the stairs and tried to talk to her but the sobbing and cries of "We're in love. You know it… why can't you love me?" just kept coming.

My mum said "Just go…" to me and ushered Eloise into the kitchen. I didn't get much Physics done in the next hour. I just sat waiting for the final act. A better man would have been part of that conversation. I wasn't that man. I was a complete coward hiding in my bedroom. I think I even put a record on to drown out the noise. Eventually, I heard, "Robby, come down now." And I did. I could see Eloise was quiet, but still very upset. My mum was pulling on her overcoat and had her car keys in her hand. "I'm taking Eloise home. Do you have anything to say?

"Eloise. I am really sorry…"

She started crying again and as Mum ushered her out with an arm around her shoulder, she looked back and said, "I will pray for you."

Now when I look back, she was a true believer and truly Christian even at such a difficult time. Then I was just pleased that she had gone. I went back to work and prayed (metaphorically, not truly) that that was the end of that. When Mum got back, she came up with a mug of tea and sat on my bed. "Son, can you see what you have done? You have broken that girl's heart. I don't know what went on, but you have done a terrible thing. Never play with someone's heart and never let anyone play with yours." She stood up and left. Like all teenagers, I never listened to my father. But I really should have listened to my mother. I learned two lessons. Breaking a girl's heart is the cruellest thing you can ever do. And for my sins I learned — God is not mocked.

Chapter 21
Insane in the brain

My doctor called me in as he had the results of the raft of blood tests. And bugger me they found I had hyperprolactinemia. He explained that while not nothing — it was not going to kill me — it was a brain tumour. He said it also often had an effect on male libido and sexual performance. I will let the institute of sexual medicine explain.

A person with hyperprolactinemia has unusually high levels of the hormone prolactin. This hormone is made by the pituitary gland and is most commonly associated with breastfeeding women, as it helps in the production of breast milk. Men and women who aren't pregnant make prolactin too, but in smaller amounts. Scientists aren't sure what role it plays in these people. When prolactin levels rise substantially in men, they can significantly affect sexual function. Research has shown that severe hyperprolactinemia (usually greater than thirty-five ng/mL) impaired libido, caused erectile dysfunction, diminished ejaculate volume, and lowered sperm count.

It may also cause severe headaches, anxiety, depression, pressure on the optic nerve may cause blindness, decreased muscle mass and body hair.

Greater than thirty-five? Mine was at one hundred and thirty-five! Now I was really worried. It should have been because the possible symptoms seemed to be a lot worse than the ones I was suffering from. And me being me, I didn't feel lucky to avoid them, I was just sure that they would get worse. It's not hypochondria. Hypochondriacs want to be ill. They are disappointed when they aren't. No, what I was suffering from was dread. But at least it explained things.

Prolactin in men rises after orgasm and could be contributing to the after-orgasm refractory period. So basically, after you have come, prolactin is produced and makes you not want to have sex again immediately. If it didn't, you would never be satisfied, and woman would be fighting you off or red-raw. But if your prolactin is high, you have in essence premature ejaculation problems but without the ejaculation. Many will say that it says a lot about me that the searing headaches, the loss of bone density, the potential renal failure and pressure on the optic nerve leading to blindness were so down my list of concerns versus the Delayed Orgasm that a scanning electron microscope would have struggled to find them. I had a broken cock and it was only going to get worse.

The doctor sent me back for a more focused MRI and they found the prolactinoma — a tumour on my hypothalamus. It was surrounded by a lacuna of cerebrospinal fluid and that was causing the headaches and explained why my right eye was getting worse and worse. All I cared about was my knob!

The treatment was Dostinex. A tiny little pill that totally fucks you up. I felt sick for twenty-four hours after taking it and if I so much as touched a drink, I got a hangover. But still, a small price to pay if it got me back to coming like anyone else. I was told to not expect immediate results. They weren't wrong about that. It seemed to have no other effect than fucking me up big style, with no apparent improvement with my delayed orgasm.

I went back after three months and the blood test confirmed my prolactin level was lowering. Yet my delayed orgasm was now so much more than a minor thing. It had become a real issue, for me at least. You can't have a quickie if you are suffering from it. This became very clear as things progressed with Kitty. Hours in hotels were great, but hard to organise as she was constantly under surveillance. So, we would meet at shops or coffee bars or for a walk by the river.

It may not sound very romantic; well, that's because it isn't very romantic, but it was all we had, and I wasn't ever going to say no to a bit of 'howsyafather' wherever it was possible. But at the same time, you can't hang around when you are fucking against a tree and there is every danger of dog-walkers. You have to get your skates on when you're getting a blowjob in a carpark and whenever you try and fuck in a disabled toilet it is almost guaranteed to bring someone in a wheelchair out of the woodwork and in need of a slash. It became a self-fulfilling prophecy. As soon as I started worrying about not coming, I wasn't going to come. The parts of my brain that control such things immediately agreed. My brain tumour had already primed the pump by filling me with too much prolactin and so it was amazingly hot fucking, but I had to fake coming. I reckon dear Kitty realised, but she didn't seem to mind too much. When it came to furtive blowjobs, she would get me all fired up, then I would pull out of her mouth and start rubbing one out. She liked watching. Then as my hand was going at lightning speed and orgasm was approaching, she would take me back in her mouth and I would come with as much relief as pleasure. But that didn't work with the quickie fuck. It got to the point that I started to worry so much that I even had issues getting a hard-on.

At home, this wasn't so much of an issue. If you don't initiate sex, especially if you have been married for twenty-five years, you just don't have sex. You read your books and put the lights out when you're ready and go to sleep. If I could see an occasion where this might not do, like high days and holidays, abstinence and edging to the point of orgasm with porn could set me up to perform once in a while. And of course, unless it was a blowjob, I could just fake it. I even got quite good at it. You make all the necessary noises and heavings and then try and make your cock twitch as you stop. The lack of physical evidence may get brought up, but you just have to shrug and say, "It must be the vasectomy and I just don't come so much any more…"

A well-balanced, rational man would have discussed it. Ask a woman has she ever thought, especially with a drunk man, "WTF, why can't he finish?" Of course, she has. There's an expectation in our culture that men will always orgasm and that they'll always ejaculate when they do. Well, both of those assumptions are untrue. But I worried that if I couldn't orgasm or didn't ejaculate, the women in my life would think then something must be wrong with them. Maybe they're not sexy enough or he isn't attracted to them any more or I'm not satisfying his needs. Or he's just a freak and I need someone who isn't. That would turn an issue into a problem that would lead to tears and misunderstanding and ugh, who wants that?

What probably would have happened, looking back is that they would have said, "I totally get it. I don't always come either, doesn't mean it's not fun. It doesn't mean I don't fancy you, it doesn't mean you're not a good lover. So why be so worried if there are times when you're not going to come either. It doesn't mean our relationship is flawed or I'm not hot enough. It just means that you're not going to have an orgasm this time and that's okay."

Seriously, would you risk it? No, that's what I thought. That's how I ended up with the world's leading sexologist. The drugs didn't seem to be helping. And I needed to try something else to get my orgasm back under control. After an excruciating discussion with the family doctor, he eventually relented and said maybe I had a psychological problem and he had a friend who was a sexologist. Not world famous, just a local sexologist. I arranged the meeting and felt a complete failure. Now I needed a sexologist! They were for milquetoast, effete, wimps (yes, I know I've used three words that all mean the same thing, but I needed emphasis). He was about my age, overweight and incredibly smug. I disliked him at first glance. At the same time, if he could make a difference, he could be as smug as he liked. I'd pay his ludicrous fees like a drunken sailor in a whorehouse on the last day of his leave.

We had a meeting and did the normal family background, et cetera. then we got down to the nitty-gritty. I told him about my anorgasmia, and he told me that this is perfectly normal as you get older. This was not welcome information. Then he told me that I could try expanding my erotic repertoire, like sex in unusual places or role play, et cetera. This was getting depressing. I was living erotic dreams and told him so and I was 100% sure that I didn't ever want to do 'role play' and I didn't want to have sex with women who did.

But not to be deterred, the man fast becoming, in my estimation, the world's worst sexologist, felt it was time to play his joker. "The ass is very erotic in men and women. You could try this with your partner…" The glint in his eye was ironical, the precursor to a shit-eating grin. It was clear to me that here was a man who loved his partner donning the strap-on and rogering him to orgasm — probably while he wore a ball gag as they role-played the 'spider caught a fly" scene from *Pulp Fiction*.

So, even in the middle of a sexual crisis, I took more than reasonable pleasure in telling him. "Anal play and anal sex are a regular part of my sex life." He looked crestfallen. I pushed him for drugs that might help. He said he'd read the Wellbutrin had sometimes helped. So, I left with a prescription for Wellbutrin. You should try it. It has absolutely no effect whatsoever. But at least you will know you have tried.

So, I went back to Dr Smug two weeks later and told him the news. He was stumped and said, "Hmmm! I don't know what else I can do. Delayed orgasm and anorgasmia have no cure. You may have to accept that this part of your life is over. You can still have sex and enjoy it with your partner, but orgasm may be rare and eventually become non-existent." That was not what I wanted to hear. Yes, yes, I know. It's not the end of the world. Except it is. And I was not ready for the world to end.

"Perhaps all your problems are predicated on an unresolved mental conflict?" Now anyone who has ever been to a psychologist or psychiatrist will know what that means. If you haven't, I will translate. "As I have no solution to your issue, rather than admit that, I would prefer you spend a considerable amount of time and a vast amount of money exploring your psyche until we find an issue that is much more troubling than this one. Then if we get past that, you will lose sight of the fact that we have never addressed the original problem, or we will say that's what caused it and through all the weeping, you will not care anyway. In essence, you will be fucked up, but on a much higher level."

As I spoke fluent psycho-babble, I saw right through this and wondered, "Is there anyone who has a more practical approach?" It was an honest question, but my mind did wander into the realms of a 'sexual surrogate'. Would he recommend a woman who had all the skills of the Whore of Babylon, who would know how to have me coming like a comet within seconds and even better, that I could pass off as a legitimate medical need and expense?

I was dragged back out of that reverie when he suggested, "There is a school of sexology that I don't subscribe to. I am not recommending it, but you could try Dr Felix. He is world-famous in his sphere" — (cue another smug smile) — "I will give you his details."

Chapter 22
The Future's So Bright I Gotta Wear Shades

I wasn't a complete arsehole. I didn't walk into school the next day holding Ann's hand. Was it out of remorse and decency or was it fear of another massive scene with Eloise? Probably all three, with decency being the least important factor. We had agreed over the phone to meet, and I told her that Eloise was "still really upset by the breakup." Not you will notice, that I had just broken up with her. That moue was not to be messed with. And we arranged to meet on Wednesday night at a pub that wasn't too fussy about serving underage drinkers. And so began the happiest months of my life.

We did everything together. We went to see bands, went to parties, stayed in. She was dead cool. And of course we did drugs together. Smoking dope was just what you did. It was a difficult drug for me, because while I can drink with the best of them, my brain was, and isn't, wired for dope. Just one toke and I am incapable of coherent speech and get an incredibly dry mouth and feel very horny. This amused Ann enormously, as she could handle dope really well and liked laughing at me being incapable of anything other than nodding and trying to take her, or my, clothes off. Sometimes I even succeeded. As we are in that department, I suppose you want an update on Ann in the horizontal. As I said, she was really cool, and I wasn't her first 'real' boyfriend. That said, she was very conservative sexually. Crazy, happy-go-lucky, trendy, open smart and 'with it' clothed, yet undressed "as shy as a maid could be." She was quiet and almost totally non-verbal. She was really quite timid and wouldn't go near me with her mouth. It started off with me thinking that she would come around with time. It also played to my ego that I was Mr Sexually Sophisticated and she the parochial maiden. Besides, I was so into her and she so into me, we were still setting almost Olympic records for doing it. Given the chance, we would be at it like knives (never understood that expression). So, while there was no swinging from the chandeliers or crazy positions, there was a lot of good solid toe-to-toe action and I learned to control myself a bit better and WTF! I was fucking a lot. And when you're seventeen, that was more than enough. I did miss Eloise in front of the fire though. Is it just me or can you hold those two thoughts at the same time? Totally devoted to one girl, but missing the other sexually at the same time? Well, I can. My sample was too small to make any kind of judgment, and generalisations are tedious and generally wrong! Now, with more of a sample to judge from, I do know how people present, and how they are horizontally, can only be judged by practical experience. There is no way of knowing without knowing. This can lead to massive disappointment or major revelations.

Sexual conservatism aside, I really liked Ann. She proved how much she was into me when we got tickets to see Iggy Pop in Manchester. I was excited. She was off the scale. Every record he's ever produced was worn smooth in preparation. Just as a side note, shagging in time to "The Passenger" is perfectly acceptable to Iggy fans, but singing along as you move your hips while lying on top and inside your girlfriend is neither funny nor clever — apparently. It just makes you "a wanker" who will be pushed off mid-shag. Eventually, I was forgiven, and on Saturday night we set off for the Manchester Apollo. We got there as early as possible, as herself needed to be at the front. The show was great despite Iggy wearing polythene see-through trousers and no underpants. Maybe that made it better for Ann, although she made an 'eeeeuugggh' face as his groin approached her.

After the show, the crowd was slow to move, and a roadie came over and asked, "Dyawanna meet the band?"

Fuck yeh! As I made to move, he said, "Nah, just you, darlin'."

She looked at me, she looked at him and as I was halfway between rage and fear, she said, "Not without me boyfriend." Now that was love. I wasn't going to quibble about the hesitation. She chose me over Jim (that's Iggy's real name. she knew everything about

Iggy). I was so flattered. She was clearly beautiful enough to be recruited as a groupie for the band, but she chose to stay with me. Only much later did it occur to me that Ann was no fool and being passed around between rock stars and spit-roasted like a piece of meat as they high-fived over her back may not have appealed that much to her. Love is blind and I was in love. She chose me, that was all I knew.

The most blissful moment of my life was with Ann. The key was magic mushrooms. These were easy to get as they grew wild all over that part of Lancashire. True story this: One of the schools we played at rugby had a pitch that was magic mushroom heaven. They had so many fucked-up kids at the school that they sprayed the pitch regularly with copper sulphate to kill of the mushroom. When we played them, the pitch was blue. Which was kind of a trip in itself. With a supply from elsewhere, we took off for the afternoon and made the "mushy brew" (Put them in boiling water. Let it cool and then holding noses we drank it. Even with nose held it tasted like a dead fish's fanny). Then we walked out into the countryside and waited. It was twilight, and the mushrooms kicked in. They aren't massively hallucinogenic, just mildly, and mood-altering too. We held hands and skipped together. Then came to a brook, about three or four feet wide and hand-in-hand we jumped it together. It was like flying! Then we did it again and again and again. I had never been so in love, or so happy. I could not imagine being any happier than this. I was right. I don't think I ever have been since.

Drugged or not, we connected. I thought about her all the time. This wasn't a crush. We were meant for each other. I was going to university, so was she, but we would finish living together…everything was possible. If you have ever been that much in love as a teenager you know where I'm going. If you haven't. Hard luck, you've really missed out.

The world was perfect. My grades were excellent. My tutor just told me "Oxford or Cambridge?" When I looked perplexed, he said, "One or the other with these prospective grades, your rugby and the reference I will write you will definitely get a place." He mentioned the rugby because I had just been selected for the county. And while that may not seem like much to you, it was a big deal back then. I've still got the red and white hooped shirt somewhere. So, I had a really smart bird, excellent grades, excellent prospects and I was loving life. It got even better when Trinity Hall Cambridge invited me to come for an interview. Dad was more excited than me and took me out to buy a suit. It was from Mr Howard, a now-defunct brand but then a respectable establishment and clearly quality, as the man had no qualms about shoving his tape up alongside my scrotum and announcing "Thirty-two and a half. Quite short for a man of your height." I quite liked the 'man' bit but didn't like the suggestion that I had short legs. I do have short-ish legs but had never realised. Not that it makes a 'happeth' of difference to this story but I have been conscious of this ever since.

With new suit and my National Coaches' ticket in hand, I set off for Cambridge at the crack of dawn. I expected the interview to be all "Tell us about yourself…what are your ambitions, et cetera." Instead, I was asked to sit outside one of the Don's chambers (Teacher's office. They are so pretentious. But I loved it). After about fifteen minutes, a kid came out looking ashen and walked away without meeting my eye.

"Mr Delaney. Come in." He pointed at a chair and I sat, then his colleague who was sitting in an armchair said, "Why do egg whites go white?" This was not what I was expecting. Thankfully, I thought I knew the answer.

"When you whisk or boil them, it denatures the protein."

He wasn't leaving it there. "Yes, true, but why white? Why not blue?"

I bluffed, "Albumin is mainly water, and when whisked the protein parts unravel and the water becomes attached to the hydrophilic amino acid and forced away from the hydrophobic parts." Fuck you, leather boy!

"That explains why they would foam but not why they are white, Mr Delaney."

Trying not to panic, I thought and said the water molecules in suspension will diffract light through them and the result will be a mix of wavelengths that to the naked eye appears white" He looked up and made a small nasal snort. To this day I've no idea if that's right. Without waiting for me to regroup, his mate said, "So if we were to hang you from the ceiling on a spring scale, then suck out all the air what would happen?"

I couldn't resist. "I'd suffocate." That was sure to get a laugh, wasn't it? Neither cracked a smile. "Very droll! What would happen to the spring scale?"

I thought to say, "It would survive" but they were a tough audience and weren't buying my comedy gold. Instead, I said, "It would come down by the amount of the weight of the air I displaced.

"At last, a boy who understands Archimedes' principle…"

I felt quite smug. Until he carried on "…but by how much would it change?" I was dancing now but he threw me a bone. "Let's just assume you are a two-metre tube of fifteen centimetres radius."

Well, I've been called a lot worse. Again, I kept this magical wit to myself and told them, "Volume of a tube pi r squared times the height, so 30x30 is 90 times 3 is 270 times 200… is 54,000, so say about 55 litres. Then say air is Oxygen and Nitrogen 80/20 so…"

"Just call it fifteen…" He jumped in, knowing where I was going.

"One mole of gas occupies 22.4 litres so about 33 grammes heavier is what the balance would say."

He looked me straight in the eye. "Are you sure? Heavier, not lighter?"

I had a moment of panic and just flipped a coin in my head. "Yes, heavier."

Again, just a snort. "Okay, now something more theoretical…" Fuck me, wasn't that theoretical? "Why does a milking stool have three legs?" I had absolutely no idea. So, I did the only thing I could think of, which was to stare had at the wall as if thinking and hope we would run out of time. We didn't. "Come now, Mr Delaney…"

"I don't know." Then I got the first smile of the day.

"Well done! Now how would go about finding out?"

I wasn't being smart, just honest. "I suppose I'd ask a dairy farmer first." They both giggled. Was this good or bad? This interrogation went on for an hour. Towards the end, we talked about grades, et cetera and they said thank you and I was ushered out.

In case you're wondering: milking stools have three legs because milking parlours and cowsheds are normally not flat. A stool with three legs can be put on any rough surface and then rotated and it will always find a position of balance. No, I don't give a shit either.

Wiser as to the design of milking equipment, but not much else, I was sent off to meet the Sub-dean or some such mucky muck. He had a nice office and was very nice. He asked me about rugby. I told him about playing for the county.

"Not in the national set-up?" He was a bit disappointed by that. Then he asked me about books, and I waffled about John Fowles, as it wasn't obvious and wasn't lightweight. Then about my social life. I mentioned my girlfriend proudly. If only I had known more about Cambridge and the general nature of the Don's predilections, I might have played that bit down a bit and played up my male friends. After fifteen minutes, he said, "Thank you for coming. We will let you know."

I went back to the coach station and got back to Manchester at eleven, where Dad picked me up. All excited, he wanted to know, "How it went?"

"Honestly Dad, I have no idea." And deep in my heart, I felt I'd blown it.

Two weeks later, two things happened. I found out I'd been accepted (with the need to get three As) and I passed my driving test. One was a huge event and the other meant I had a university place. Having a driving license changes everything. I felt invincible. Now I could borrow Mum's car and go out. No more buses or lifts. This was real freedom. I could go anywhere at any time — as long as Mum let me borrow her car. What's more, I can confirm that with two people who are young enough, flexible enough and willing, it is possible to have very satisfactory sex in a Mini, even if one of you is 6'3".

Chapter 23
One night in Paris

The logistics of two married people getting away are not simple. First, there are dates and cover stories. That's relatively easy. It's the small things that are tricky. You have to book your own flights and then how do you get seats together? What if we meet people at the airport? What if we know someone on the flight? I sorted this by getting her to tell me her seat and moving mine to be next to her. Then arranging to meet at the gate at the last minute. We would both scout around for anyone we knew and if there was someone, I would change my seat. As it happened, we were both nervous, but it all went off fine. There was a bit of canoodling on the plane but while it had never stopped us in public before we were strangely restrained. We talked instead. Only for an hour, yet so much came out. Gordon was very successful, but a drinker when not working. Drunk, he was very 'not over her affair' and was insanely jealous and suspicious. The jealousy you can argue about is a vice that he should try to conquer. Suspicious, he had every reason to be. Now I truly understood why he tracked her every move and generally kept her on a short leash. She told me she was unhappy in her marriage, but he loved her and was kind and generous and that she could deal with the situation as it stood. This from a woman you're on your way to Paris to 'take the relationship to the next level with'. Whether it was that, or just general lust or the fact that I liked her more and more, I don't know. I just made the right noises and couldn't wait to get to the hotel.

I'd abstained for days and hoped I would have no 'delayed' issues. We landed, taxied, exited and taxied to the hotel. Kitty had to check in as Gordon had booked it. This somehow seemed wrong, but I got over it. We went up to the room. I started to kiss her as soon as the bedroom door was closed. She didn't push me off but before things developed, she pushed me away and announced we needed to get settled. She unpacked, hanging dresses and putting her stuff away. I dropped my bag and tried as casually as one can to put a tube of lube by the bedside. She pretended not to notice, which I really appreciated as I would undoubtedly have blushed.

Unpacked and settled, I moved in again. This time things started to heat up for real. As my shirt was coming off and hers already was, the phone rang. We let it ring but then Facetime started. It was Gordon and we panicked. I grabbed my stuff, but where to go with no shirt, no shoes and no time?

In a Brian Rix moment that will always make me laugh even though it was serious and potentially calamitous, I grabbed my bag and clothes and climbed into the wardrobe. I'm tall and the wardrobe wasn't built for the fuller figure and so hunched like Quasimodo among Kitty's frocks I had to listen to every excruciating word. He had Facetimed ostensibly to see her and check she was okay and chat.

He asked to be shown around the room. "The room looks nice. What's the bathroom like?" He really was checking up. Oh, fuck! Was he going to want to see what the wardrobe was like? That was bad enough, but hearing another couple talk was awful. His professions of love made me feel bad for him. I suspected that this would put the damper on our sex life. If not that, then the cramp that was developing as minutes passed in the wardrobe would. Eventually, he hung up and she opened the wardrobe. I love Kitty's laugh. It's bawdy but feminine. But this wasn't it. She was belly laughing like Sid James in a *Carry-On* movie. God, I loved her in that moment and joined in. A close shave, a narrow escape, and a comedy cliché may not be the most romantic of moments, but I swear it brought us even closer. Nonetheless, she was spooked and as I had heard on the call, she was due to meet her friend Abi in the bar. This was part of the cover and had to be done. The plan was that she would cut Abi short and I should come down in an hour if she didn't come and get me beforehand. Then we could have a drink. She got ready for Abi. I lay on the bed, I looked around and saw that the bottle of lube had been on the nightstand and now it wasn't. Without missing a beat, she had moved it mid-call and put it out of sight. She was a smooth operator all right. I lay there and watched her. She looked even better when she didn't know she was being watched. She had grace and moved in a way that enchanted me.

She went for her drink. She called in while she was at it, so Gordon could say hello to Abi. Then I asked the reception to call me and let me know she was in the bar. It was one of those moments, you walk into a swanky bar and there's a beautiful girl sat on her own and she looks thrilled to see you I was happy. I was almost too happy to notice the looks of envy or respect from the guys in there, but not that happy. Like I keep saying, I really am that shallow. We had a few drinks and ordered some food. I ate it and Kitty looked at it. She only seemed to eat salad when absolutely necessary and got all the rest of her calories from chocolate, which she then hated herself for eating. I thought it was a foible then, but later realised she had a very unhealthy relationship with food and even later, with relationships. That's all for later. Let's get back to what you're really interested in. We chatted and relaxed as the drinks kicked in. By my standards, I was quite abstemious. I wasn't going to leave my best game in the bar. Trying to be cool and not too eager, I bided my time. As ever, she took the lead.

"Let's go to the room. I believe I have a promise to keep."

"L'addition s'il vous plait" was out of my mouth before she'd even finished the sentence.

And she kept her promise. What more do you need to know? You're so predictable. We went back to the room and it was exciting. It was always exciting, but this was a new level. This was a trip away and it was more than just a sexual tryst. I was falling, and if what she was saying was true, so was she. This wasn't about some new sex variation or being naughty — it was a way for two people who had had a lot of sex to somehow take things further. Sodomy and communion are rarely mentioned together but this was how it felt. Kissing led to undressing — again she never failed with lingerie — I will now never see a Basque and not think of Kitty in Paris. I tried to take my time, but the 'quickening' was overtaking us both. We started fucking and it was so great I didn't want to stop, but if I didn't, there was no danger of delayed orgasm — just the opposite in fact. That was a welcome relief. But she preferred hard and fast and if I didn't slow down, I would not be putting any lube to good use. As ever, Kitty saved the day. "Yes, harder. You're going to make me come" and I did, but just in time to keep my powder dry, she came and said stop.

I was frantic with lust and breathing heavily. "We're not done yet," I panted.

And with a gleam in her eye, she made a beckon towards the nightstand and with a phrase you don't expect from a gentil (not non-Jewish gentile, French, gentil, elegant and high-born. We *were* in Paris) woman, said, "Don't you want to fuck my arse?" She rolled on her front and I needed no more convincing. It was, and probably still is, one hell of an arse. I took her bum in my hands and surprised her for once. Easing the cheeks apart, I started tonguing her where, from my objective judgment of the reaction, she had never been tongued before. The writhing and moans were clearly a positive sign as was the "Fuck! That's amazing, don't stop." So, I didn't for a while. Then I reached for the bottle. I smeared a large glob into my palm and slowly worked it into her. I had done my research online and wasn't going to muck this up. Once two fingers could slip in without any adverse reaction, in fact, they were getting very 'verse reactions, I smeared my cock and positioned it. Then, gently and slowly pushed.

She tensed slightly and I murmured in her ear, "Okay?" and got an immediate "Oh yes, but just go slow." The sensation is different from anything else. At least any other sex act. First, there is resistance, but somehow it was stimulating my cock to just get harder. Then it started to move in. A tight ring around your cock, the same pressure all around. But not the soft grip of a vagina, nor the smooth glide. It was grip and it felt great. I stopped as the head went through, and she tensed again. "No. Don't stop now." I advanced until my cock was fully in and I was lying flat on top of her.

It was only then that I saw the hotel bedhead was a coppered mirror. It was subtle but clear. I saw her face and our eyes locked. I started moving gently and could see there was no pain or even discomfort. She was enjoying this. Kitty was always expressive when we were fucking, but she took it new heights. As I started moving in her she groaned and looking me straight in the eye. "Now fuck my arse!" As I did, she started writhing and pushing back onto me and growled, "That makes my cunt feel amazing, ugh ugh, do it, don't stop, I need to feel you shoot your fucking cum into me." The grip, the novelty, the lack of feeling I was being indulged, and the amazingly earthy commentary meant that despite all efforts to the contrary and the one time I might have liked a bit of involuntary delay, I was quickly coming to the point of no return and with the unimaginative and unnecessary exclamation, "Oh fuck, I'm coming."

She writhed some more and said, "Aaargh I can feel it." And I'd swear on a stack of Bibles she came too. But you never know, do you?

Both heavily breathing and spent, I started to pull back "No! Don't move, just lie on me." I didn't know if this was a romantic or physical necessity. Lying still, and my cock still hard in the tight grip of her, I kissed her neck and shoulders how she liked me to. In the bedhead mirror, I again caught her eye.

"Fucking hell, that was something else," Was all I could muster.

"Get me some champagne from the minibar and we can do it again later if you like."

I got up as discreetly as I could and went to the bathroom to clean up — thoroughly. You can go from vagina to anal but never back again. Unless yeast infections and cystitis are your things. Freshly scrubbed and with a towel over my arm I delivered the champagne and gently wiped away all lube and gently kissed her bum.

Her face down still and me sat up. I couldn't resist a post-match analysis. "That was amazing but was it really okay for you?"

She reassured me it was "…far from painful, in fact it was amazing for me too. I didn't expect that. It made my cunt ache and I've never had an orgasm that way before." Just as I was preening, she did one of those 'Make you happy and sad at the same time' comments. "Your dick is the perfect size for my arse." I tried my hardest to let it go, but while I liked being optimum girth-wise, I couldn't help thinking that perhaps she had knowledge of the whole range from other men. I did not like that thought. Still, I was here in bed with my lover, sated after sodomy and if I played my cards right, an encore could be on the cards. She finished her punditry by looking a little coy. How could anyone be coy after what we'd just done? But she did and said, "I really liked what you did with your tongue…"

I gave the only reply possible in such a situation. "Let's see if champagne improves it?" It does. Once you've warmed it up in your mouth.

We then lay in each other's arms and talked. The bullshit that you do. Nothing worth noting, just close, special words. A code in a way, just finding new ways to reassure each other that we were now more than just fucking. Making love sounds soppy. Soppy, yes, yet in our own earthy, physical, how we like it way — it was lovemaking.

We were getting sleepy. Bear in mind this was the first time we had slept together. It seemed odd getting out of bed to clean our teeth and her to take off her makeup. She wanted the light out before she would come out of the bathroom. Then she told me she needed the left side of the bed and "Darling I can't have anyone touch me when I sleep."

We kissed passionately, and she rolled away, and I pretended to fall asleep too. I'd seen her orgasm from anal sex but without makeup, it was a bit early in the relationship for that! She sleeps with her legs drawn up and hands under her head. Mouth closed and breathing so gently you could imagine she was in a coma. She looked so beautiful and so blissfully unaware of it. I had a very hard time to stop staring and nod off myself.

In the middle of the night, I rolled over, and it was obvious she was awake.

"I'm sorry, am I keeping you awake?" I am a restless sleeper; I always have been.

"You're awake now…" That was left hanging. But not for long. Soon we were wide awake and rolling around, you get the picture. If you don't, then I'm not spelling it out. All I will say is that we were toe-to-toe and it was loving and caring and still delightful. I didn't want to be greedy and was lost in this moment. I was surprised when I felt her hand on my slippery cock and she moved it down as she raised her hips up. I was a bit confused at first, but then realised what she was after. I found the lube and soon lost my virginity in the missionary position for anal sex. It is absolutely the most wonderful sexual act you will ever enjoy. It's perfect. Or at least it was for us. Take my word for it. Try it yourself if you can. But not with Kitty. That's our thing.

She knew she would be called again, so as soon as we woke up, the bed was made with only one side showing signs of occupancy and I went down to breakfast to get us a table. She came down thirty minutes later looking great but also looking unhappy.

"I've just had a big row with Gordon. He says he doesn't believe I'm here to shop with Abi. I have to fly back, or he will fly over." We had coffee and I ate while she watched. We talked about the options. There were none. She arranged a flight back that day, rather than stay in a hotel on my own, and not this one as she had to check out. She had to at least do some shopping with Abi for her alibi. Making the best use of our time, we finished breakfast quickly and headed back to the room. I was disappointed she was going, but her "pissed off with husband sex" was something to behold. After all manner of variations, the problem was I was getting that delayed orgasm sensation again. If we stayed fucking, I could fake it and the lack of evidence could be put down to the tank being empty. Then she said, "I want you to come all over my tits" This should easily be accomplished with me pulling out at the last moment and moving up her body or her blowing me. The only way I could do it, though, was to go porno. I sat astride her as she sucked my balls and I cranked it out like a madman. This took time, but she wanted what she wanted. Eventually, I signalled that she should pull back and watched as I shot over her beautiful breasts. Considering it was the third time in twelve hours, I was pleased with the display. But it was hard-earned.

Thinking we would shower again, I was surprised when she demurred. "When he meets me at the airport, I want to still be able to feel and smell you on me."

I had a shower. I didn't need to punish anyone, and I didn't want to go home smelling of anything. I just phoned ahead to say my meeting finished a day early and I was coming home. This wasn't unusual and wasn't questioned.

At the airport, I hung around in the baggage claim area to give her plenty of time to get clear. I learned a lot on that abbreviated trip. Yes, some women really like anal sex. It can be truly amazing. And pissed-off wives have some strange ways of punishing their husbands.

Chapter 24
Tears dry on their own

In between all the study, the rugby training, and playing and going out with mates, I'd noticed Ann was getting more 'Arsey'. If you are not conversant with the vernacular of North-West England that means grumpy. It must have been that she wasn't getting enough of "Golden Bollocks" attention, so I tried a bit, but not much, harder. I was really pleased when Ann suggested we "go away for the weekend." This was a genius idea. I had enough money from my summer job to just about afford it. She was a cool girl. "We'll go halves, of course..." And so, we booked a B&B in the Lake District. I borrowed Mum's car and we were set. I envisaged forty-eight hours of raucous sex, interspersed with beer in country pubs and a bit of walking. Ann, it transpired, envisaged a huge amount of walking, dope-smoking — she was stoned more and more, and perhaps a token amount of sex. We arrived at the B&B with me full of high expectations and Ann a bit glassy-eyed from the joint she had smoked in the car. The landlady was everything you would expect from someone in the British service industry that relies on the goodwill of customers — she was very unpleasant. Unpleasant as only British B&B landladies can be. Scowling at our temerity to give her our money, she grumpily showed us to a room. It was okay. And I dropped the bags and she said, "Breakfast is from seven-thirty to nine." And walked off.

I flopped on the bed and gestured for her to join me. "God, is that all you think of…"

Well yes, was the answer. I was in love, and I liked sex very much. She opened the window and sparked up a J and sneered at me. Something was up? Joint finished she said, "Let's go for a walk" and so we did. She was now stoned and grumpy, and now I was stoned and monosyllabic too. Eventually, we got fish and chips and then a few drinks in a pub. She warmed up a bit and at around ten-thirty, we went back to the B&B. I had high hopes. After all, this was my first dirty weekend away. She flopped on the bed and said, "Ahhmm really tired, can you just leave me alone."

I had no idea what I'd done. Sex in the morning was delivered as a duty, not a joy. I knew her well enough to know that. A wiser man would have left her alone then too, but I was stupid. Bad sex set the tone for the day. It was shit. It rained, we didn't speak much and went to bed early.

"I don't want to, Rob. Please, can we not. I really do love you, you know, but I just can't." I was a bit disappointed, but that was okay. Love is never easy et cetera, and as a sop, she fell asleep spooning me. I hoped her hand would eventually move down to my dick later.

It didn't. We got up the next morning and drove back. I dropped her off and as I was going, she kissed me on the cheek. That was all. Now you can see a train barrelling down the tracks, can't you? I didn't.

Schoolwork was getting more intense as exams were only a couple of months away. So, we only saw each other on Fridays and sometimes Saturdays, when our respective groups of friends would meet. Sundays were study days and she wasn't doing my course, so she didn't want to do it together and she was always stoned anyway.

Jimmy and Greg kept pushing me to go out with them and keeping me and Ann apart. It was weird. The next weekend she said she was away at an aunt's and Jim said we weren't going into town, just to the local for a few pints. It was all very weird. On the Saturday after the match, I insisted we were not staying local again. "Fuck it! Rob, we're not going into town. Ann's seeing Flan." It sounds funny seeing it there. 'Ann's seeing Flan.' But at the time it broke my fucking heart. Flan was the local drug dealer. He'd already 'done time' and had a fearsome reputation for violence. I tried to leave and tell them "I was going to 'brass' 'im!" They knew better and held me back. Jim and Greg knew I was no match. All three of us would be no match for him and his henchmen. I couldn't believe it. I started ranting.

"Look, it's bollocks, she's just a friend, she scores off him.

"Rob, we didn't keep you out of town to avoid him. We've kept him away from you. He's after you. We told her she had to tell you. She was supposed to in the Lakes. But she didn't." I couldn't cry in front of my mates, although all I wanted to do was curl up in a foetal ball and wait to wake up and discover this was just a nightmare. It wasn't. We went and got 'leathered 'at the local pub for a change. They walked me home, pissed as a parrot. And threw me on my bed.

I gave them half an hour head start then got up and walked the five miles, drunkenly to Ann's house. It was like a teen flick. Really that pathetic. One in the morning drunkenly shouting her name. Lights went on. Faces appeared at the door. Ann looking scared. She and her dad were holding Flan back. "Go home, Rob," she shouted over her mum's shoulder.

I couldn't help noticing that her mum was wearing a winceyette nightie and her hair was in curlers. I don't know why, but I laughed as she walked towards me. She looked back at Ann furiously, "You haven't told 'im, have ya? You'll feel the back of my hand for this, lady!" Then to me, ever so tenderly, "Get yourself home, lad. There's nothing for you here. I'm sorry!" And she kissed me on the forehead. It was a truly kind thing she did, and it took me totally off guard. I felt tears welling up and rather than let anyone see, I turned on my heel and walked away. I did eventually stop crying. But I suspect it was dehydration, not mastering my emotions. By the time I got home, heartbreak had turned to anger.

I was in a weird headspace on Sunday. Hangover, tired, and my mind going a million miles per hour. I couldn't sit still, I couldn't concentrate. I started to get Mum's car keys to go and confront her about twenty times and shouted silently, "Fuck her and fuck him!" just as often.

Then I heard a letter being posted through the letterbox. There was no mail on Sunday! I saw the back of Ann walking quickly away from my house. Letter in hand, I ran after her. I grabbed her arm and she didn't look sad or hurt or sorry, she looked angry. Angry! Where the fuck did that come from. "Just read the letter." She pulled away.

I took the envelope and tore it up and threw the pieces on the ground. "Fuck you and fuck him! And when he's in nick and you've got two kids and a council flat, your life is shit and you see what a huge fucking mistake you've made, just remember this! Fuck you and fuck him!" Then the anger she had shown dissolved. I was mystified.

"I'm sorry, but you and me is not what I want … you're really, I dunno, not for me."

Rather than listen to any more of her, as I saw it, traitorous bullshit (and on reflection, slightly bizarre bullshit), I walked back in. Once she'd gone, I went back out and picked up the bits and taped it back together. It was all platitudes and apologies. After all, she was only seventeen too. What it did have, though, was a lock of her hair. Which was weird and the last line, "This is a lock of my hair that represents the part of me that will always love you." Even then, heartbroken, it struck me that 'represents' was a weird word to choose and that a strand of a dead bit of yourself was the bit that represented undying love. A good metaphor in a way. I put it all straight in the bin and moped. For about two weeks I moped. That's a lot of moping. Then, I moved on to much more extravagant, self-indulgence.

Working in the States, I learned the expression 'turnaround is fair play.' I'd done the same to Eloise and some would say that what goes around comes around. I couldn't accept it. I was the better choice. I would have loved her forever; I was going to be something in the world, yet she chose a convict! It made no sense. But it did what boxing and rugby had failed to do. It toughened me up. My capacity for love had been cauterised. This would never happen again, and it didn't. Until it did.

Chapter 25
I was born again

We were both vain about our bodies, and Kitty liked hearing compliments about hers. But they had to be true. Or at least not identifiable as me just trying to flatter her. That was a sin that she did not forgive. Not for what was said, but for not giving her the reassurance she craved, but would never admit to. Simple flattery was a back-handed slap. This wasn't too much of an issue as she did, I suppose, still does, have a delightful body. So, there we were, again naked, post-coital and relaxed I was running a hand along her hip and looking at her. She caught my eye and looked quizzically at me. Without thinking I said, "Regardless of having had two kids, you have a spectacular body..." She started crying. It took me a moment, then it hit me. I held her tight and had the sense to say nothing. Eventually, she told me. The story of a baby she had carried to term, his being still-born and being taken from her too soon. The heartbreak, the pain and wound in her heart that would never heal. I could tell you in detail. But if you don't get it from those details, all the minutiae in the world won't help you. If you have lost a child, you know; if you have a child, you can get close and if you haven't had either, you will never, ever understand. I just held her close and whispered, "I'm so sorry." Which was true, and what else is there to say?

Eventually, she pulled away and dried her eyes and said, "It's all right…" I pulled her close again. It wasn't me who started taking things further. Even I wouldn't be that insensitive. But she seemed to want to blank out the last ten minutes. So, in that emotionally charged state, we followed the inevitable path to making love. This time it wasn't fucking. It was warm and passionate but loving and caring and I suppose cathartic. It was slow languid sex, not hard and fast. We moved together and at risk of sounding melodramatic, it was a real coming together. We felt each other, and it was a physical yet spiritual thing. I was kissing her passionately and then gently kissed her neck as we were joined at every point.

What I heard was "I love you…" so with all the pent-up emotion and restraint I had felt for a while, I pushed even harder and blurted out "God, I love you, too." It was then I realized that she had mid-sentence and simultaneously finished her thought with, "…doing that." Aaaaaggghhh! But now wasn't the time to stop. So, I didn't, beads of sweat on my forehead as I refused to let this delayed orgasm bastard get the better of me. I eventually came inside her.

Rolling over, she looked at me and gave a gentle laugh. I knew why. I mumbled, "I think that maybe… I shouldn't have said that." I may even have blushed.

"Did you mean it?" This was a critical moment. I have never had a head for heights, and this was jumping off a cliff.

I teetered on the brink for a moment and then said, "Yes, sorry, but I do. You don't have to say anything. And don't just rebound and say it too. I know it's against the rules, but I really do love you, Kitty."

She laughed again. And gave the best response possible. She kissed me with a passion that normally comes before sex, not after it and when we broke the kiss she said, "I haven't really thought about it. No, that's a lie. I've thought about it quite a lot and I do think I love you — a bit." That was enough for me. It was out there. And she didn't say she didn't. Or did she? Again, I will never be sure. Because I'm not exactly sure when it started to happen. When did I go from an ardent lover to being in madly in love? All I knew for sure was that right there and then, I had fallen hard, and I could only hope, no pray, no needed, her to feel the same way.

Chapter 26
London Calling

It's no cure for heartache, but rugby helped, by distracting me. I also seemed to be getting into more scraps on the pitch. Can't imagine why? And drinking reached new heights of self-inflicted damage. Jimmy set me up with other girls and I tried. But not much. They all had one basic failing — they weren't Ann. It didn't stop me shagging, then behaving increasingly badly until they broke it off or just didn't bother calling. It didn't help. There was a disconnect in my brain. It made the yearning worse, not better. Just to be clear, there was no conveyer belt of girls. I wasn't that hot or that much of a catch. But my scowling indifference meant some girls weren't interested. Others, with troubles of their own, I suppose, saw a kindred spirit. Casual sex was just that. Not much good to either of us, really. Just a way to show solidarity. I liked it well enough and there was a protocol in these things. After a couple of dates, a girl would have to show some interest and reciprocity or call it off. And there's something really rather wonderful about being given a blowjob out of politeness rather than affection.

Schoolwork was of no interest. I was in a self-destructive spiral. I think somewhere, I thought that if she could see what she'd done, she would come running back, or if she saw me with another lass, she would be jealous and come running back. Neither worked for me, or on her. I was angry and confused and started down a path of blaming all women for what one had done. It took me years to see that they weren't all like that (just most), that really Ann was just looking out for herself like we all do, and that I really needed to stop being such a needy little wanker.

I battled my way through the final months doing virtually nothing but laying on my bed feeling sorry for myself, wallowing with teenage angst or going out drinking and being horrible to girls. The exams didn't go badly, but they didn't go great either. In one paper I don't know what happened, but Ann came into my head and I sat thinking about her, then twenty minutes had passed. I still finished the paper. I didn't really care if it had made a negative difference. If only teenage heartbreak wasn't so delicious. Being a tortured soul, the smell of burning martyr followed me everywhere. I was such a clown.

I finished in June and then had two months to wait for the results. I was slowly getting over Ann. No, not over, around. When I wasn't a snarling, miserable, self-absorbed cunt, I was worse, or drunk or both. I could do this because I had found a summer job in a factory. This paid a proper man's wage, so I was really in the money. Every day I clocked on and spent eight hours stacking slabs of twenty-four cans onto pallets. Six slabs per layer and eighteen layers per pallet. Then a forklift driver would take it away and the process started over.

There were breaks, of course, and these were strictly enforced by the full-time staff. For me, though it was money for old-rope and really built up my shoulders and chest and so helped with rugby. The 'real' money, though, the same money as some got to raise a family, did not help. I was out of control.

This level of out of control is totally sustainable when you are seventeen going on eighteen, and training hard at the rugby club. Now, a ten-pint bender would have me laid up in bed for forty-eight hours. Then, we would do that on a Friday night and meet at the club for a match at twelve the next day. Maybe with slight indigestion, but with a hangover that had been seen off with a massive fried breakfast and about a half-gallon of tea so tannic you could stand the spoon in it.

The weeks passed, and in August it was results time. I needed three As for Trinity Hall. I got my computerised slip form the school secretary and I had got two As and two Bs. I couldn't even really fuck up and be able to blame it all on Ann and a broken heart. I missed by a whisker and so would go to my fall back, Queen Mary College, London. Frankly, I didn't really give a fuck. But term would start in mid-September and I had to get sorted with all the planning. It's funny to think that now it's all taken care of by special teachers at school, by parents and by the university. Not then, or at least not for me. No one knew what to do. Eventually, I filled in the forms and then found out that because they weren't my first choice, Queen Mary College would not let me have a room in the Halls of Residence. I set off to London a week before term to find a room. Traipsing around East London was not exciting or scary. Just really fucking dull. The third 'flat' on my list was a bedsit in Leyton. The first two were too expensive. This one was a back-bedroom in an old Victorian house. Through the common entrance hall, you walked to the back of the house. It had a kitchen, well, a cooker and a sink en-suite as they now say. It was actually just separated from the bed bit by a bit of plasterboard. There was a back door which opened onto the garden and you turned back up the side of the house to the lavatory. It was £65 per calendar month and I took it. These days Iraqi refugees would cry, "Oppression, torture…" at such digs, but what did I know? I just needed somewhere to drop my stuff. Actually, it was all right. A shithole, but at eighteen you don't need much.

So, in September of eighty-one, I arrived at university still a bitter and twisted boy. Determined to fuck as many girls as possible, and equally determined to not like any of them. Kinder souls may say a heartbroken, teenage misfit, who needed the solace of friends and family. I'm more in the "what a self-obsessed whiney, little cunt" camp myself, but you decide. Self-analysis is like looking in those fairground mirrors, you never get the real picture.

No ivory towers and romance for me and next to no interest in academic life. I decided to enjoy myself. The first day of "freshers week" involved getting a bank account, getting a student card, getting all the other stuff sorted and most importantly, getting your grant cheque. Americans especially, and kids of today even, find it hard to believe that university for my generation cost nothing. Actually, it cost less than nothing because, on top of all tuition fees, Her Majesty's Government also paid you a Student Grant. In 1981 it was £1820. Paid in three instalments. Hit that with a stick, you Yanks, with hundreds of thousands of dollars of college debt.

I had £50 quid, from my dad. Not an advance from him, a gift. I was really touched. Deciding to ignore his advice "to not blow it all on the first day," I advanced to the student bar and ran into three guys who I had met signing up for my courses and a library card. Andrew and Mark are still among my closest friends to this day. The other was is and I suspect always will be an Uber-knob. I won't tell you his name as it's not fair to insult a man who has no chance of a comeback. So, I won't do that to you, Sean. We got a beer and chatted about sport and music the way dogs sniff each other's arses. It was a feeling out and testing of credentials. Having established heterosexuality and acceptable band choices and that for two of us at least, rugby was a superior form of football with the beauty of the Bolshoi ballet and the nobility of boxing, we planned our evening. There was a band playing, and we would go together.

Then we looked around for girls and saw girls looking around for us. Then and now it still strikes me as odd. I wanted to 'meet' as many girls as possible but always, lads find a pack to hunt with first. And often, but not always, girls are suspicious of the lone wolf. My new mates all had rooms at the Halls (of Residence) so they headed back, and I went to my digs. We met later, had pints, talked to girls, watched the band, had an in-depth discussion on the musical influences and merits of the band. More pints and more groundwork with the girls and went home. In those days the pubs shut at eleven and the tube stopped soon after. A big night out was a serious commitment to staying out until six when the tube re-started or walking home. The next couple of days followed the same pattern. Logistics, buying textbooks, meeting tutors, drinking in the bars and watching bands.

I wore my 'northern chip' very proudly on my shoulder. I wore a National Coal Board donkey jacket, checked shirt, boot-cut jeans and work boots or big heavy clod-kicker shoes. I was downing a pint of bitter and scowling. It was my default look. In came a student with floppy blond hair, cavalry twill pants, a dress shirt, a mustard waistcoat, and a checked sports jacket. He had a signet ring on his pinkie and brayed as only private schoolboys ever could. I loathed him on sight. He came over and we were introduced. He seemed unaware that my dismissive "Hi" and turn away was his last chance to fuck off and avoid "a fucking good hiding." Instead, he kept talking to me. This bloke could not take a hint. I turned back and decided to give him a verbal pummelling if not a physical one. I looked him up and down and he did the same to me, and looking me in the eye with a glint I can still see now, he said, "Clearly, one of us got the dress code wrong!" I belly-laughed and he public-school-brayed and I got my first posh mate. Through him I sated my taste for posh girls. At least the ones who wanted to sample a bit of rough before marrying a public-school educated lawyer, doctor or banker.

After the first few weeks, people started shedding the friends they had made by mistake and forming stronger ties with the others. I had joined the rugby club with Andrew and Mark. We hung around together and drank and chased girls. Well, I did, Mark had a girlfriend back home and Andrew was just escaping from religion and was a bit shy. This isn't a book about my friends, though. Maybe I'm a snob, but I suspect most people who read shit like this have been to university. That's why the university tales I have will very much match yours. Except you were there for yours, and so they will be better. I'm just trying to work out how I got to where I am with my heart and my cock, so let's just stick the juicy bits, shall we? Well, I'm going to anyway.

Alice.

At the end of the first week, we went to the Rugby Club disco. It was 'fancy dress' rather than turn up in a toga (Thank you, *Animal House*). I decided to be post-ironic before post-ironic was hipster and went as a rugby player. The kit was cool then. The shirts were heavy cotton and the shorts had front pockets. I wore my club socks out of respect but replaced the boots with high-top trainers. Sure enough, there were a few costumes and a mass of togas. Male and female. I talked to a tall girl called Alice who was nursing something noxious in a plastic glass and wearing her bikini and a sarong. I think she was a little drunk. Why? Because when I asked her to hold my glass when I wanted to light a cigarette, she pouted and said, "Can I have one?"

I lit two and as I passed her hers, she said, "It's simple, you scratch my back and…" I passed her drink but with both my hands full "…I'll stroke your balls." An odd expression, I know. You can't make this shit up!

What I can tell you is she was a good as her word. Now this very subtle body language was not lost on me. So soon after she had stroked my balls, we quickly headed out of the disco to her room. Clothes came flying off, but as a serious sportsman, I had double-knotted my boots. The laces were a complete pain, so the boots didn't come off, even as Alice climbed on. So began my first university fuck and very nice it was, too. She was writhing around and making the right noises and it was all developing nicely. Then in burst her roommate with half a dozen be-toga'd players. As a defence mechanism, she pulled a sheet over us both. Her roommate asked, "Alice, who is that?"

Alice very eloquently replied, "Fuck off! Fuck off all of you!" I couldn't help giggling, but I was anonymous under the sheet.

That was until I heard Mark shout, "It's Rob. I recognise the boots". Much caterwauling later, they did indeed fuck off and much to my surprise I was still hard and still in Alice. She moved to get off me, but I held her hips. She didn't try any more, and we resumed where we'd left off. Soon she leaned forward to kiss me and grinding away she brought herself and me to a very satisfactory conclusion. *So, this was all it takes at university*, I thought.

I was still in no mood to have a girlfriend and clearly didn't need one to have sex. We got dressed and re-joined the party. Alice wasn't clingy. In fact, quite the opposite. Which, even though I didn't want it, was a bit disconcerting. Andrew came over with drinks and said, "Here you go, Mark, and here you go 'Boots'." A stupid fucking nickname, but one that stuck for years. Every now and then Alice and I would get together for attachment-free sex. I liked her and she liked me. Not enough for anything else, but it worked for us. At least, I think that was how it worked. If not, sorry, Alice. You were lovely and I was just a stupid boy.

We couldn't afford many drugs and they weren't as readily available as they are now. We smoked some dope and occasionally I scored some speed. Cocaine? We were students. Nobody could afford coke. So really that just left sex and music. I spent my time continuing to be a self-obsessed and whiney. And chased girls and played rugby and listened to music. Like I said, a standard university education. Just slot in your drugs of choice and sport/leisure activity.

I slept with a lot of girls. But not that many. Not that I was that charming or good looking, it was more that the girls were experimenting too. Slowly couples developed and some stayed together but there was always a pool of singles looking for each other. I didn't have it all my own way though. Desperate to just fuck and fuck over girls, I was blind to the fact that maybe I wasn't the only one.

Addie

Addie was truly beautiful. She had it all. She had a beautiful face, a beautiful figure and she is, without doubt, the most beautiful girl I have known. Not just biblically, I mean the most beautiful girl I have ever known. Sorry, the rest of you, but it's true — not even room for discussion. She was a goddess. So, what the fuck did she see in me? I still have no idea. We met in the least romantic setting you can imagine, the biology lab. By a sheer fluke, she was working opposite me and I was blown away by her looks. I tried to be cool. This was impossible as she was so gorgeous. Then I tried to be funny. "So, do you come here often?"

She looked at me like I was an idiot and said, "No, this is my first biology lab." Have you ever noticed that when a joke falls flat that it just gets worse if you try and explain why it was actually funny? Mid-explanation

I realised this. I came to a bumbling stop and she saved me with, "Shall we get a drink later?" I agreed without hesitation, but sure that it was to compare course notes or to get my advice about the best Tube passes or anything that wasn't romantic. We duly met in the student bar, had a quick drink then and she waved hello to some of her friends. I was totally blindsided when she said, "Shall we go back to mine?"

I couldn't believe my luck. At chez Addie we soon started kissing, and undressed she was even more beautiful than dressed. That is so rarely the case. Think about it. You know I'm right. I had never been so sexually aroused and inevitably disgraced myself in a very short time. She was very sweet about this and we cuddled. Then as I was gathering my strength for round two, she told me she had a busy day the next day and I really should go. I was crestfallen but hoped to establish my credentials ASAP. I was paranoid she'd think I was a bad shag. All the evidence certainly pointed in that direction, so I couldn't blame her.

The next day I hunted for her, with no luck. Days passed and when I did find her, she told me, "I've got back together with Andy." He was a very cool guy, I couldn't deny it and so, that, it seemed, was that. The good news for me was that he was often a terrible boyfriend and my role was to be used to remind him that he wasn't the only game in town. This happened on a couple of occasions and I did, I think, a better job between the sheets. I adored her, she was so gorgeous, and the side benefits were glorious. The only shock came when we met up a few years after university and offhand, I mentioned how crazy I was about her and she told me, "Really? You never took me seriously, you never really tried. I was mad about you too. I just thought you weren't that interested." I'm still confused about Addie.

Finnula

You'd never guess from the name, but she was Irish. All dark Celtic, lyrical, lilting voice and kind and soft. I met her at a party, and I suggested that we go back to mine as I had some dope and we could share a joint. She said she hadn't smoked a joint before and I reassured her she was in safe hands. When we got back, I skinned up on an album cover and we smoked while I put something soft and lyrical on the turntable. We were on the sofa, and the bar heater was on full and she said she liked the sensation of being stoned. We chatted some more and soon were kissing and she started unbuttoning my shirt. I returned the compliment and said, "Let's go to bed." She wobbled a bit towards the door, and we made it to my room. It was cold — this was student accommodation — and we got under the covers and then took off our clothes. She was even more fingers and thumbs than me. But we got there in the end. It was lovely and dreamy, and I was hard as a rock, and I met no resistance as I slid into her. We moved together and she murmured, "I'm not on the pill." I knew how to decode that. We kept on going and she had a dreamy look in her eye as she tried to focus on me lurching above her. I am sure that before she was ready, I was, and needing to get the timing right, I lurched in and then pulled out and came all over her belly. After a decent period, I got up to find some tissues but came back with a discarded t-shirt. As I wiped our tummies clean, she was already fast asleep. I soon joined her. I woke up the next morning — and she was gone. I didn't even hear her leave. I didn't have her number and it was Sunday. On Monday I went looking for her. When I eventually found her, she wouldn't talk to me. I said "Hi" she looked at me for a moment and just walked away. To this day, I worry, did I take advantage of her? I truly didn't think so at the time. She was totally into everything we did. But there is always that nagging doubt. She never spoke to me again, never let me ask, never mind explain. It haunts me.

Julia

It wasn't all so gothic. In fact, sometimes it was comic. Some bright spark decided it was a great idea to have a beach party the week before we broke up for Christmas. Why not? Girls would be in swimwear and it was indoors, and we were all smart enough to get changed once we were there. In my cuts-offs, espadrilles and a wife-beater vest and straw hat, I fitted right in. I was talking with a girl I fancied who soon made it clear she was waiting for her boyfriend. She asked me, "Do you know Julia Mycock?" I didn't but didn't snort like a buffoon at the name either. I was introduced to Julia. She had on a sarong and a bandana around her head and she looked like a serious beach goddess. I made serious progress by not making any cracks about her surname mostly and keeping it light and fun. I thought I was 'in' and so when my friends said, "Rob, we're off," I waved them away. A little later I offered to walk Julia home. She didn't object. As she changed into winter clothes, I searched for mine. My wanker flatmates must have need laughing themselves to sleep — they had taken everything except my raincoat. I had no option but to walk her back freezing my bollocks off and when we got to hers, we kissed a bit and then she said goodnight!

I explained I'd missed the last tube and was stranded. She said, "Well, you'd better come in then." Bingo. Or not after some very pleasant kissing, my advances were rebuffed. At the second attempt, she was a little less subtle.

"Fuck you? Really? I've only just met you." Well, I'd met girls who didn't have these ridiculously high standards. I slept with her, badly, me in an armchair, her in a bed. Then, while it was still dark, she woke me. I had high hopes, for a moment, only for them to be cruelly dashed. "It's six. The Tube is running now, and you have to go, my mother is coming to pick up my stuff to take home."

Not even a cup of tea, never mind sexual intercourse. And just to prove there is a God and he hates me, it had snowed overnight. In espadrilles and beachwear, I struggled to the tube station. Shivering, I was so glad to get into a train. People stared and moved away from the lunatic in shorts and vest and straw hat. Even so, I hated getting off the other end and back into the cold. When I got home, I was near hypothermia and once my circulation had returned, I plotted my revenge. It never came to anything though. Come on, it was a funny trick to play. I'd have done it. The point if there is one: I would risk death by freezing to secure a shag. And yes, I did see Julia again, and no, we never did.

Lou

There's always the one who got away. And Lou got away, or do I mean escaped a truly awful fate. She was cool, smart and fun. Like us all, she had her own shit to deal with but we always got along really well. I wanted to get along more than well. She didn't. For me, she had potential to be the one. I really liked her and fancied her like mad and respected her. Yes respect. I would never have used the word then, but respect was what it was. Maybe that was what she didn't have for me. After all, I was a stroppy, moody, abrasive drunk who didn't respect her enough to not try and sleep with her friends. I can still see her dancing in a red dress. Hip swaying in a way that didn't lie, long before Shakira educated us about them. The long and short of it, it never happened. Not even a kiss. As a matter of principle, I insisted all her boyfriends were complete knobs, and ironically most of them were. This is intriguing, because by that measure, I was perfect for her. You never know, but the smart money would have to have been on three days of mad passion, three weeks of joy, and then three months of misery and then onto the next one. We will never know. Or at least I won't. Lou was smart. She knew a trouble when she saw it.

There were other girls at college. You know who you are. I assumed that because sex was unimportant to me then, it must have been unimportant to them too. You all brought something to my life and thank you for that. I was an idiot. I hope you can look back and laugh. I hope I never hurt anybody. If I did, I am so sorry. Really sorry. Not just for the appalling behaviour, bad sex and lack of awareness. I'm sorry for not being smart enough to realise I was playing with people's emotions, while only thinking about mine. I'm sure I wasn't the only one. But that doesn't make it right either. For any girls who might think they messed with me. If you did, I didn't notice. So, no harm done.

I graduated from university with an Honours degree — older but no wiser. I was still unable to fathom out women, or how I felt about them. Pathetic, isn't it? Internalising anger and insecurity only helps it grow and become harder to control. I was still no nearer getting over Ann. Or rather the after-effects of Ann.

If only they had anger management people in 1984. I suppose they did, but I never saw one until much later. Fucking and fighting were my coping mechanisms. I didn't realise until a professional told me my issue wasn't hurt or anger — it was shame! Some direct their anger outward, while others focus it inward. Each moment of anger provides a powerful distraction from experiencing shame. Shame, when toxic, is a paralyzing global assessment of yourself as a person. When severe, it forms the lens through which all self-evaluation is viewed. Everyone experiences shame at some time, but not everyone experiences it like me. It takes a lot of energy to protect yourself from shame. Most importantly, it leaves you prone to anger. Anger that results when natural desires for love, connection, and validation are inhibited by the impenetrable barrier of shame. Cheers, Ann.

Chapter 27
Sex and drugs and rock and roll

In my last year of university, I shared a house with five other friends, or four friends and a girl called Lorna. And yes, just the once if you were wondering. A drunken, not very satisfactory union. What can I say? We were young and it happened. But that is not the point. A guy who moved in was a friend of a friend. He was an Australian medical student called Pete. We had the two attic rooms in the Victorian shambles we called home. He dubbed us "the Penthouse boys." Back then *Penthouse* was more synonymous with a porn magazine and porn was just filthy, not morally reprehensible as we now realise. We became good friends, due, I think, to three things. He had a hugely generous nature and was eternally optimistic. He had a dark sense of humour and a really annoying girlfriend. So, he often needed to escape, and going to the pub with me was a great escape. This was not a truly viable proposition for students at the time as pubs were expensive, especially if you drank beer in the quantities we liked to. This was as much as you could ship on board until they threw you out. That, of course, included getting a double-round in when at

10.50 they called "Last orders, gentlemen." One of the few times I was ever called a gentleman.

Pete had a solution to this dilemma. Drug trials. He was studying at Bart's (St. Bartholomew's Hospital), they ran drug trials and would pay you what seemed at the time, the 'riches of Arabi' to take part. £300 to spend two nights and three days in a hospital with free food. We couldn't leave the premises either so that also meant we saved money. When you were finished, they paid you cash in hand. So what if they were giving you an experimental drug and taking blood samples every four or six hours? Actually, it was a bonus because it was normally nurses who drew the blood and nurses were normally girls and so it was a chance to flirt and maybe even pull. Not during the drug trial. The nurses had integrity, even if we didn't. Or was it because they knew the drugs we were taking? My first drug trial was for beta-blockers. You didn't know if you were in the placebo group or what dosage you were being given. Being young and dumb, we just took what they gave us and waited to see what happened.

I am reasonably sure I was not in the placebo group. Neither was Pete. After the first dose at six that evening, we were feeling mellow by seven and by eight I was positively chilled. They took our blood pressure and it was seriously low. But not dangerously so. The next dose was at midnight in bed and I slept like a baby. This makes me wonder what we were taking because all today's commercial beta-blockers tend to keep people awake. Anyway, the next morning, I got out of bed to pee and nearly fainted. I just about managed to stay upright and filled the bottle by the bed and got back under the sheets. Still feeling amazingly calm and happy, I called Pete in the next bed. He woke up and before I could ask him anything, he looked at me with eyes almost rolled back in his head and slurred like some Victorian opium addict, "Mate, the Penthouse Boys are beta-blocked!"

When the nurse came to take our blood pressure and blood, she asked, "Any side-effects?" We both insisted not. She did look a bit concerned about how low our blood pressure was though. After she had gone, we had a quick confab.

"These drugs are cool, can we nick some?" He assured me this was very unlikely and what's more, that if our blood pressure continued to be so low, we would definitely have our dosage reduced and might even be kicked off the trial. This was double jeopardy. No drugs and losing money. We concocted a plan. This involved exercising before the scheduled blood pressure and blood regime to ensure it gave artificially high readings. It worked and with apologies to Bart's and the drug company and anyone whose health has been impacted by my fraud, we walked away feeling very mellow indeed, our pockets full of cash and walked straight into a pub to get a lunchtime shine on. Lunchtime ended with us getting home at eleven-thirty having stayed in the pub all day (the pubs around Bart's had a special license and didn't need to close at three as most others in London had to). The next morning was not good. I don't know if beta-blockers are contraindicated with alcohol, but fuck me, the hangover was a right bastard. Why apart from nostalgia do I mention this? Well, Pete was responsible for introducing me to lying in drug trials, impotence, and my wife. In that order.

There were seven teaching hospitals in London. The rules when recruiting people for drug trials was that they had to screen out anyone who had been in a trial within the last twelve months. Systems were not computerized then, and if they were, they didn't cross-reference. So, we were incredibly cavalier and were willing to take just about anything. It was great money for doing nothing, as we saw it.

Once, we were recruited for a trial of a tricyclic anti-depressant. I had no idea what they were and wouldn't have cared if I did. I hoped the anti-depressant part meant it would get me high. It didn't, but on day two I awoke, for the first time in living memory, without morning wood, no morning glory, no piss-proud cock or any form of nocturnally induced tumescence. This did not worry me, but Freud would no doubt have noted that I noted it, nonetheless. The nurse came around and did the necessary with bloods and blood pressure and asked if I had noted any side-effects. I really didn't want to say, "Actually, I didn't have a boner this morning and that's not normal." Instead, I said nothing. As we were locked away and had nothing to do but read (there was no daytime television then), my mind soon went to matters carnal and I went to look for somewhere private to relieve the tension, as it were. This was duly located, and I started my normal routine. But nothing happened. The Red Army simply would not advance into the peninsula. I totally freaked out. I mean freaked out! They had given me drugs that broke my penis. I was only twenty and very much did not want a broken penis. But what to do? If I walked off the trial, there was no guarantee that they would fix the problem elsewhere. Maybe it was only temporary.

I found Peter and asked if there were side effects to tricyclic anti-depressants and he said, "No, not really. I mean, there are some very rare ones. But nothing we need to worry about." I wasn't about to tell him about my failed wank, but I was seriously worried. So, I pushed him some more. "Nah mate, headaches, nausea, some people get a dry mouth."

I mentioned my lack of morning tumescence and he looked really concerned "Shit, yeh! It's really rare but they can induce erectile dysfunction." I was beginning to discover that adrenaline is brown. "…But it's not *normally permanent*. It should be okay again in a few months or so." I was seriously worried now. As you may already have guessed, Peter was a complete and utter wanker.

I laughed this off, saying, "Yeh right! As if?" But I was not in the least bit as blasé as I pretended. He left me hanging until the next round of dosing. Only then did he tell me the truth. For twelve hours I experienced being a eunuch. I understood the loneliness of the emasculated, the despair of the impotent and the feeble nature of my hold on sex. I was literally going out of my fucking mind. I was so relieved when the sadist came clean. I was too happy to be angry with him. But I wasn't going to take any more risks. I pretended to take the two next doses and then spat them into my hand. The next morning, normal service had been resumed and I made damn sure by finding a private space more than once. I kept my pills and actually ground them into Pete's food on a day I knew he was going to see his girlfriend that night. I have no idea if my fiendish revenge actually worked. One, because he would never say, what boy would, and judging by the trouble she had getting him up the stairs, he'd shipped on-board enough beer to mean he could barely raise a smile, let alone anything else.

Nonetheless, we stayed close and when I graduated, we got a flat together. And that's how I met the woman who was to become my wife. Only decades later did I remember about the vile effects of anti-depressants. Had I remembered, I might have noted Tofranil is a tricyclic anti-depressant and saved myself a load of trouble and a truckload of angst.

Londoners now may not be aware of what a shithole Hackney was in the eighties. "Beirut with JobCenters" was how one comedian described it. That was quite generous. It was horrible. It was also really cheap. To try and make Hackney less of a shithole, or rather make its deepest shitholes a bit shallower, the council gave cheap housing to students, nurses and the absolute scum of the world. Pete was still a student, and so with a bit of lightweight fraud about my status, we took the lease on a flat on the Kingsmead Estate. The 'estate' was in fact twelve blocks of five storeys, low-rise flats with piss-reeking stairways, boarded-up windows and cars up on bricks, but why focus on just its good points? These blocks often feature in London crime dramas. You will see the Kingsmead when the hero or heroine police officer has to go and find a scumbag at home. It was grim, but as I said, it was cheap. We had a kitchen and a front room with a gas fire, a bedroom each and a toilet. I mention the toilet, simply because it is important as a cipher of Pete's eccentricity. I would often find him in the kitchen on a weekend morning to find him making a pot of tea, toast with marmalade and jam and a newspaper at the ready. He would then put it all on a tray and take it with him to the lavatory. I looked aghast the first time, and his response was hard to fault. "It's just better use of time and it makes it a nicer experience." Hard to argue with apart from total and utter disgust.

I was working as a labourer in a theatrical warehouse. The money was pretty good, especially when you factored in the low rent we were paying. There was one extra benefit of working as a labourer in a theatrical supply company. There were plenty of young girls who wanted the bohemian life of treading the boards. Or at least working in the theatre. I was their bit of northern rough and I didn't mind at all. Once they realised I had a degree, and didn't think a thespian was a dyke with a lisp, they often got tired of me fast. But that kind of worked for me too. I still wasn't looking for anything beyond casual fun, lots of laughs and hopefully raunchy and high-impact sex. It's how I met Joanna and I have had a huge love and respect for the theatre ever since.

It also meant I could also subsidize our drink and drug habit. Just to be fair to the mad one, he was very alive to this and had his pride. If I was caught financially patronizing him, he would make some grand fiscal gesture like buying a bottle of champagne. Then for days, he wouldn't be able to go out, so he would stay in and study. Or stay in with Justine. The studying was fine with me. But having Justine around — not to be encouraged.

As for Justine, how can I explain? Well, firstly her name was Bernadette, but she didn't like that, so she adopted her middle name when she arrived at medical school instead of art school. But she definitely wanted to live like common people. She was the extremely middle-class daughter of bourgeois parents from the outskirts of London. She made out that she had rejected all that and was a committed feminist, environmentalist and strident socialist worker. You either agreed with her or had your ear talked off. Even if you agreed with her, she would challenge you to somehow prove it. She was quite pretty though, yet this was the first time I had known a pretty girl that I just could not fancy. She drove me mad, but not in any way that developed any sexual tension. It was just tension. Okay, push me if you want. I suppose, in a real pinch, I would have fucked her

Another angle on Justine. I don't know what it tells us, but it tells us something. Joanna was to put it simply, an ace fellatrix. Off the scale, porn-star quality. This was fine by me and I wasn't so stupid as to broadcast the fact or she would have had a pack of baying men after her all the time. Yet there was a downside. She was never really keen on anything else. Being young and foolish, I didn't go with the flow and instead pushed her for full-on sex. Why? I don't know. It's a forbidden fruit thing, I suppose. Rather than have the conversation with Joanna like a grown-up would, I mostly accepted her view of our oral extravaganzas, "I love doing it and you love it. Where's the problem?" And that's where I should have left it. Instead, over several pints with Pete, I told him of my, dare I call it, problem.

Firstly, of course, he told me this was no problem. In fact, for most men, it was a dream. Then we started drunkenly analysing the situation. Maybe she loves the reaction it gets, loves the power that it gives her? She also knows she is really good at it. So, it's a way of competing with other girls. She thinks it's not such a big deal compared to having sex. "Maybe she just doesn't like intercourse, because you are shit at it?" he also helpfully offered. Then he quizzed me about what she actually did that made it so fabulous. No, I am not going to tell you. Google 'How to give a brilliant blowjob'. Joanna probably posted it. What I will say, is that she made it a performance and she was never rushed. In fact, she challenged me to hold on for as long as possible and as I did, she rose to the challenge and she made sure there was plenty of eye contact. She liked to see me, see her, doing it.

The next night that Joanna was over, and we retired to my room for obvious purposes and Pete and Justine went to theirs. Things proceeded slowly. When you know what's coming, you don't have to rush, and that for Joanna was all part of the game. Eventually, I was laying back on the pillows, my legs spread wide and watching my cock slide into her mouth, while I maintained eye contact and she maintained a hand-grip on my balls. It was delightful. It was then that I saw my door was slightly ajar, which was unusual when sex was on the cards. I glanced and considered getting up to close it when I saw a slight movement. Staying on message with Joanna, I ran my hand through her hair and groaned. Encouraged by this, she eased off as she wanted to be in complete control. I looked over again and the door was even more open, and Justine was crouched down watching. I should have stopped and told her to fuck off. I didn't. Then I saw Pete's head higher up in the crack. This was getting weird. As I was losing, shall we say, momentum, Joanna felt the need to raise the stakes. She got on her knees and said, "I want you to fuck my mouth." I'd never heard this before, but I kind of got it. So, holding her face, I did. It had the desired effect. But as she saw the inevitable coming, she stopped me and started jerking me off while tonguing my balls. "Tell me when you're going to come," she said, and a short time after, I raised the alarm. She moved up and quite literally engulfed me. I can't understand how she didn't gag, but I was beyond the point of caring.

When I was done, she eased off my now incredibly tender cock and quite matter-of-factly said, "When you do that, it goes straight down your throat and you don't have to taste it." Please note she said 'you' not 'I'. Then laughing her head off, she looked straight at the door. "Yes, I saw you and I saw Pat see you. It was actually quite hot." She really did love theatre and knew how to play to an audience.

Writing this, I have just felt the cold wind of hatred from a million men swirl across me. The men who dream of such a problem. The great unblown! Sorry, guys. Proof for you at least, your life doesn't really suck. Is that any consolation?

Chapter 28
In the year of the cat

As soon as I was out of Dr Smug the sexologist's office, I called and made an appointment with the world-famous Dr Felix. The first consultation was set, and I was excited, maybe a solution was at hand. I could be twenty-five again, totally at ease with sex and able to come as quickly or as slowly or as often as I wanted. Well, it was worth a try. As I arrived for my appointment, I saw that the doctor's office was in an apartment block, which I thought was a bit dodgy, until I saw all the brass plaques for all the other doctors. Dr Felix had discreetly titled himself as Psychotherapist rather than 'Last hope of sexual losers' — which was nice, I thought. I went up to the fourth floor and went into his waiting room. I sat down and waited. Unfortunately, I was early and so had time to look at the leaflets and posters. "Depression is a disease that needs understanding" fair enough, no issues there from my side. "Female orgasm. Why is it so elusive for so many women?" Interesting, but not my field. At the same time, it convinced me I was in the right place. "The Sexocoporel Annual General Meeting" all looking good so far. Then I saw it. 'Paedophilia. You can control it.'

Fuck me! If anyone else comes in this waiting room they are going to think I'm a fucking pedo! If I see someone else, will they be a pedo? I was seriously pondering whether I should explain that "I just have problems coming, I'm not a kiddie fiddler," to anyone I saw. It was nerve-wracking. Then I heard the consulting room door opening and caught the briefest glimpse of an attractive woman. Sometimes it's good to know your worst instincts never let you down. Why? Because even with that merest glimpse, I was distracted to thinking.

Well, I'd have a crack at making her orgasm given half a chance…

A couple of minutes later, I was greeted by Dr Felix or "The Cat" as I came to think of him. He was so not cat-like and so not sexy. He looked like someone who would be the agricultural implements experts on *The Antiques Roadshow*. Jumbo cord trousers and a plaid shirt. Half-moon glasses on a red cord, balding and, well, frankly fat and not handsome. I could see why he got into the sex business as a pro. Because as an amateur, I wouldn't fancy his chances. Nonetheless, besides my uncharitable thoughts, The Cat turned out to be a really, exceptionally nice man who changed my life.

I walked in and saw the standard psychiatrist set up. Two armchairs facing each other and a clock facing his chair. We both sat down and he explained that this first session would take two hours and then he would decide if he could help. Well in for a penny… and off we went.

The first ten minutes was easy, he just wanted the family background and medical history. I told him all that and my history of the prolactinoma and the anti-depressant story. He looked up and was visibly angry! "Anti-depressant for delayed orgasm? That is odd… crazy!" He got out his medical compendium and started looking for the Tofranil and got even angrier.

"A urologist thinks he is qualified to give anti-depressants with no psychological training. Maybe I should prescribe you some diuretics… And the we can see what he thinks of me?" This was a distraction, but I was warming to him. Who wouldn't warm to a doctor who will openly criticise other doctors? He also realised we were getting side-tracked and so he wrote some notes and declared, "I will look into it and get back to you…"

Then we started talking about my delayed orgasm and anejaculation. He told me, "Delayed orgasm can lead to the avoidance of sex and relationships. If you are left feeling frustrated or disappointed every time you have sex, it's understandable that you'd tend not to engage in sexual activity."

Yes, to the frustration but no to the avoidance. He continued, "With D.O. (we were already into abbreviation), your partner may feel that you don't find them sexually stimulating enough, that they are bad lovers, or have an inadequate body. This is most likely not the case, but identifying and discussing the actual cause of the problem can be sensitive and far from simple. Don't you find?"

Damn straight. Talking about it with your red-hot lover or your long-term partner. Maybe some men are good at that shit. I would just feel like I was a eunuch. "Yes, it's difficult," I replied. Then he said he had a checklist we needed to go through to rule out some causes.

"Fear of causing pregnancy?"

"Nope, had a vasectomy years ago."

"Religion? You said you were raised a devout Catholic."

What crossed my mind was his use of 'devout'. Why are Catholics always devout but Protestants are always staunch? You never hear of staunch Catholics or devout Protestants. Was I avoiding the issue? Perhaps?

"Well, my background was religious, and sex was dirty. But only if you're doing it right, as Woody Allen said. Although sex quotes from Woody Allen have a darker overtone these days."

The Cat did not laugh.

"Feelings of shame?"

"Not proud of my affairs, but it's never been an issue in the past."

"Strong cultural or religious beliefs about sex?"

"I don't think so."

"Stress or depression?"

"I have always been stressed, my whole professional life."

"Sexual trauma?"

"No, the monks were violent, but they never tried to rape me."

"Relationship difficulties?"

"Hhhhmmmm! Yes, a wife and a mistress." He scribbled away at that one.

"Fear of feeling out of control or vulnerable — relaxing and 'letting go' does not always come naturally. D.O. may be a physical manifestation of psychologically holding back?"

"That's it, the feeling is that I can't let go no matter how much I want to."

"Negative feelings about the look, smell or feeling of semen?"

"No. No snowballing. I don't love it, but it doesn't bother me either."

"Snowballing?" he asked.

"When you come in a girl's mouth and she kisses it back into yours."

"Oh, I've never heard it called snowballing." And he scribbled furiously. I felt rather pleased to have widened his vocabulary.

"Fear of losing physical control during orgasm, particularly the fear of sudden incontinence?"

"Absolutely not."

"Okay. Good," said the Cat. "Now we need to look at your sexual history." It was not what I expected.

"So, when did you first start masturbating?" Blimey! He didn't beat around the bush.

"Eleven, I can remember the very first one."

"Continue…"

"I found my elder brother's copy of *Emmanuelle* and reading it made my cock hard. I was rubbing it while I read, and this got more and more exciting and some white stuff came out."

"What did you do?"

"Well, as soon as I could, I did it again."

"So how often did you masturbate?"

I didn't know what the correct number should be, so I told him the truth.

"Probably about three times a day. Sometimes more." I looked at him, not knowing if he would be appalled or disappointed.

"That's good."

Good? Why is that good? Is he a lunatic? He saw my questioning look.

"It means you have a strong libido. The libido generally falls as we get older, but you were lucky enough to have a high starting point." Then without a blink, he asked, "How do you masturbate?" Blimey again. He really wasn't holding back. I looked at him quizzically.

"How do you hold your penis? What movement do you make?" This was truly information I had never shared with anyone. Kitty had seen it in action, but never asked specifically. I showed the Cat the action. It looked like I was gesturing to call him 'a wanker'. He didn't blink and just noted

"Thumb and fingers jerking?" Then he threw a curveball.

"Do you hold your breath when you orgasm? Triple blimey! I'd never really thought about it. So, I thought about it and said "Yes! I suppose I do."

"When you masturbate…" what more could he want? "…what position are you in?"

"Generally, lying on my back on a bed."

"Hhhmmm, and when you are having sex, is this a position you use?

"Not often. If a girl likes it. But it's not my preference."

Moving off topic slightly, he then explained, "No, it's not a good position. Most women only like it because they see it in films and believe it is empowering. Most, though, prefer sex from behind lying, kneeling or standing, and face-to-face lying down. These are the best positions for men too." He was very emphatic and as he was a world-famous sexologist I wasn't going to argue.

We got back to wanking.

"Now, as a man, how often do you masturbate?"

"If I don't have sex, I tend to masturbate."

"So, if I understand, you have sex or masturbate every day?"

"Yes, until this issue started happening."

"That is quite a lot for a man in his fifties. Maybe try and cut back."

Then he went on, "And when you ejaculate, how is it?"

What the fuck does that mean? I thought. *Does he mean how does it feel? What happens?*

Thankfully he came to my aid. "How many pulses of semen?"

Aaahh! Now I get it.

"It used to be more, but now three or four, but recently the intensity has been reduced."

"Hhhmmm, that's normal with age. We can surely fix the intensity problem, but lower ejaculate volume is normal. It will increase if you reduce the frequency."

Well, that was good to know. Then we got off the wanking subject.

"So, when you are having sex, take me through your issues."

I explained that there was no set pattern, but that arousal led to foreplay led to penetration and until recently I would vary intensity and speed to match my partner and when it was time, I would increase the tempo and orgasm myself.

"But now sometimes, often, I start to feel that I will not finish, and this becomes a vicious circle. I get concerned, my erection softens, so I worry more, and it becomes self-fulfilling."

He laughed. The fucker laughed. Not nastily, but enough to make me think he was an insensitive prick.

"Now you know how it feels to be a woman sexually. Men are much more physical in this regard than women, much more in the brain. If a woman gets into the loop you describe, it will always have exactly those same results for them."

This was interesting but no use whatsoever. He must have read my face.

He gave me some statistics. "Delayed orgasm is experienced by over twenty-five percent of men over fifty and rises to thirty-five percent into the sixties." I suppose I took some comfort in knowing I wasn't a total freak. At the same time, this didn't help me feel any better. "It's crazy, men don't talk about it," he said. And I suppose those figures are quite shocking or at least they were to me. Men talk about everything. Everything, that is, apart from serious discussions of sex. It's because we are all scared of either falling short or revealing a weakness. As I mused, he quickly went on.

"The good news is I believe we can resolve your issues. It will take time, and you will have to do a lot of work with me." He wasn't going to suggest doing things together was he? Before I had the chance to tell him I just wasn't that sort of boy, he continued.

"There must be a proper balance between the parasympathetic nervous system — which controls the body at rest — and the sympathetic nervous system, which controls the body's 'fight or flight or freeze' response. In other words, the performance of your penis rests on a reflex loop. At the top of the loop, sensory information is processed either in the spinal cord or brain and then received by the penis. And then, at the other end of the loop, the spinal cord or brain tells the penis what to do next."

I was totally confused. So he made it simple.

"We will work on both the psychological and physiological triggers. Exercises to break your bad habits. Also, a series of very specific muscle training and physical movements to get you back to the natural movements and break the bad habits you have developed."

He went on. "You may well remember, young men generally try to overcome the reflex loop and stop orgasm happening too early. This becomes learned and can lead, in time, to situations like yours. You have mastered the 'fight or flight or freeze' response so well that the other side, the parasympathetic is overwhelmed. You have a prolactinoma, plus stress, compounded by the stress of your delayed orgasm and the SSRIs. It's good that you came so soon." He was foreign, the awful pun was lost on him.

"We have much work to do. But we have to stop now. Until our next meeting, I want you to work on the stress in sex. One game you can try is not having sex! You play the game the one who gets the other to beg for more to take things to the next stage is the winner. But you must not have sex. Try this for a few weeks. You can masturbate, but try not to, and absolutely not together. Together, it must be just the game. This will eventually lead you to relax about orgasm rather than anticipate it." It sounded like a terrible idea. But heh ho! Give it a go. And you know what. It really isn't as bad as it sounds. It is not great, but it did play a positive part in the process.

Then he stood and said, "When shall we next meet?"

"What? Can't we just continue until I'm fixed?" is what I wanted to say. But I just lamely got out my diary. But now at least there was hope. I left happier than I went in. Nobody saw me, so nobody thought I was a pedo!

Chapter 29
Bad Luck

I've had some strange nights. I've been off my tits in many bars around the world. I've sat in a whorehouse in Spain that provided 'Lookalikey' whores and just had drinks. They were very expensive, the drinks and the whores. I was a wingman to a friend and despite, or maybe because of my vices, I have never had any interest in 'Commercial sex'. Yes really! I don't condemn it; it just doesn't work for me as a concept. But perhaps the strangest night I've ever had was in a Thai Karaoke bar in a suburban town swilling down brandy with a man who had just caught me going away for a weekend with his wife. Joined the dots yet?

Kitty and I met at cheap local hotels for a few hours as often as we could, we walked by the river and snogged in carparks. We met in coffee bars and made use of the disabled toilets, even a self-service tanning salon once or twice. The hotels were fine, but be it the pressure, or my brain tumour or something else, I often just couldn't come when we were having a quickie. All of it was wonderful in its own way though. Helping her with the shopping because it was the only cover she had for being out, was frustrating in one sense, yet it was also a chance to talk about anything and everything. The sheer mundanity of it made it so easy and the way she looked at me made me feel warm — like a kid. I was getting deeper and deeper in. She announced she had a chance to be at a fashion show in London for two days and more importantly, two nights. If I could make it, we could go together. During the day, she had to be visible and spend time with friends, after that we would be on our own. After Paris, we knew we had to be uber-careful. I was only to WhatsApp if she contacted me first as her phone was often checked and I was to make no efforts to contact any other way. It was just too dangerous. I watched my phone like a hawk and tried to be available for anything at short notice.

She didn't make it easy though. She sent raunchy messages. Once after leaving a hotel and going our separate ways, she sent a picture of her fingers on her clit and the message: "Today was literally fucking incredible. But I need more. Come to my house at three." I duly did and fucked her against the garage wall while the cleaner was pottering in the kitchen. Did she like the fucking or the thrill or both? Or really did she truly love me as she said in another text: "I've never felt this way about anyone before. Physically we are amazing together. At the same time, I love you and I also want to be sexy and wanton for you. I want to be your tart if you want me to be or your tender lover if you want that too. IRDLY!"

IRDLY! I Really Do Love You. I loved reading that more than the sexy bit. Pick the bones out of that lot. I felt much the same. It was madness, but what glorious insanity. Sex was always there but it was more than that now. Much more than that. Despite the constant surveillance, we managed to arrange to take the train together. I would join one stop down the line as she would probably be dropped off as a courtesy and as a double-check. Radio silence had to be observed and I said I would find her in her seat once I was on board. I stood on the platform really excited, not sexually, well a bit, but by the thought that we would be going away together. Like a couple. We would do shit together, not just sex, things that couples do, go out have dinner, get drunk, go dancing. I didn't care what.

As the train pulled in, my phone buzzed and WhatsApp announced, "Darling, Carriage 5 Seat 28." It was the other end of the train but not a problem.

I sent back a simple "See ya in two minutes." And in those two minutes, she had started to cry and had her phone to her ear. She gestured me to be silent and I waited as she whispered into the phone. After an agonizing couple of minutes, she hung up. "Gordon cloned my phone. He knows it's you. He knows what we're doing."

The train was already moving. The next stop was more than an hour away. She was gently weeping, and I was just sat there in shock. I tried to comfort her, but it was on a packed train. Of all the things she might say,

I was shocked by what she did come out with, "I'm so sorry, my love." And then we did embrace and fuck anybody watching. "I'm so sorry. He wants me to stay on board and for you to go back. He wants to talk to you." This was all getting a little surreal. The best I could do was the reply, "What do you want me to do?"

"I don't know. What can we do?" Then her phone rang again. No prizes for guessing who. She was whispering onto the phone and started crying all over again. Eventually, they stopped talking. "We need to get off at the next station. He says we can talk and then he wants to talk to you. Then he will talk to me, and if we can both convince him it's over, he will have me back."

My answer was not exactly imaginative. "What do you want me to do? What do you want to do? I love you, Kitty, we can make a go of it. It's what I want. Like I said, what do you want?" That went on in a loop for it seemed to last forever.

Then the train pulled into the station, killing the conversation for a moment. We grabbed our bags and got off. Outside the station, there was a hotel. There's always a hotel outside the station. Thankfully, this one was quite swanky, not a fleapit. We walked over and left our bags and went to the bar. It was empty and so we had a waiter before we even sat down. To this day I don't know why but I told him, "Two glasses of champagne." We sat and I leaned in and kissed her. It was warm and close and not sexy. The drinks arrived and we started where we left off. "What do you want me to do? What do you want to do? I love you, Kitty."

And I really believed her when she said, "And I love you as I've never loved anyone. It's different. Not just the physical stuff. There's something I can't describe. It's just something I've never felt before."

I told her that if that was true then we had a chance, we could make it work. We kissed some more and then came the bad news. "We can't! I can't do this to my kids. You can't do it to your family. Carrying all that baggage, it would weigh us both down. We'd be at each other's throats in a couple of years."

I disagreed and we talked more, and she cried. And I felt like crying. Her phone rang again. I don't suppose I could blame him. I nursed my champagne for fifteen minutes and when she came back it was all logistics. "He wants you to call when you are on a train, he will meet you at the station. I'm to carry on to London."

I told her we couldn't talk here, and she looked askance. I walked to the reception and asked if they had a room. They did and I walked back into the bar and waved a key. "We need somewhere we can talk in private and figure it all out. That's all."

I guess you know us both now. That wasn't all. There was love in that lovemaking and tears and a huge amount of talking. She could not end her marriage like this. We had to stop, and this was the last time we would see each other or talk. There was a lot more crying. I don't know that I stayed dry-eyed either. Then ninety minutes later we checked out again. I put her on the next train to London and as she left, I gave her a tiny scrap of paper. The length and width of a cigarette, I had torn it from the top of the room service menu. IRDLYAIAW (And I Always Will — do keep up!). She cried again and I saw it go into her purse not just thrown away. I wonder if it's still there?

The train pulled out and I called Gordon. It was a brief, terse call as I told him my train would get in at 7.38. Then I had to figure out how I was going to explain getting home two days early myself. This was made easier because my cover story was that I was flying to Barcelona for a conference. I lied that I was calling from there and that a huge food poisoning outbreak had meant it was called off and I would be on the first flight back but, "Don't wait up, darlin'." I received nothing but sympathy. That just made me feel worse. Then back on the train and figuring out how to deal with Gordon.

He's not Scottish. So really, his parents have no excuse for calling him Gordon. Maybe they loved the Thunderbirds? Anyway, he's an Ulsterman and that did make me think that maybe he had a gun. I know it's ridiculous, but you try putting yourself in my shoes. True to his word he was there to meet me, unarmed as far as I could see. What the fuck do you do in that situation? Shake hands, not shake hands? I settled for a non-committal, "Hi."

It seemed to do the job and as he turned his back, he said, "Come on, let's get a drink." We walked out of the station and into a pub. "How's your health?" I looked a little confused. "Kitty told me about your tumour…"

"I'm okay. It's no excuse for anything." He was throwing me off track. I expected rage and recriminations not polite inquiries about my well-being. He likes Scotch, so I said I'd have one too. Armed with two triples and no side-arm, he tried to find a space to talk. But the place was rammed. "This is pointless," he said. "Let's find somewhere quieter." And with that, he downed the scotch and we walked out again. The only place that was open and quiet was a Thai restaurant. In we went and as they had no scotch, he ordered us two big brandies. We sat and started to get serious. "Rob, I need to talk and be clear. I know you are a good guy. I know you're not just some wanker. I'm not going to turn this into a character assassination…" Assassination was a word that jarred, but I just let him talk. "I need to figure out how to hold my family together. I can't do that unless I know it's over between you and Kitty."

I looked him square in the eye and said, "She has made it totally clear that it's over." She wasn't that emphatic at all. It just seemed the right thing to say. That she had ended it and I was very hurt.

"Is it over in your mind too?" He was no fool.

"Gordon, after all, that has gone on, I don't expect you to believe a single word I say, but yes, it's over."

It was then that it got even more surreal. The huge plasma screen in the restaurant lit up and two Thais waitresses started singing Karaoke to a song I had never heard before. Maybe it had been a big hit in Bangkok.

We talked more and had another large brandy. He wanted details, of course. No not like that. He wanted to know how long it had been going on. I lied and said, "I wasn't keeping a diary."

Then the killer. "She's amazing, isn't she? Do you love her?"

How to handle that? No, and I was a twat, just fucking his missus, but yes, and we are in another world of hurt. I side-stepped better than I ever had in my playing career. "It doesn't matter either way. She's told me to never contact her again and forget we ever knew each other." He sat and processed that.

The manageress of the restaurant came over with the brandy bottle and having totally misread the situation offered us the microphone and pointed to the screen. It was It was Chris Rea's Fool if you Think it's Over. So we sang a duet. FFS! No, we didn't. Although,

So we sang a duet. FFS! No, we didn't. Although, all said and done if we had, it wouldn't have made the night stranger.

"Maybe later," I said to the woman.

Gordon laughed and then immediately moved off at a tangent. "I like you. You're a good guy. I know you're a good guy, a cool guy." Then boom, again. "When did you first notice her?"

Rather than think fast, I just told him the truth. "The first time we met."

"Yes, she can have that effect. I think she noticed you, was more the point. I saw it and hated it!" Where the fuck was this going? He then started telling me about her. All about her. It was strangely not awkward — two guys who loved the same woman, talking about her. I let him do most of the talking. (I can hear Kitty laughing at that. She always insisted I could never shut up and listen.) And I let him set the pace on the drinking. He wanted it to be a sprint, not a marathon. So, we were on our fourth triple in less than forty-five minutes and I was starting to really feel it. After he had finished telling me about his amazing wife and alluded to me being one of a few, if not many, 'mistakes' she had made, he ordered more drinks and looked me straight in the eye. Or as straight as we could both manage by then. "Can you keep away from her?"

I immediately said "Yes."

"Do I have your word?"

"Yes." That was the tough bit. I am a selfish, thoughtless twat. But even a selfish, thoughtless twat can have a code. Somewhere inside me, when you give your word, you keep it. This time I wasn't at all sure I meant it.

Then he shook my hand and said, "Let's have another drink." So, we did.

He was getting drunk. He had to be, because I certainly was, and I was bigger and heavier. After a few more pleasantries, I can't remember what they were. He said changed tack again, "I have a Head of Security.

He's ex-SAS. He told me once he works off the books too. I have thought of having you thrown in the back of the van and letting him dole out some medicine..." He expected me to be scared I suppose.

But pissed and never any good as the recipient of threats, I simply said, "I've been beaten by professionals before, and a couple of amateurs. If you decide to take him up on his offer, tell him to do it right. You'll only get one shot." Boom. That took the wind out of his sails. Helped by a gut's full of hard liquor, it must have sounded more convincing than it did to me.

More drinks and him asking me if "Miranda knows about this?" I told him, no, and he moved on to, "Who else knows?"

I told him the truth. "If anyone else knows, then they didn't hear it from me. I'm not proud of myself!" This seemed to hit the mark and he ordered yet more brandy and the bill. Weirdly, we argued over who should pay. Social convention prevails even when you are two men pissed in a Thai Karaoke bar discussing the affair of your wife/lover. He'd invited me so he paid. Drinks downed and bill paid, we swayed to the door. Then he got his car keys out and offered to give me a lift home!

With another shred of decency coming through again, I could see he was pissed and upset. I could not let him do it. I snatched the keys and he scrambled for them. "Gordon. We are both pissed. You're not getting into a car." I walked off and he followed me. I said,

"C'mon, we can share a taxi." Reluctantly he agreed. It was a mistake; we should have taken two different ones. In the cab, the drink took its full effect and he started to look sullen and I could feel his anger rising. He was mute in the back of the cab and so as we got close to his house, I said to the cabby, "Just down here on the left, it's number one-forty-seven." Something flashed across his eyes and I realized my blunder. We got out and I asked the cabbie to wait a minute. I walked around to say goodbye and he had a cold fury in his eyes.

"You know exactly where to stop at my house and what number it is, you cunt!"

"Gordon, I've been to your house with you before…"

He poked me in the chest. "More than once, eh? To fuck my wife, you Taig cunt!"

I pushed his hand away. "If you want to finish it like this" — I spread my arms wide — "Then take your fucking swing!" I wanted him to hit me. Then it would be okay. Then it would be all sorted out. I'd fucked his wife and he knocked me down.

He didn't swing, but he did sway. "Put your arms down."

I didn't. the cabbie had his phone out, ready to call the police I suppose. "Fuck you, you Taig cunt, fuck her, fuck you both…" Then he lurched towards his gate. I got back in the cab and went home.

(BTW, anyone not familiar with Ulster slang, a Taig is a Catholic. Quite why that was so important to him; I really have no idea. The rest I understood completely.)

I got home. Miranda was on another night with the Samaritans There was food in the oven and a nice note on the counter. This was getting stranger and stranger. I just got into bed. Drunk, lover-less and I thought that was that. Until my phone rang. It was Kitty. She was calling on the hotel phone. "Are you okay? I've just had Gordon slurring down the phone."

I told her I was drunk too and a little of what happened. "Well, he carried on when he got home. His daughter found him across the kitchen table with a whiskey tumbler in his hand."

I told her I was so sorry and gave her my side of things. I told her I still loved her, and she said, "I love you too. But it's over now. I'm hanging up or I will just cry even more…"

I shouted, "Please don't…" Click. She was gone.

Weeks passed. In a way, I was okay with it all. We'd had our moment in the sun and a big dramatic end and normal life was a tad boring but relaxing at the same time. I missed her. I missed her a ton. But yet…

Then my phone rang and I didn't recognize the number. "I'm at my mum's. I can't really talk…"

In a whispered conversation we both checked each other was okay and eventually agreed to meet when she got back. She said she would let me know when but now it would have to be exclusively at her house and only when Gordon was away. She was being monitored now as if MI6 had her under surveillance. So, it wasn't over after all. What was she thinking? What was I thinking? Let's face it: we weren't thinking. Love may be blind, but it definitely makes you stupid. What it did do was start the happiest six months of my life.

Chapter 30
Galvanized

Now I knew what was waiting for me, I walked into the Cat's waiting room with about thirty seconds to spare. This was deliberate as I didn't want to sit under the 'pedo poster' for a second longer than necessary. My saviour walked in to get me and after a brief "How are you and how are things?" we got back down to business.

We started with more theory. He explained, "You must learn to control the perineal and pelvic floor muscles. By exercising them we gain more control and can contract them and speed up ejaculation and strengthen it.

"So, please stand." We both stood.

"We contract the muscles at the base of the scrotum and to the anus." I never thought I would be doing this with another man, but what the hell.

"Can you feel it? "That's it. Squeeze the lemon!" I giggled. I mean, who wouldn't? But he kept a straight face and said, "Yes. Not too hard not too little. Squeeze… Can you feel it at the base of your penis? Good."

I went to sit down and he gestured no. There was more to come.

"Now tense your buttocks." So I did.

"No, not like that!" This was getting weirder by the minute. I was tensing my buttocks wrongly.

"You are moving the thighs. Do it like this. And he showed me. Okay, so I tried again. And he was pleased and nodded his approval. Tip, for anyone interested. The right way to do it is as if you are trying to stop someone pushing something up your bum, using only your butt cheeks as defence.

"Yes, we must also strengthen pelvic floor muscles for the power of the ejaculation. Aging weakens the muscles involved and when this happens, semen doesn't spurt, it dribbles, and orgasms may provide little pleasure."

If it was going to give extra power to the ejaculation too, this was worth investing in. "You should do this every day. Thirty times. Preferably twice a day. But it must be every day. So, muscle memory gets established. This will help with the delayed orgasm and in time add intensity to the ejaculation." I took him at his word and have done them ever since. In fact, I'm doing them right now.

Next, he told me we had to work on relaxing. This was counter-intuitive as it was the issue that was making me anxious. He kindly helped me to understand.

"Anxiety messes up sex. Anxiety triggers stress which is exactly the opposite of what needs to happen for sexual arousal to continue uninterrupted. Arousal is under the command of the 'rest, relax and digest' response. It can be short-circuited if the stress response is triggered. The stress response is designed to overrule the relaxation response to keep you alive in times of danger. It sounds paradoxical, but you have to be relaxed to get sexually excited. You, Rob, when you are stressed, have a freeze reaction — sexually."

So we did some breathing exercises. Simple diaphragm breathing. Just like they teach you in yoga classes and just like they teach actors at drama school. If you breathe the way you breathe when you're relaxed, it hoodwinks your body and brain into being more relaxed. I was sceptical. But it was worth a shot and actually, it was quite relaxing.

"Thirty times a day every day — minimum."

Then he brought me back to wanking. "Last time we discussed masturbation. Over time men develop very personalized styles of masturbation. Often these do not mimic intercourse or fellatio, which is wet and warm and gentle. You showed me your style and it is quite vigorous. Some people have called this the 'Death-grip'. If you do it a lot, and you don't use lube, it can get disassociated with sex. Why? Because the typical vagina feels too loose, in comparison with the Death Grip. Then fellatio provides insufficient friction to produce an orgasm."

This took time to process. Then I realised he wasn't stopping there.

"I've counselled men who work their penises harder than any woman ever would. You must stop this. When you masturbate, use lube and make your hand like a vagina or mouth. This will re-associate it with intercourse."

This information is solid gold for older guys. If you still rub one out from time to time or even often. Lose the death grip and use lube. Believe me, I have moved on and while it takes time to change the habits of a lifetime, the results are hugely beneficial. Sex and masturbation are no longer different physical sensations, or not totally anyway. One becomes the mimic of the other and, frankly, you get back to the excitement of sex in the physical, as well as the erotic, stimulation.

"And don't lie on your back. Masturbate in your sexual positions." This really was getting to be comical. I was fifty-four and being taught how to wank by a highly paid expert.

There is no denying that it is much harder to wank in the positions that you have sex, after decades of lying back. It just didn't feel right to be kneeling up pretending to be going at it doggie style. But the professional advice is 'wank as you fuck'. Again, it joins the two back together. It works

And with all that, he told me our time was up and, "Next time, we will start very specific exercises. Until then, have sex but don't try and orgasm. If it happens okay, but no trying." As he walked me out the door, he bid me farewell as no one had ever done before: "Remember, always masturbate with lube like a vagina."

Chapter 31
Brown-eyed girl

Sometime after the Joanna scenario, it must have been a Saturday night. Pete announced, "Nurses' disco?" I was tired and knocked about from rugby and just wanted to go out and get drunk. Discos have never been my thing. I'm a useless dancer and I don't like it. They are noisy. This is not a problem as such. I like loud music, but my limited success with girls comes from talking to them, not strutting my stuff on the dance floor. So, I said, "Nah, mate."

The immediate response was "Rob, there are only two certainties in life: death and nurses!" Maybe I should have stuck to my guns, but his argument was compelling. So off we went to St. Bartholomew's' Medical School nurses' disco. If I had stuck to my guns, my life would have been so very different. So would Miranda's.

It wasn't a sumptuous location. Don't for a second imagine Studio 54, or even a small-town night club. It was the medical school bar and common room with a man with turntables, a glitter ball and all the curtains drawn. Tables were pushed to the edges to make a dancefloor and that was that. We paid our £3 at the door and walked in. It was a single man's heaven. Seventy-five percent of the people there were women between the ages of eighteen and twenty-three. They were all dolled-up to the nines and the other twenty-five percent were the male nurses and medical students and me. We were in the eighties, so male nurse equated to hairdresser or florist so "Definitely probably almost certainly queer" and so no competition.

"If you can't pull here, you can't pull, mate," said Pete. This was challenging because all the girls were there to dance. Not my strong suit. So, I hung around the bar and watched for a while, nursing my pint, and shout-talking to Pete and any of his mates who I happened to know. The feeding frenzy was starting, but I bided my time even as I saw couples pairing off. At last, I saw a chink of light in the darkness. Two girls were talking to a guy and one of them was drop-dead gorgeous. I edged closer trying to figure out my next move as she turned and caught my eye.

So in a moment of inspiration I said, "Stop playing gooseberry, why not come and talk to me?" She clearly didn't hear and moved closer and I said it again.

Her reply was not what I expected. "That's the worst chat-up line I have ever heard." I was dying on my arse here. All those years of not giving a fuck and pulling like crazy. What was wrong with me? "Try: can I buy you a drink?" she said. So, I did. And she told me she would like a gin and tonic. And that's where it all started.

We talked and she explained that she wasn't the third wheel in the conversation. In fact, the lad was a former boyfriend. (I liked hearing 'former') who was trying to 'get back with me'. Her friend was there to give moral support and ensure he understood. I looked around and couldn't see him. So, we chatted on. She was spectacular. Not 5'7" and not willowy. That was a good start. She had smiling brown eyes and auburn hair, and a delightful figure. Slim but rounded and a fantastic arse (sorry, 'Mind, but it's what I noticed at the time). She was very, very pretty and so full of beans. I suspected a bit drunk too. It all augured well. Then impending disaster struck.

She said, "Come on, let's dance…" There was no way out as she dragged me physically to the dancefloor. En route, I warned her that I wasn't much of a dancer. She was not to be denied. And to the Celtic tones of Van Morrison, she glided while I lurched and towards the end of the song she suddenly stopped and said, "Well, you weren't lying about your dancing skills."

We walked back to the bar and as Van sang on, I asked in lip-synch with the music, "Would you like a drink yooooooo, ma brown-eyed girl?" What was I doing? *FFS, Rob! What is wrong with you tonight?* That was so cheesy. It deserved her to dry-retch into her own mouth and simply never talk to me again.

Fortunately for me, this actually brought on a belly laugh, through which she sputtered, "You have the worst chat up lines — ever!" and she was right. I was never this uncool, but rarely had I been so taken by a girl. She made me nervous. Back at the bar, we talked some more, and I looked for any and every way to drag her somewhere to kiss her. She knew how the game was played and was determined to stick to verbal communication. The lad from earlier reappeared in front of us and without acknowledging me, looked her straight in the eye and said, "I'm leaving. Are you coming?"

Her reply was, "I'm having a drink with Rob."

To wind him up, I played nice: "Hi, what can I get you?" Turning and seeing me six inches taller than him and his ex, blowing him off in public, he said nothing, turned on his heel and left. With a bit less self-control, it would have been a flounce, but to be fair, he just about kept it under control.

"Was it something I said?" This diffused the awkward situation a bit, but not a lot. After ten minutes she explained that she should probably find her friends as they were going home together. I asked where she lived and she said Hackney.

Bingo! I thought. On parting, we agreed to meet at the Kings Head pub opposite the Hackney Hospital the next night. Half of me thought she was off to find 'the demi-flouncer', the other half that she was just being polite in agreeing to meet. A little crestfallen, I found Pete and some lads and we proceeded to get hammered. I could have chased other girls, yet somehow my heart wasn't in it any more. That didn't hold me back on the beer.

The next day I woke with a raging hangover and wasn't altogether sure I would recognize her when I got to the Kings Head. I knew she was very pretty, but I could not picture her face. The day passed with much tea drinking and reading the Sunday papers. Eventually showered and shaved, I had to go to the pub. Pete was with Justine. That meant standing on my own at the bar. This would add public humiliation to insult if she didn't turn up. Thankfully, a medical student mate of Pete's was there. He was loud and boorish and a bit of a dick. At the same time, he was giving me cover so I bought him a pint. I kept looking at the pub doors as eight o'clock came and passed. At ten-past, she walked in. Well, at least I was pretty sure it was she who walked in with her ginger friend. She started scanning the room and eventually saw me. She smiled and walked over.

She giggled and said, "We were all a bit drunk last night. I wasn't sure I'd recognize you!" Phew, it was her.

I could bore you with the conversation, but you've suffered enough. It all went fine, and I discovered she lived with two other nurses in a block only two hundred yards away from mine and Pete's shithole. (We'd gone metric in the UK in 1965, but it never caught on for weights and distances). We had a few drinks, we told tales and laughed a bit, and when it was time, I walked her home. She grabbed my arm as we walked, and we linked all the way. I liked that. At her door, we kissed, and she politely didn't invite me in as her flatmate was sleeping or some lame, but acceptable excuse. We planned to meet again midweek.

We will get to the sex. Just cool your jets for a few pages. Or skip ahead. But it won't be what you expect. Another date and nothing much to report really except that she was always so kind and fun and upbeat. She was a nurse off-duty, as much as she was when she was on-duty. She mentioned that she liked to swim, and I said, "Me too." Then she mentioned that the hospital had a swimming pool that no one used at weekends and with her nursing pass and we could go and swim together. How could I refuse? I would at worst, get to see her in a swimming costume and who knows…

So, at eight-thirty on Saturday morning, I met her at Barbican Station — the nearest Tube to Bart's. She was coming off a night-shift and even though she should have been exhausted, she looked fine. Yeh, you heard it before, I mean like fine wine and fine dining, fine. Now, all this may have been because it was also the first time I had seen her in a nurse's uniform. I know it is totally unacceptable objectifying, but back then, Bart's nurses' uniforms were sexy. Not, Halloween sexy nurses costume sexy, I mean properly sexy. They wore black shoes and stockings; tights were tolerated, but they were supposed to wear stockings! Don't believe me. Ask a nurse from back then. Apparently, it was a hygiene issue. I bet the person in charge of hygiene was a bloke.

Over that was a blue-grey gingham tunic. Very not sexy until it was waisted with a big thick belt and a nurse's watch worn on the left breast. A small card hat rounded it off at the top with the hair up under it. When worn by a shapely, pretty, twenty-two-year-old, it was enough to get any red-blooded boy a bit hot under the collar. It certainly worked for me. But the cherry on the cake was the cape. For walking around the streets, they had to cover it with a cape of navy blue, held in place with scarlet ribands. She was waiting with a friend, also dressed the same. I seem to remember feeling that if my troislistic fantasy was to come true now, I could really die happy. Not a very noble a thought, I know. But come on! Two nurses dressed like that! But the threesome, you will be surprised to learn, was not in my fate.

Her friend left after a brief "Hello" and Miranda said, "Have you got your cossie?" Being the suave sophisticate I am, I held up my supermarket carrier bag. Inside was a towel and trunks. So off we set. It was well hidden, that pool. Down subterranean corridors and through numerous swing doors but then suddenly, a pool, twenty-five metres by fifteen. We had gone metric in pool sizes. She pointed me off to the gents' changing and said, "I will see you here in a minute" and giggled.

I speed changed. Why? Think it through? If she got in the water first, I wouldn't get to see her in the Miss World Swimming costume section of the show. At the same time, I didn't want to be in the water as it looked cold and a bit dick-shrivelly if I needed to get out. I waited at the doorway and waited… and she came out and I was, to say the least, a bit taken. Boy, could she fill a one-piece. I walked up to her and went to kiss her. She looked me in the eye, dipped her head to one side and then the cow pushed me in.

"There will be plenty of time for that after we've had a swim." I laughed and she dived in like a mermaid and started swimming her lengths. So, I did the same. I'm not a great swimmer, but what else can you do. I wasn't going to bomb her and standing in the shallow end seemed a bit lame.

Eventually, after what seemed an eternity, she said, "That's my twenty-five lengths," and swam over to me and we kissed. Not a huge amount as we were in the deep end. But kiss we did and then we got out of the pool and kissed some more. A lot more in fact, as there was no one else around, no lifeguard, no caretaker. The poolside was a bit exposed and I ushered her toward the changing stalls. Then I did something really sexy. I mean really sexy. I rolled her one piece down to her waist. It is one of the sexiest things ever. Especially when the breasts revealed are as really delightful as they were. A one-piece swimsuit rolled down to the waist is just aesthetically and erotically perfect. It became a beach fashion in the South of France a few years later and when I was on holiday in St. Tropez, I had to spend so much time face down in the sand to hide my approval that my back was like mahogany and my chest light blue by the end of the fortnight.

Our kissing continued and my hands went to her breasts. That's when she got a bit nervous and skittish. She pulled me off her and said, "We'd better get changed." I walked back to the gents looking like a Dalek. We met back at the doors and I suggested we hit a greasy spoon for a bacon sarnie. This was inspired. At least it seemed inspired judging by the look on her face. With a mug of builder's tea and a bacon sandwich in her hand, she looked super content and she ate ravenously. I love women with a good appetite. Or rather, I hate the salad movers who go on and on about what they eat and their weight. With one exception. Kitty was just like that and it didn't bother me. Clearly, love is blind, or at least myopic to dietary foibles.

We headed back to Hackney on the bus. And I invited her back to mine. She counter-offered that we should go to hers. Why not? It was only two-hundred-yards difference. As we walked up the stairs I said, "I know, keep the noise down, the girls are sleeping."

The reply I got was a giggly, "No, they're both doing earlies, they won't be back before 4 this afternoon." I thought this meant my luck was in. I was wrong. There was no luck involved. She had it all worked out. She was very cool. She was very pretty. She had that nurse's uniform back on and she was in total control. In we went and she rinsed out her costume, hung the towel, took off her cape and took me by the hand and led me into her bedroom. After all my college dates, I felt reasonably confident I could give a reasonable account of myself. And I think I must have because we became a couple very quickly and had a very physical relationship. And for all you dirty buggers, I could give you chapter and verse. But I'm not going to. She eventually became my wife and mother to my kids so I feel I will draw a veil over all the intimate details. Isn't it enough to say that for a huge time I was faithful to her? Not out of any sense of duty or honour. No, it was simply because she was all I wanted. Sex was never our issue. Well, not until it was.

Chapter 32
I love the way you lie

Meeting up with Kitty was never easy as she always had to be 'somewhere'. Her phone would ring and it would be Gordon 'just checking in'. If she didn't have a totally credible excuse, then it would be carnage. As a result, we would meet on her shopping trips or in coffee shops where she could be with the ladies. I didn't mind. Even without the sexual tension, I enjoyed being around her and we would talk and laugh and kiss. One day we were in a toy store as she needed to get a gift for a friend's son. I was useful, as I've never grown up. I had strong views as to what an eleven-year-old might want, rather than what his mum might like him to have. Anyway, with the present bought, we had a coffee and 'billed and coo'ed' at each other.

Then we kissed and it got quite passionate. It was her, not me, honest! She stood up and gestured to the toilets. I wasn't sure that this was a good idea after all the Cat's advice, but I wasn't going to say no either. I gave her a twenty-second head start, then followed. Into the ladies' — they are always cleaner than the men's and the passionate kissing got more intense. I lifted her skirt and she unbuttoned my fly. I was still unsure about this and my semi-hard dick reflected that. So she squatted down — no kneeling in a toilet — and started sucking me. Even though I knew this wouldn't produce results, it did firm me up and so, very romantically, I turned her around, hitched up her skirt and pulling her panties to one side shoved my cock into what was a surprisingly wet pussy. We went at it hammer and tongues, minus the tongues. Yet somehow, I just knew I wasn't going to come. I knew her body well enough by now that she probably wasn't going to either. She knew me too well, too. She started wriggling and making the right noises and I played along. As she faked her orgasm, I made the spastic gestures of the hips and thrust as hard as I could and said "Oh fuck! Fuck. I'm coming." But didn't.

We held each other for a few more moments, then rearranged our clothes and kissed and walked out of the cubicle as bold as brass. I knew what I'd done and what she'd done and I would bet a lot of money she knew too. As we walked back to our cars she stopped me, kissed me and said, "I really do love you!" I just had a huge smile on my face and felt warm and happy and special and all those other soppy, sentimental feelings we laugh at in other people. I loved her, too. It was bizarre, two people faking orgasm was lovemaking at its height. A coming together with no coming together.

Then reality hit back with a bang, or rather a ringtone. "Hi, yes, I'm just getting a present for Kristen's boy…"

I walked away. People are always more natural when they don't have an audience. When she hung up, we kissed and went our separate ways. I didn't care that my cock didn't work. Well, I did, a lot, but somehow not so much.

Chapter 33
It's all about you

Having remembered to always masturbate with lube like a vagina — I mean, what could be sexier? — I was back with the Cat and he asked me how things were. And the truth was good and bad. Sometimes there were no problems and other times the same issue. Before we got down to practical business, I got another theory lesson.

"You have said you are competitive and results-driven: we call this the Delivery Boy attitude. Lovemaking involves giving pleasure and receiving it, but some men believe their first job is to give it. It can happen that when a man pays too much attention to his partner's experience, and not enough to his own, he loses erotic focus, which can interfere with ejaculation and orgasm."

We marked that one down as an almost definite, probable maybe.

"You must value your own pleasure. You're more than a delivery boy. You too, deserve erotic satisfaction and have every right to ask for the stimulation that produces it. If you engage in vaginal intercourse, it may not provide enough stimulation. You may need a very vigorous manual or oral stimulation." And the zinger! "If so, ask for it!"

Now that's a tough one to broach, don't you think? "Darling, your vagina, while lovely, no longer delivers the vigorous stimulation I require to orgasm so…" I would instinctively duck for cover at that moment. Not many women that I know would handle even the most diplomatic dissing of their vag' very well.

"You had some issues with anti-depressants. These are notorious for impairing ejaculation. Unfortunately, even though you took them for such a short period and have stopped, the effects on libido and ejaculation can be long-term — even permanent." I wanted to cry. "But as you have episodes where this isn't a problem, I think this is not a major issue." I wanted to cry for joy.

"Other drugs also impair sexual function." Again, the questioning look.

"Just alcohol and occasional cigarette," I lied.

"Alcohol is not your friend here…"

"Isn't not being able to orgasm when you're drunk just normal?" He agreed and we moved on.

"Now let us talk of erotic context. The myth is that men can function sexually under almost any circumstances, while women can enjoy sex only under several pre-conditions — a nice dinner, flowers, clean sheets, and a man actually interested in what they have to say. But men also have pre-conditions for satisfying sex, and as men age, the context becomes increasingly important. You may need particular conditions. Identify yours and work with your partner to provide them."

So, no more carpark blowjobs, disabled toilets, up against a tree, in the tanning salon or myriad other quickie spots. That was disheartening.

We did more lemon squeezing and buttock tensing. Then he spent a huge amount of time on the breathing again. It was very important, apparently. "No, not through your nose! Do you breathe through your nose when you're making love?" Clearly, for him, making love and fucking were the same thing. They're not. I suspected he was not in the mood for that discussion, so we moved on.

"In the beginning, the exercises of breathing have to be practiced like a daily gymnastic for ten to fifteen minutes and carried out slowly to feel them well. Now you have mastered this, we will move on to doing them in other sexual postures and mobilise the muscles we use in sex to get your body back in the correct orientation. But until then, I want you to really acquire them and practice them during masturbation and sex if you can." We were back to wanking. And that was that and we set a date for our next meeting.

Chapter 34
Kissing the Tortoiseshell

"Seven Seas" by Echo and the Bunnymen has no relevance, beyond the fact that the song was the one we used in my first ever TV commercial. You see, I got out of the warehouse and landed a job in an advertising agency. It didn't pay as well. The upside was that it had a career path of sorts. That said, if I'd stayed at the warehouse, well, I suppose I might be area manager by now. The real upside was that it sounded cool. And it was. I started by working for six weeks in each department. Production, media, account management, finance and then creative. I bless the Lord for this. I am one of the few people left in this business who knows the fundamentals of the other disciplines. It means I understand what they do and don't see them as the enemy, or stupid or pointless. Anyway, my final stint was in the Creative Department where an old Art Director had lost his writer and said he would take me under his wing. I got lucky. I flourished under that wing because he was such a talented guy. Thank you, Mike. You taught me well. After six weeks he asked to keep me and the Creative Director said okay. I got a raise and a business card that said "Copywriter" on it. I was off.

Now I had a great girl, a job with prospects and everything was going well. Miranda had changed me. I wasn't chasing girls to prove a point — I really liked her. Sex was something to be enjoyed, not a performance. We were setting new Olympic records for doing it and sexual variations were as much about getting closer as they were about variety. It was, though, a very high-voltage charge. Nurses have seen a lot and they, are, well, earthy. I think that's the polite way to say, my girlfriend was open to anything and dynamite between the sheets. Life was good, the future was bright.

Working with Mike made being an advertising copywriter fun, and I was flying up the learning curve. He was a terrific mentor and as he was a grown-up, I didn't fall into the traps of being more interested in how cool the job was, rather than doing the job. Soho pubs were full of young teams who were determined to be cool creatives. This was much more important than the work itself. Hanging in the right bars and working with flavour of the month directors and trying to date models. Good work if you can get it, and I wanted it. But Mike kept me on the straight and narrow. Well, to a degree. So now I didn't just have a job, I had a career. He told me I had a talent for it and gave me a great bit of advice. "Before you learn the tricks of the trade, learn the trade, son!"

I read books about advertising. I studied the award shows to figure out how ads worked. What was the underlying idea that made that commercial so fantastic? What insight made people choose Pampers over Huggies when they were, essentially, exactly the same? I got good at what I was doing, we won awards and I got raises and promoted. But this story isn't about my far-from-illustrious career. Just to say I was growing in confidence in a job that I liked, and it paid well. Professionally, life was good. I also had a girl that I liked. I wasn't going to fall in love, but I was definitely dipping a toe in, and might, in time, have step into it, albeit very carefully. My job meant there were plenty of late nights and working weekends on new business pitches (Watch *Mad Men* and forward-wind twenty years and you will get the picture). Miranda was a nurse and so worked shifts. It was perfect. We couldn't see too much of each other. Our schedules made that impossible. The result was that every date was looked forward to, and so was exciting and fun. We slowly became closer and closer. Liking and sex came together more and more. We got very comfortable with each other and each other's bodies. Wasn't this how it's supposed to be. It certainly felt that way. It wasn't the Vronski/Anna Karenina stuff of madness and insane passion. It was warm and close and loving, just not actually love. That was perfect for me.

Then the double-whammy. Mike announced he was moving back to Australia and Miranda qualified. For her, that meant she was now going to live out her dream and travel for a year. I didn't try and stop her. I wasn't going to propose marriage and I was pretty sure she didn't want me to. The result was, I had to find a creative partner and I was soon to be single again romantically, too. She was only going for a year, she said. Now bear in mind this was 1985. Cell phones were around but looked like bricks and were expensive. So were international calls. We talked a lot about it. We agreed that it was "silly to make promises" and if, when she got back, we both wanted to pick up where we left off, then that would be great. And anyway, the post worked, and we could send letters. We told ourselves it was a good test of our relationship. Being apart would give us perspective and all the other nonsense you tell yourselves in these situations. I saw her off at the airport. She was with her friend and traveling companion and really excited to go. Nonetheless, she had tears in her eyes as she kissed me goodbye and I was truly sad to see her go. If all that was true, why did I call Anne (not that one another one, this one had an e) as soon as I got home? Miranda was in mid-flight and my resolve to wait for her didn't even last until she landed.

Chapter 35
A Natural Woman

After months of Dostinex, my next blood work came back that my prolactin was in the normal range. That was great, the Cat was pleased to hear it, but the Delayed Orgasm was still an issue. On the flip side, I'd started to get to like our meetings. Things had started working. Not perfectly, but there were definite signs of improvement. Remember, I was still married, and in a long-term relationship, you really need to work at the exciting bit. After twenty-five years, we'd done everything either of us had ever wanted to do. We'd done most things that only one of us wanted to do, and we had a routine. Everyone has a routine. Don't try and deny it. For some women, it starts with the dreaded 'hand'. The one that women fear, every so not-subtly moving across the mattress to delicately touch a shoulder or hip that is acknowledged by both parties as a silent yelling of "I want to fuck." If the gentle caress isn't enough, then the snuggling up commences. This is a sham of 'I just want to be close to you' gesture and actually means "If you don't want to fuck, you can blow me…" Women are much more subtle. They just make a simple facial gesture and we know what that means. Or they grab your cock, or in fact do anything that doesn't signal they don't want to do it and generally, we're in. But it rarely has the emotional intensity of the early days when you'd rip each other's clothes off. The excitement of doing it in the carpark or at a friend's house. In the morning you might get started and have your partner recoil from a kiss and say, "Whoa…morning breath." And you go and clean your teeth. Cleaning them in the sure and certain knowledge that you will be rewarded with sex, but it is a bit of, if not a passion killer, a passion cooler. And before any of you go off into a "That's such a phallocentric, macho bullshit view." It isn't. Women like sex just as much as men. The rider on that is that it isn't always with the man they are with. How do I know? Because the Cat told me. And he is an expert.

That said, the Cat then explained that we also needed to re-train my body to bring all the sexually important muscles back into play. He asked again about sexual positions. Once I had told him he said, "Good, we start with 'a Leverette', so much nicer term than your English 'Doggie style" — an ugly name for a beautiful sexual position. Good for you and good for her if it is done well."

Where the fuck was this going?

"Stand and rest your knees against the edge of the chair. Now show me how you make love like this." So I did.

"No. Not like that. Not thrusting. Like this." Then he stood up and showed me the 'pro' style.

"You see, we roll the hips. The thighs don't move. This makes the penis arch in the vagina and rub the G spot. Very good for the women. Now you do it again."

It was surreal. I tried again and so there I was in a doctor's office. With my knees against the front of a leather armchair, 'air-fucking' in doggy style.

"Yes, better. Roll the hips back as far as you can. Feel your back arching…" Then bugger me if he didn't take hold of my hips and help. This was seriously weird. I guess a measure of how desperate I was is that I was keen to impress him. We continued. And with the Cat as my carnal ballet instructor, I was getting the hang of something that for forty years I thought I already had the hang of.

"Good, better! But no thighs…" and just as I was thinking I had the knack — "Now we breathe. Out as you roll in. In as you roll out. Yes, good…" and so it went on for fifteen minutes. Small alterations to my style and concentrating on breathing then. Who knew doing it right was so nuanced? I didn't. Did you?

"Yes, you feel it? Yes? Now, when you are ready, you start to tense the buttocks and squeeze the lemon…" I wasn't going to do that with him, but I followed his drift.

We stopped. His instructions: "You must practice this every day. Practice and practice so that it becomes normal during sex. Masturbating while doing this is very good practice."

And what is undeniably true is that it is the weirdest wank you will ever have. Standing, knees against the edge of the bed, rolling your hips and rubbing one out. At first, it was just too fucking strange. With practice, however, it was easier and, well, how can I put this delicately? Once I factored in the buttock tense and lemon squeeze, I had to wipe down the headboard. And my bed is a king-size!

Chapter 36
Perfect Day

I have no idea what it's like to be a spy. But I bet it's sexy and exciting. That's how the next six months with Kitty were like. We had to be so careful about anyone finding out about us. But I was madly in love. Lucky Strike extra, when I first put the Cat's work into practice it didn't just work for me. It got a serious response from Kitty. "Fuck! What was that? That felt amazing." I didn't tell her I had a trainer. I was still too shy for that. To my shame, I also put it into practice at home. We lived together, there were bills to pay and so there was no hiding from the fact I was seeing the Cat. Miranda thought it was, "Stupid. There is no issue, you're just getting old and you've always been sexually obsessed. We don't have to sex all the time. Just relax and go with the flow." This strangely mirrored the professional advice.

All I wanted sexually was Kitty. But if sex simply stops totally at home, then it would be an issue and the reasons would be pretty clear. Was I a coward or discreet or sensitive or just a selfish wanker? Dunno, but I kept on having sex with them both. One with love and unbridled passion and the other with tenderness, care, and duty. I was also sure Kitty and Gordon had not suddenly become celibate. That was more of an emotional dilemma. I hated the thought of her having sex and hating it. At the same time, I hated the thought of them fucking and her loving it. Find your way out of that moral maze.

We met, mostly at her place. It was the only place she could be without being surveilled. When the coast was clear we would meet and really make love. It was amazing sex as well as loving. That had a multiplier effect that was new to me. Love or great sex. Or loving the sex because you were in love or loving the sex because you couldn't give a fuck. That was all part of my history, but this was new. This was great. What I liked, even more, was lying entwined with her and holding her. Once she asked me the oddest questions. "Do I have a sexual aura? Don't ask why, just tell me." I replied nervously. This was another minefield on a razor's edge on a volcano.

"Now, remember I have had no formal psychological training. To me, the woman with the sexual aura may not be the prettiest in the room, but she will be the most attractive. And so, yes, your attractiveness is disproportionate to your looks."

She gave me a harsh look but gestured, 'carry on'

"Not that you aren't good-looking. Firstly, you got dealt a fair hand by nature and you make the best of all you got with a keen eye and great style and, let's face it, a big bank account. Your obsessive dietary issues and a healthy dose of vanity compound that." She laughed. It was a bit forced. But I thought, *Well, in for a penny, in for a pound.*

"As for sexual aura. Paradoxical. That's the keyword. You have an aura of naughtiness. It's very sexual, but it's also challenging and iconoclastic. You're not a femme fatale. It's not dangerous 'amour fou' stuff. It's more the challenging/disparaging part. 'I know how the game is played. God, you're pathetic. I dangle sex and you pant like a dog who's seen me pick up the lead and say "Walkies"!' And just like with a dog, it puts you in charge and makes you the generous giver. Around that though, is more than a hint of vulnerability."

I was on a roll.

"I think your sexual arrogance is a thin veneer you project: 'I will never admit to weakness, but I've seen bad things and I'm not as tough as I make out. I'll show you just enough to confirm it, but if you dare pity me, I will crush you.' And then there's the raunchy 'For god's sake it's only sex…and I'm very good at it' earthiness. It all adds up to a heady brew. Some of it is authentic and just you, the rest is an M.O. that you have developed like a nervous tick. It's your paradox. You love that it works, but hate that it's *that* that works. Your sexual self-esteem is so much higher than your actual self-esteem. That's your aura. I think maybe that's why sex in the mirror is so hot. It confirms everything you are thinking. That's not the whole you. There's other stuff of course, but that's outside the aura. So yes. You have a sexual aura, you amplify it consciously and the irony is that it works — but not to get you what you really want. Honestly, I say this all because I think it's true. Not to hurt or to flatter or to impress. I'm mad about you. So maybe it's just the meanderings of a half-crazed, lovesick loon. How's that?"

"I fucking love you, Rob!" She kissed me so hard it had the desired effect and the Cat earned his fees and then some.

It was the best time ever. Another summer, thirty degrees, lying in her bed, just showered. Talking, sated and totally connected. She looked wonderful, she felt delightful, naked and in my arms. It was not her body or her aura that entranced me. It was the real Kitty. The one I like best of all, the one I so rarely got to see.

Now, I can accept that love feels different for everyone. Yes, with Kitty, the sex part and the physical attraction was there, but I'd had that before. Looking back, the signs were all there. If only I'd realised earlier. Well actually, I reckon even if I'd realised earlier, I was already falling too fast to put the brakes on. I loved Kitty. I didn't just like looking at her. I couldn't stop staring at her. I loved how she moved, I loved how her face crinkled up when she was thinking, I loved how she bit her lower lip when she was really turned on. Eye contact was a serious communication tool. The scent of her, the texture, the feel of her, I could pick her out of a crowd in a darkened room.

I've done a fair number of drugs and being around her was like getting high. Halfway between a line of coke and a doobie. And I guess that combination explains why I acted like a drug-addled fool. I could not get her off my mind. Her happiness was incredibly important to me. If it meant giving her up to ensure she would be happy I would have done it. Is that true? I certainly felt that way in a mad romantic, hypothetical way.

What it did mean in practical terms was that I was willing to go out of my way to make her life easier and happier. Calls and texts and quick coffees. Helping with the shopping, running errands. They weren't a chore. I wasn't just happy to do it. I wanted to do it. She bought me clothes and little gifts and was just as chatty by text and call. It wasn't clingy and annoying — it was a delight. I was happy. That said, if I'd seen anyone else like that, I would have called them a pussy-whipped wimp!

I wanted to protect her. I would have loved the opportunity to beat the fuck out of someone who offended her. Almost praying for some twat to get heavy in a bar or on the street. Not to impress her, but to show her how I would take a bullet for her.

I was stressed at home. Not by guilt, well, yes, guilt, but also because I had to constantly battle between being a good guy at home and hiding what I was doing on the away games. This hadn't happened before. Previous encounters meant virtually nothing to me. The smoking gun proof, though, as I look back, is that the things that would drive me mad in anyone else were just lovable little quirks with her. This schizophrenia manifested in many little ways. I'm a bit of a Howard Hughes on the personal hygiene front. So was Kitty. The difference was with her, if she was sweaty from the gym or having a heavy period, I didn't care. Nothing about her was anything but attractive. Even gross smelly messy stuff.

I'm a stickler for time-keeping. Kitty is always late. It never bothered me. She wastes money on clothes and some of them never even have the tags taken off. I'm extravagant but thrifty, waste normally gets right under my fingernails. She idolizes her kids and is incapable of disciplining them, whereas I am a Victorian dad and would never take any shit from mine. Yet none of this annoyed or frustrated me. It was quirky and lovable and oh God, I was so blind! Yet it was so great. It felt wonderful.

I looked it up much later. Or rather, a mate told me. "You're a biochemist. Look up limerence." So, I did.

Limerence is a state of mind which results from a romantic attraction to another person and typically includes obsessive thoughts and fantasies and a desire to form or maintain a relationship with the object of love and have one's feelings reciprocated. Just be warned — Limerence is a motherfucker.

After all that had gone before, how could I not see it coming? I walked out of her house that afternoon the happiest I'd ever been. No, it's too melodramatic to say it all went wrong then. That took a few more visits. But it was that day that I was spotted leaving by the cleaner as she arrived. I just waved as innocently as I could fake and kept walking. A week later Kitty texted me.

"Gordon knows you were here. He has been paying Sylvia to keep a watch on me. He is adamant it's all over now. Stay away and I will let you know what's happening."

I called, fuck the consequences but she was immovable. "Let me sort it out and I will call you." I was scared and pleased and twenty-seven other emotions but the over-riding one was that this might be the start of something much more than an affair.

Chapter 37
Since you been gone

While Miranda was away, we talked occasionally on the phone and we wrote to each other. I saw other girls. We had said we'd made no promises. I never mentioned them to Miranda or even hinted at them. She was similarly discreet. I guess that meant that we were both in the same boat. We hadn't met anyone better.

It kind of felt like cheating on her, but it didn't stop me. At the same time, our letters and calls were getting more intense and serious. I don't know why, but Rachel was my wake-up call. She was pretty and pretty wild. She worked at another agency and we met at some awards show or other. It was a formal event. I was in a tux and she was in a ball gown. The tables were for twelve and had big draping tablecloths. I had a new creative partner, Jack. We were up for an award and bugger me — we won. We went up for the 'take and shake,' as it was known. There were no speeches, you took the award, shook the man's hand and waved to the audience and then waved the award like a man winning the FA Cup. Then back to the table and stand the award in front of you. Yes, showing off. After even more drinks, the dancing started, and Rachel came over and sat in the empty seat next to me. I was hammered, she was getting there.

We went and did a line of coke in the toilets. That led to heavy petting until someone banged on the door. We went back to the ballroom and talked coked-up shit for a bit, but we both had that look in our eyes. We started kissing and it got a bit hot and heavy. Then she said the strangest thing. She looked me in the eyes and said, "There's something I've always wanted to do…" She looked around and at the right moment, slid from view under the table. I thought she was just mucking around and would never … then I felt my zip coming down and my cock slide into her mouth. It should have been a schoolboy fantasy moment. It wasn't. It was just embarrassing. I tried to shake her off as it were, but she stuck to her task. I tried to come, but I was drunk and coked up and there were people everywhere. Maybe it was my first venture into delayed orgasm? I didn't know what to do.

Thankfully, Jack came back and said, "Want a drink? You look weird, you all right, matey?" He sat down and as he pulled his chair in, he collided with Rachel. She started laughing and he looked under the table. "You dirty buggers…" He started laughing too and she re-emerged and bold as brass started fixing her lipstick. A strange sense of honour prevailed. I couldn't just brush off the woman who had been blowing me under the table. And she was pretty, and she was clearly sexually adventurous.

So a while later we left together and headed back to my place. She went to the bathroom, and from what I heard, she had been desperate to pee for some time. Not a very sexy start, but what the hell? I was now in full Tony Bennett style. Tux off, bow tie hanging loose, top button undone and then not so Tony Bennet, drunk and lying on the bed. She came through with her dress half-off and joined me. She held up a bottle of Johnson's baby oil and said, "Look what I found."

We got naked and started oiling each other up. She rubbed my cock between her oily tits, I rubbed oil all over her arse and started fucking her from behind. Aided by baby oil, my finger slipped easily into her arse. She liked that. Alcohol and Charlie may have held me back from coming but it didn't have the same effect on her. She was like a fucking mongoose with a snake. She came and came again. Then she suddenly stopped me. "My pussy is too sensitive now. I need pain." This was getting weird. Really not my thing — pain. "Shove it really hard up my bum. Make me scream."

I realized I'd grown up. It may have been many men's fantasy, but not mine. I lurched up and pretended to feel sick. I ran to the bathroom. And made retching sounds. Rinsed my mouth used mouth wash even though it wasn't necessary and as slowly as I could, I went back into the bedroom. And said, "Maybe later…" and pretended to crash out. Pretty soon she fell asleep. I could have woken her. I just didn't want to. There were clearly some sex things I just didn't want. The thought of inflicting pain was horrible, beyond a turn-off — it was hideous. I climbed in beside her and eventually fell asleep myself.

The next morning, we did fuck. Out of tradition, I suppose. It would have been rude not to. It was a simple toe-to-toe missionary fuck and I suspect we were both glad to get it out of the way. Whether she had forgotten about the night before or was too embarrassed to mention it, I will never know, but we were both happy to let it go. I made her breakfast and as kindly as I could, I said, "Last night was crazy and fun, and you are gorgeous, but I've got to tell you, I'm kind of committed to someone else. She's coming back in a few months and…"

Whether from relief or defence, Rachel said, "That's fine, I was wondering how to tell you I have a boyfriend…" After another cup of tea, I called her a cab. (I couldn't let her do the walk of shame in her ball gown.) A peck on the cheek and a big smile were the last I ever saw of her. What I'd realised was that I wanted Miranda. I wanted back what we'd had before she left. I didn't want meaningless sex, however hot and raunchy. At the same time, I hoped that the future would be meaningfully hot and raunchy.

I was celibate for six whole weeks and met her at the airport. Even after twenty-four hours in-flight, she looked fantastic. We were all over each other in the arrivals' hall, car park and in the car. We waited until we were home before we got joined at the hip, as it were.

After a John-and-Yoko-style love-in, I asked her the one
big question that had been on my mind, and I needed the
answer. It was clearly unexpected. She was surprised
when I brought it up, she looked worried, pondered for
a few moments and then said "Yes."

Three months later we had the full Morning Suits
and 'all the women in hats wedding'. I was happy. I
knew it wasn't like in the books and movies. I thought,
*This is what love is. Ann was a teenage idiocy, the books
and movies are just make-believe.* We honeymooned
and once back, started a lovely, warm, simple, 'just like
in the movies' married life.

Eight weeks later, Joanna called out of the blue. She
was going to be in London and "Did I want to meet for
a drink?" I told her I was married now and without
hesitating, she said, "Does that mean you've given up
drink too?"

It hadn't and when I told Miranda and she said.
"Go, go and have fun, she seems nice from what you've
told me. I'm working a night shift and I don't really
want to meet her anyway, to be honest."

So in week nine of my married life, I met back up
with Joanna. She was fun and we laughed and laughed
about Pete and Justine and drank. And then she told me
how she had split up with her boyfriend and teared up.
Then we had another drink and I tried to console her and
then and then and then… She blew me in a Superloo at
the end of Blackfriar's Bridge. It even had a comedy
moment. The doors automatically spring open after ten

minutes. In a moment of dexterity that amazed us both, I managed to re-shut the door haul up my pants and come down her throat at the same time. As soon as that was done, I realised I was three things: I am totally unreliable, a stupid selfish cunt and I never wanted to do this again. I saw Joanna into a cab and never called. And for seventeen years was a totally faithful husband. Faithful because I wanted to be, not because it's what I should be.

Chapter 38
At the edge of the world

My next meetings with the Cat weren't that strange. Well, not strange by our standards. We did our exercises in breathing and lemon squeezing and he polished my doggie-style somewhat and then got me to lie on a rolled-up camping mattress as he perfected my missionary position sex. Weight on forearms and knees. Feet splayed, face looking directly down into your lover. Breathe, or rather pant out as you go in and vice versa. "The breathing is very important."

Besides all that, I had something much bigger to worry about. Kitty and Gordon were going for a weekend away to 'sort everything out.' I didn't know what to make of it. Maybe this meant the end for me and her. Surely there could be no act three. She had always managed to find a way back, so I prepared myself for the worst. It would be the end. In a way, it also calmed me down. I would leave home for her, but the thought of having to sit down and tell Miranda that was what I was doing was horrific. She loved me, she needed me, she always said I was her best friend. So, while I wanted a new life with Kitty, I was saved from all the downsides if they decided to make a go of it. Miranda was working, so I was home alone at midnight when the phone rang. It was Kitty. She was drunk. "I'm having a mojito with a nice man called John. How are you?"

For fuck's sake, what's going on? "John, I'm just stepping away for a minute, order me another mojito. It's all over. Gordon wants a divorce. No options. So, I'm getting drunk with John. We can talk tomorrow."

"Don't you fucking dare hang upon me. Where are you? I'm coming to get you."

"Nooooo, bad idea! Anyway, it's the Beaulieu Spa and you're fifty miles away.

"I am getting into a car. I will be there in an hour and if John lays a finger on you, I will get very physical with him and then deal with you!"

"Tough guy. John, my lover is coming to beat you up!" She sobered up for a moment "Really Rob, I'm fine. Just a bit drunk. Gordon is passed out upstairs. I'm just having fun. Don't come."

"Fuck that! I'm on my way."

I could see how I was being played and tested. I should have just said, "Okay, goodnight." I knew, though, that that would probably mean she would at least cop off with 'John' and maybe even fuck him. Why was I in love with such a promiscuous lunatic? Well, I'd have an hour of driving to figure it out.

Once I was on my way, I texted, *I will be there in an hour*

She texted back ten minutes later. "You're sweet but I'm okay. John has an annoying laugh."

I texted again — nothing for minutes. My imagination was torturing me. Then my phone rang as I was speeding down the M4. "Hi, I need to keep my voice down, can you hear this?" It was like a rhino fucking a warthog. "Gordon pissed and passed out! I'm back in the room."

"Shall I come?"

"Please don't. I've sobered up a bit and if Gordon knows you are around, he will go mental. We can talk tomorrow. But it's so lovely that you would drive out here. Thank you, darling."

"Are you sure you are okay?"

"Yes, you were right to be a bit concerned. John walked me out of the bar and tried to kiss me. But I pushed him off. Don't know what I would have done if you weren't coming…" and then she giggled. She was, she is, mad. Even in a crisis like that she needs constant affirmation from men. I was in love with a lunatic. Eventually, we agreed to meet the next day. We hung up. She went to bed. I was excited, confused and scared shitless. Fuck. This shit just got real.

It was a beautiful summer's day. She texted me and we met a quiet bar with a terrace. She climbed out of the cab and held me. And we kissed. She cried as she explained: Gordon was adamant, it was over!

This stunning realization of what we had done hit Kitty like a punch in the guts. She always thought she would be able to turn it all around. Now she realized this wasn't going to happen. I said, "So, shall we give it a go? I love you and hope you love me." She grabbed me and said yes! I was ecstatic. I ordered champagne, for me. She had a vile hangover and so was only drinking mineral water. I should have seen it as a sign. Nonetheless, we spent a few hours making plans and kissing and talking the shit you do when you are in love. Then reality set in again and she had to pick her kid up from school. I had to go home and figure out how I was going to break the news at my end. Being the courageous man I am. I went straight back to the house — and acted as if nothing had happened.

The next day we met at a cheap hotel and after getting the inevitable out of the way, we lay on a bed and talked. We knew so many of the same people Kitty suggested that if I moved out it shouldn't be for her. "Gordon has told the kids about you. They are really angry and are adamant that if I don't drop you, they will live with their dad and don't want to know me any more" She started crying. "I can't do it, Rob. I can't lose them." I tried to convince her that they would come around in time. She wasn't so sure. We talked and talked and agreed that after a few months "…we could act like we found each other" and go public.

It seemed like a good idea at the time and I think I jumped at it because it saved me from telling Miranda I loved someone else. Weird, I know, but it felt it would be easier to say, "I don't love you any more…" than saying, "I don't love you any more. I love someone else." Nonetheless, we were just so excited about the future and how it was all going to be ugly at first, then perfect. It was all just surreal. Gordon was still at home but had moved to the spare room. I was still at home and acting like nothing was unusual. To move things along, I got practical. I found an estate agent with a small studio flat for rent and took it the next day. I arranged to meet Kitty there, and again it was like the first days of a romance. A shitty studio, no furniture. Tiny kitchen and a bathroom. That was it. But while I didn't carry her over the threshold, it felt like that. We kissed and were thrilled. She started planning it all out. "Bed there, table over there. I've got a load of kitchen stuff and…" It was joyful.

And no, we didn't. There was no furniture and well, now I come to think of it I have no idea why we didn't christen the place there and then. But we didn't. Instead, we went for lunch and talked more. I gave her a key. It seemed important that it was our place, not mine. Then we laid our plans. I was going to take a day and sort the place out with a bed and a table and all that other stuff. We couldn't meet for a few days, but we would on Friday. I would have to go away for Friday night and she would make her own excuses. This was all getting very real. Still covering my tracks at home, I escaped to Ikea and filled the car with the basics. Then plodded across town and got the stuff into the studio. Normally that would already have me sweaty and fucked-off. Flat-pack furniture does that to everyone, doesn't it? I had a huge smile on my face. Kitty had already been in and brought flowers, she'd got pans and all kitchen paraphernalia. There was all the bedding we would need, and she'd even filled a fruit bowl and put bottled water on the side next to a card. "Let's be happy in our bolthole — can't wait to see you. IRDLY XX". I worked like a Trojan to assemble the bed and all the other stuff. When it was all done, it was surreal. I had a new place, our place. It was tiny and shitty, but it was full of hope.

We both kept our home pretences going. A few days later we met at the studio. Kitty was late, but what did I care? She had her overnight bag and we were going to be left in peace. She changed, we went out for dinner and everything was just perfect. We kissed over the restaurant table and talked about the future and how mad we were for doing this and how mad we were for each other. Halfway through we got the bill and left, eager to just get 'home'. That's how it felt, even if it was just a shitty studio with an Ikea bed. It was one of the best nights of my life — and I've had quite a few smashers along the way. And draw your own conclusions — no more smutty details. Excellent, if you're still wondering.

Chapter 39
Fate up against your will

I am a good dad. A bad husband and shit person, you could argue by now. However, while not faultless, I set the bar really high for myself as a parent. It means you miss out on a load of stuff the new-age-peer-parent-friend gets. Yet the price they pay is so much higher.

I took being a dad seriously. Like religion and believers, so many parents don't do the basic research. Not me, I read books about it, thought hard about it and was determined to be a good one. While there are plenty of opinions, there is also a fair number of simple truths. Children need to feel loved — not simply be told "…love you" at the end of every mundane conversation. If they feel it, you don't have to say it.

Children and teens really crave boundaries, limits and structure. At the same time, they also need some healthy separation from us. If you slip into that friend role, it's virtually impossible to lay down the law and set limits.

Heh! Do it how you like, just accept that your 'friends' way is, by any professional standard — wrong. I have seen people who take on that "friend" role with kids. The boundary issue is bad. Even worse — the over-sharing. It is dangerous because it really gives kids the message that you are vulnerable and need *them* to be strong for you. My first rule: I take a bullet for them; they never take a bullet for me.

With me and their mum, the truth is, kids should not be involved when parents struggle within their relationships. Even when I had to bite my lip so hard it was a figurative open wound, I tried to avoid rows when they were in earshot, never mind in the room. Yet inevitably they would hear sometimes. That's not so bad if it teaches them about arguing, and that all couples get into it now and again. What you can never do is involve them in the argument. I have never explained our quarrels, just left it at, "Sorry you heard that. Don't worry about it. We will fix it. Not your business, when it is, I will tell you."

Then, as kids grow up, the psychologists will tell you they need to "individuate." Psycho-jargon for become less dependent on you and so make their own way. Kids who aren't able to do this are mostly the ones who over-compensate, rebel, go off the rails and blame you. Or they go the other direction and idolize you, never leave home or learn to function on their own.

As painful as it was for me sometimes, you have to cut them loose. Because that's how they learn to function in the world. If you are their buddy, they will have a hard time flying solo.

Why do I mention all this? I fucking hate it when I hear "I would die for my kids" or," I would do absolutely anything for them." Always from the ones who blithely doing what suits them and rarely making any of the sacrifices they actually should make.

You know what? I'm going to brag about something other than sex for a minute. I'm thankful and a little bit proud that my kids are happy, well-adjusted adults now. They love their dad for all his faults and we have a relationship that is warm and loving and caring — but we're still not friends! A fact that we are all happy with.

Why do I mention all this? Because I was so in love with Kitty that I did let them down. There's no denying it. By my standards, it should never have involved them.

But secondly, here's a dark and dirty secret that you may find illuminating.

My first extra-marital affair (well, technically, second, if you've been keeping up) wasn't with a woman.

The first years of married life were idyllic. Everything was a joy. All the little pleasures were magnified because we enjoyed them together. I felt lucky. Not just to have such a great wife who was fun and sexy, head-turningly pretty and seemed to think I was pretty great too. I grew up. I learned so much from Miranda about real kindness and caring — because she is both kind and caring. It's her default position, not a pose. For her it is effortless. She was calm when I was brash. I liked her calm, she liked my brash. She was frugal; being a nurse in London does that to a woman. I was extravagant. We counterbalanced each other. She didn't like some of my friends and just told me so. She wasn't threatened or jealous of them. She would be convivial enough when meeting was inevitable, but she encouraged me to see them on my own. "You will enjoy yourselves so much more if I'm not around." Other stuff that one of us liked but the other didn't — we just did alone, too. I watched rugby in the pub and she made dinner as she couldn't see the point in thirty orcs chasing a ball about. She loved animals and volunteered at the dog pound and while she did that, I stayed home and made dinner. We talked about everything, no secrets, no tensions and any arguments were just passing squalls. You get the picture — it was bliss. Best of all, she worked shifts and I worked crazy hours. So, we had plenty of time alone and when we had time together it was almost like a date.

She taught me to have some perspective as well. I came home one night angry and frustrated from work and gave her all the details of the office politics, why I was right, how the client was an idiot how we were letting a great idea die on the vine… after about fifteen minutes I finished and saw she was trying to sympathise, but I knew that look in her eye too.

"Anyway, how was your day, beauty?"

Her eyes filled with tears and she hugged me and said, "A baby died in my arms today." I held her while she sobbed, for the baby and the mother, not for herself.

They call nurses angels. That was the first time I saw it was true not just cute.

Despite that tale and other horrors from hospital, after a couple of years, we talked about having kids. While there was no conscious decision, we stopped worrying about contraception. Which, it has to be said, is a major boon to your sex life. And this was a sex life that was definitely already booming. Now, for us, sex could be totally spontaneous too. Not surprisingly then, we had two kids, within twenty months of each other. The first just happened, the second was a conscious decision.

It's an old cliché, but trying for kids is ever such a little bit of a turn-off for blokes. I really don't know why. In our single years, a woman saying, "C'mon, let's have sex now," would be a dream come true. Yet hearing, "I'm ovulating, let's go," just isn't.

It didn't stop me and I do remember laughing my head off after one encounter seeing Mind with her knees up to her chest, presumably to give the swimmers a downhill start. She looked me in the eye and said, "Have you been, you know…" and made a wanking gesture. I refuted this allegation. And she said, "Well, you weren't exactly copious. Either way, I want you ready to go again in half an hour." Like I said, nurses are great. They are so earthy. From then on, I added to my sexual repertoire the goal of trying my hardest to be copious. Oh, the romance of it all.

The pregnancies were pretty standard. A bit of morning sickness and food cravings — I once saw her eat two four-packs of jam doughnuts and start on the third. Two made it back into the cupboard. I walked through later eating one of the leftovers and got a right bollocking. "You selfish sod! You know they are all I can eat at the moment!" I felt so guilty I went and got four more. All that and more of standard pregnancy stuff went on. If you've been there, you know it. If you haven't, it will bore you rigid. So, I will just say, it was lovely. I watched her get bigger with something we had made together and even more, I loved the idea of becoming a dad.

Many say childbirth is wonderous for a man. It wasn't for me. It was horrific. Seeing someone you love in agony is awful. The helplessness, the total inability to do anything but hold a hand and say "Breathe…" I hated every second of it. No, actually, looking back there was one lighter moment.

When Miranda was fully dilated with our first, the midwife said, "Now you're at ten centimetres, when the next contraction comes, I need you to hold your breath and try to push the baby out." Full of gas and air, she duly complied with a small breath held as the next albeit mini contraction arrived. She gave up after two seconds, looked the midwife squarely in the eye and said, "No! that isn't going to work." And then lay back on the bed like a petulant child. The midwife who had heard it all, but never heard that, looked confused. I laughed and loved her more in that second than I'd ever realized. Anyway, the next big contraction came and nature took its course and we, or really, she, was delivered of a bouncing baby boy.

That's when the miraculous part of childbirth hit me. When she was holding him freshly weighed and scrubbed (seven pounds, six ounces if you're counting), their eyes met and I saw two people fall madly in love. I rejoiced in that. Unlike some fathers, I wasn't envious of him moving me one down the pecking order. If anything, I was envious of her. The bond between a mother and a child must be incredible. I can only imagine. What must it be like to have something grow within you, to be truly part of you? Weird I may be, but I would love to have a baby, even the labour. To go through agony and have such a reward surely makes it even more worthwhile.

Joe's sister Milly was born twenty months later. Same story and same result. I was a good dad even then. I bonded with them and loved every single minute of it. Fuck off! Are you delusional, or you haven't had kids? Nights of teething and colic and all the other bits are hard, but you somehow feel you are putting in the hours that validate the experience. At the same time, when it was happening night after night at two in the morning, I just silently pleaded for the little bastard to stop crying and go to sleep.

Generally, it was great. I did the right things when they were babies. I dived into housework, I cooked and did everything I could to get Miranda to rest and to give her the time and energy for the kids. My big treat was bath time. Anyone who uses a baby bath is missing one of life's real pleasures. Get in the bath and then get them in with you. The purest, simplest joy I think I've ever felt. And once the girl could sit up I could have them both in with me — double bubble!

At risk of a tangent on a diversion (relax, I will get back to the first affair soon enough), I was having dinner with an American client and his wife and telling this tale, when she hit me from so far in the left field, I think I really did look at her slack-jawed. "So, you wear a swimsuit in the bath!" It wasn't a question.

I eventually replied, "Of course not! It's a bath." I swear she looked at me like I was a child-molester. What is it with people and genitals? I will never understand her issue. If I was kiddie-fiddler, would a swimming cossie stop me? Or did she think the sight of my Johnson would scar these children for life? It was pointless to argue the point though. She would never see mine, viewpoint that is, and come to think of it, genitals too.

The wider point, kids were a joy. Every stage brought its own little wonders and treats. It changes a marriage. For us, it changed it for the better. The real practical change was that there slowly developed a tacit understanding that while I was fully engaged as a parent, I was the provider/enabler, their mum was the primary love/caregiver. That worked well for years. I took so much pleasure from the kids. Playing, reading to them, watching shit plays, freezing on sports grounds et cetera. Again, you either get it or you don't. The separation of roles did mean I left most of the heavy lifting to their mum though.

One highlight I suspect is worth telling: When our daughter was seven or eight, she wanted a disco birthday party. So, I put together a playlist and got some lights and ten little girls had the time of their life gyrating away to the sort of music that actually made me feel slightly nauseous. But you do what you have to do. Then I was dragged onto the dance floor by the birthday girls. Rather than get a bad back, I picked her up in one arm and her friend in the other and jigged about a bit. Then Tilly looked her friend in the eye and said with complete conviction, "See, I told you my dad was REALLY strong." I was thrilled. Then as I thought that through: *Really? Silly compliments from little girls make you all puffed up? What is wrong with you?*

At the same time, my career kept on an upward trajectory and I liked that. Yes, I missed so much when I was away for meetings or on shoots or working late and weekends, et cetera. I knew I was missing out on loads of special little moments. At the same time, I was giving them everything they needed. No smell of burning martyr, just a sense of purpose and focus. That was good for me and good for them.

I don't know when it started, but that slowly morphed into something far less virtuous and a much more dangerous place. I started having an affair.

There was no conscious decision on either part. We kind of stumbled into it. Neither of us knew where it would end up. We didn't care, or at least we didn't think about the consequences. I thought about the job all the time I wasn't with it. I loved it, I wanted to make it happy and loved all the special little signs of affection it gave me, like a bonus or a raise or a promotion. We went to fancy locations when it was just me and her, the best restaurants, rubbing shoulders with models and actors. More than that, the job understood me, we were perfect together… all right, you get the picture, I was having an affair with my job.

The problem that I didn't see, was that, as my grandad had told me years before, "You can't ride two horses with one arse!" What's worse, my mistress was very demanding, she wanted all my attention and put me under enormous pressure to give it to her. Miranda started coming second, more and more. I wasn't doing it consciously, but a night out was punctuated by "I just need to answer this email." Or, "I need to take this… won't be a minute." Weekends were never spent fully at home. I seemed to have fallen into the habit of 'just popping into the office for a few hours.' I left home early and I never got home before eight at night. I knew she was a woman who needed to feel loved, but I never seemed to have the time. It was always something I would get to when things eased up a little.

When I was home, I was stressed, distant, quick to anger and just to make me a joy to live with, I was resentful of the fact that she wasn't overjoyed by the material wealth and opportunities that I busted my pick to provide. I wince as I remember, sullenly walking behind her and the kids at Disneyland, taking calls and answering emails and like a total twat. Then angrily pointing out as she looked disapprovingly, "… This is what pays for all this, and the nice house and the private schools and everything. So get off my arse!" She looked as if I had just given her a body shot that my old cornerman would have got a chubby over. I just carried on emailing. I suppose in its own way, I was telling my mistress, "My wife just doesn't understand me…"

In all that, though, I had no interest in other women. Or rather I noticed them, but never ventured beyond noticing. I loved my wife; I had the kids and I had my mistress — that was enough for me.

Another thing I hate is dinner parties. I like having friends around for dinner. Being relaxed, eating, laughing and drinking are things I love. Scrupulously tidying to create a false impression that this is how we actually live is just stupid. Sweating all day to make lavish meals, while pretending that it was all easy is right up there too. But when you have children and so do other people, dinner parties are what you do. Or it was what we did, and so did many others in our circle of friends. Sometimes it was fun. My mate Quentin always turned his dinners into raucous drink-fests and claimed his rule was that "A dinner party is only a success, if someone gets drunk enough to try and dry-hump the hostess in the kitchen." I never did any dry-humping, but I did need to be wheel-barrowed out of his house a couple of times. Alongside other diners — male and female, I might add. Other evenings were just dull and generally the food was not worth the effort that the bad chef had obviously put into it.

It was at one such evening, that people got fed and drunk and slowly filtered out of chez nous in the early hours. Miranda was more than a bit drunk which was unusual but not exceptional. I told her to go to bed and I would load the dishwasher and tidy up. I was bagging up the copious number of empty wine bottles when her phone buzzed. I thought nothing of it. I kept cleaning the surface and then it buzzed again. I picked it up and saw a message from Graeme. Probably a 'Thanks for a lovely meal' job, although the convention seemed to be that it was the wives who sent them to each other. I clicked on it. "I couldn't stop staring at you." That was a bit off, but there you go. Scroll down to message number two. "I can't stop thinking about you. I need to see you again. Soon! I love you."

My first reaction was "Silly sod, he's going to be embarrassed when he realises that he sent that to Miranda." I put the phone down and continued to get the kitchen ship-shape. Something nagged away at me, though. I picked up the phone and there were no other messages from him. In fact, no other messages at all. Then I looked at her sent messages. There was one earlier in the day. "Be discreet tonight. Eyes will be on us. XXX." And then the world came crashing down. I simply couldn't believe it, yet I couldn't deny the obvious either.

I wasn't angry, I was homicidal. I knew this was dangerous territory. I was drunk and I really wanted to hurt someone. Another hangover from boxing. When you get hurt, you throw every punch you've got or you will get pummelled. No time to think, just throw shots. Thankfully for once I didn't let instinct take over.

Instead, I sat on the sofa and just felt numb. If I went up to bed, there would be at the very least, shouting and screaming from me and presumably weeping and lying from her. I knew I wouldn't be able to be reasonable and the kids would hear. I was visibly trembling. Was it rage or fear of what I was capable of? That scared me too. I needed time. I poured a ridiculously large scotch into a tumbler and anaesthetized myself until I fell asleep, or more likely passed out.

The next morning despite a hangover from hell, I was clear-headed and resolute. I went upstairs and was greeted with a loving smile from someone I used to know. I threw the phone at her. "Seems he wasn't as discreet as you advised." I pointed to the kid's bedroom and said quietly, "No denials, no explanations and not a fucking word until they are out of the house. Now I'm going to see him." She looked ashen and started to speak. She must have seen the look in my eyes, because when I hissed, "Not one fucking word!" she stopped. I was out of the house before she even got out of bed.

Miranda must have called or messaged because he was in front of his house waiting for me. I knew I was going to beat the fucking daylights out of him, but he took me by surprise. He cowered. Really cowered and started pleading with me, "Please don't. Ann is inside." I grabbed him. He didn't even resist. Fist raised I was about to hit him but he started fucking whimpering! What? I couldn't hit him. It would be like punching a kid or a guy in wheelchair. Then he started moaning "I'm really sorry, really, but she made all the running, I couldn't…" No one is that scary, I certainly am not. He was just pathetic. "You even so much as speak to her again, I will fucking end you! Do you understand?" He blubbed something that sounded like agreement. I threw him to the ground and he fucking curled up like he thought he was going to get a kicking. All I could think was: Mind, an affair, I get it. But with him? Fuck me, is that the best you can do?

Just to prove once again, that all comedy is based in tragedy, His wife, Ann, saw me over the hedge and said, "Hi Rob, lovely night last night, thank you. Want to come in for a cuppa?"

I didn't.

When I got home, Miranda was up, dressed and looking scared. I pointed upstairs questioningly. "They're still asleep." Was the reply. I was still shaking with anger or was it disappointment in her, or that I hadn't leathered him?

"I don't want to hear a word of your fucking lies or reasons or apologies. You didn't just fuck him, you fucked everything! And Yeh, by the way, you broke my fucking heart. Happy?"

She started saying "I'm so sorry, I can explain…you were so distant, I resisted him for ages and …" Again, I cut her off. "Not a fucking word! When I get back, you need to have decided what you want to do. But seeing as I just left your wanksplash of a lover cowering in his driveway, I doubt he will be suggesting you two run off into the sunset. So, make some decisions. I will be back… when I'm ready."

I walked off to drink myself stupid — once the pubs were open anyway. I walked around in a fugue for a couple of hours. My phone kept ringing. It was Miranda, I ignored it. Once opening hours arrived and after a couple of pints with chasers, I had an epiphany of sorts.

I had been a really bad husband for years. I really did love my kids and they would know the reason for the split if I left, or if I threw their mum out. I wouldn't tell them, but they would eventually find out. I couldn't let that happen. Call me a chauvinist of you like, but you know I'm right. Thinking that way about their dad would be bad enough, but about their mother! I wanted to hurt her, to make her feel my pain at the same time, I knew I had to fix things. And I would be a liar if I didn't admit that I also know that people will always ridicule a cuckold. Yes, you do, why are you trying to deny it? In the stereotype scenario, there's a demon shagger, a slut, and a wimp husband who clearly can't satisfy the slut sexually. There was no way I was letting the kids see me and her in those roles, and that fucking cowering cunt as some Don Juan, would just be salt in a haemorrhage.

I walked home, a bit pissed but not very. It was a lovely summer afternoon. We sat in the garden while the kids had been sent to do their homework. Miranda would not be stopped from giving me a cascade of apologies and those thinly veiled apologies as justifications. You know the script. "I don't know what I was thinking, it was idiotic, a mistake, just..." I stopped her.

"Look me in the eye and tell me it's over."

"Rob, it was stupid…

"Just yes or no?"

"YES!"

"Do you still love me?

"YES!"

"If you ever see him again, we're done. Do you understand?

"Rob, please can we …

"Do you understand?"

"YES!"

"Then we will see if we can fix things."

She looked surprised like a woman getting a last-minute pardon after the noose was already around her neck.

"Never for one moment think that anything I've done, or how I've been, will ever justify what you did?"

"I know, I'm so sorry, let me explain…forgive me"

"No. You don't get to do that. You're sorry you got caught that's all. You don't get to lie and twist and make it less than what it was. And I'm not doing this for you." I pointed to the kid's rooms. "I'm doing this for them… not you! Forgive yourself whenever you want. Okay, you're forgiven. But absolution? Not you've come to the wrong church for that!

"Please Rob, let me just explain…

I got right up in her face, "Not. Another. Fucking. Word — Ever!"

From that day, in fact from that moment, we carried on as if nothing had happened. Every now and again, normally when I was drunk, I would rant and rave about what she had done and punish her by never let her explain anything.

And besides, what's to explain? Men care about the sex more than women. If a woman told her partner that she loved someone even more than them, but it was one hundred percent platonic, that's not great, but it's okay. We can deal with that. But if they'd fucked, all bets are off!

It's the reverse for most women. Sexual jealousy comes second to the emotional kind.

Then also, if you were watching carefully — I never let her admit it. Of course, they fucked. You'd have to be an idiot to think they didn't. But they never admitted it. So maybe, just maybe they didn't. Of course, they did — I just never want to know for absolutely, definitely, categorically sure.

What I did know was that love, like silence, once broken, is never mended. We did some excellent repair work; most people would never see the cracks. I couldn't miss them.

And that's how much I love my kids. Would I do anything for them? I don't know until I'm tested. What I did do was bury my ridiculous pride for them, hide a broken heart from them, ignore and hide their mother's betrayal and put a brave face on it — anything to keep them safe from things that would hurt them.

If you think that's noble — it isn't. I did it for me, not just for them. If I'm not a good dad, then what am I good at? Confrontational sport, selling people shit they don't need and shagging. And probably not that great at shagging judging by the fall-off rate.

If you think it justifies anything I subsequently did, you are falling into the "But what about…" trap of moral equivalence bullshit. I got what was coming, I suppose. Then I dealt with it. Writing this now, my biggest regret? That I didn't hospitalise that wanker! Yes. It does say a lot about me.

A few weeks later, after our seventeenth anniversary, I went to America.

I wasn't looking for an affair. At that time, my job meant I was virtually commuting to New York every other week — for a week. I worked with Laurie who was an Account Director, by day. Outside of the office, she was a fashionista. Everything was about style and clothes. Now, American men are terrible dressers. Actually, so are most American women. I am vain, there's no point in denying it. Consequently, I take too much care about what I wear and how I look. This made me a desirable target for Laurie. Added to that, I was married, lived on another continent and understood the unwritten rules. Like I said, I wasn't looking for an affair, but back in the hotel bar after a long day, drinks turned into another drink. The rest of the team slowly left and when it was just the two of us, some strange semaphore took place and we ended up in my room. I'd been faithful for seventeen years and so it was fun and different doing it with someone who did it differently. It was really good sex. Not cosmic for either of us, but really very nice. She left in the early hours and I went to sleep. When I woke up, I had the strangest feeling. I expected to feel really guilty. I didn't. I felt fine. Not smug or self-satisfied and not ashamed or self-loathing either. More in the American sports vernacular, "No harm. No foul." I went into the office and Laurie and I had a very grown-up chat and at lunchtime went back to the hotel to fuck some more. That became the pattern whenever I was in NYC. I didn't ask about boyfriends, she didn't ask about my family life. It was a very civilised affair that went on for years.

It's true what they say. Cheaters, cheat. Once I had done it once, I had fewer and fewer qualms about doing it again. I wasn't one of those lascivious Lotharios who are always on the lookout. But if the girl caught my eye and I caught hers, well, why not? "No harm. No foul." So along the way, there were others. While it's a cliché, it's just simply true: they meant nothing, well, virtually nothing. Yes, I know. Hypocrisy and sanctimony are bad colours on me — and anyone else.

Chapter 40
Movin' on up, movin on out, time to break free

I was scared and excited. Either or both at any given moment. Miranda had been away at her folks with our youngest, so I was all alone. I saw Kitty every day or almost. It was all becoming very real.

We were going to make the big step, we were really going to do this. As some sort of a prelude, we arranged to go out with some mutual friends to see a band. We weren't going public. Even a twat like me wouldn't do that until I'd broken the news at home, but still, people aren't stupid, and I wanted to be out with her, not always furtively tucked away somewhere.

We had planned it one afternoon when we were both free. We lay on the bed in the studio. It wasn't sexual — it was just warm and tender. We talked and at one point she said, "But I can't jump out of one relationship and fully commit to another…" I said I understood, and we would take it one day at a time.

You heard it, didn't you? I simply wasn't listening. Anyway, we would go out on Friday and because I was leaving home on Saturday, she wanted to be out of town so she was flying to Milan to meet up with a couple she knew from university.

I wanted her to stay but she was insistent, and it sounded right. "You can't leave home and come straight to me. It would just be too cruel. You'll be free, I will be free and to everyone else we will have just found each other."

The Friday night out was a humdinger, we laughed, drank danced and it must have been obvious to the friends what was going on even though we kept up a pretty pathetic pretence. Drunk and laughing, we fell into bed and even though it was a drunken fuck, it was glorious. We fell asleep together. I remembered to leave her in her foetal sleep position and when we woke up, I went out for breakfast. It was rom-com material. Then she had to get to the airport, and I had to stiffen the sinews for the worst conversation of my life. If you've done it, you know, if you haven't, it is excruciating. Hurting someone you loved, maybe still love. Crushing someone who has almost always kept up their end of the deal. Someone who hasn't seen it coming.

I picked Miranda and our girl up at the airport and it was just small talk until we got home. Dinner tasted like cardboard, but once we'd eaten, I sent the lad off as "We need to talk," She never saw it coming.

Pouring herself another glass of wine, she gave me a smug look and said, "We need to talk, do we? What stupid thing have you done or what stupid thing are you planning to do?" This wasn't going well, and we hadn't even started. I told her that we had drifted apart over the years and she immediately came back with, "Yes and I want to fix that, too. Your brain tumour and all those sex issues have been awful for me as well, you know."

I insisted it was more than that. There were fundamental issues in our marriage that meant… It was all lies. I wanted to leave to be with Kitty, but I couldn't tell her. I was afraid to. It would hurt her even more than the bullshit I was spouting, and Kitty had insisted that I mustn't mention her. I lied and lied. She cried and cried, and I picked up my bag and left. Mute and ashamed, I stood at the door and she looked at me and simply said, "How can you do this to me?"

I've never felt so bad. In the little studio apartment, I'd rented a month before, my phone kept ringing. Each time it was Miranda. I simply couldn't talk any more. I sent Kitty a text. "It's done. I love you. I have to switch my phone off now. See you tomorrow."

I was sad but not. It was a relief but terrifying. Exciting and awful. Every paradox you can imagine. The next day I went to a coffee-shop for breakfast and there was a strange unreal calm. Kitty would be back tonight and even though she had to get home for her kids we would have time to talk. Her train got in at nine. She walked off the platform and looked terrible. She looked at me and we hugged but something was wrong. This should have been the moment. Our moment, where we could start looking ahead and plan all the great times we were going to have.

"So how was Milan? Did you have fun?" She looked like I had just gut-punched her. What the fuck was going on? Was she ill? I asked, and suggested she just go straight home.

Instead, she just said, "Let's get a cab." The conversation was strangely stilted in the taxi. Not just because the driver was listening. I didn't push it. I just assumed she was exhausted after a massive night with friends. We arrived at the studio and in an ever so domesticated way made her a cup of tea and we sat on the bed. I hugged her and she hugged me back with an almost scary passion. "Oh, Pat, I've done something really bad." I looked at her with an inquisitive face and replied: "It can't be that bad, tell me!" "Realising that it was really happening with Gordon and it was because of you, I felt so angry, I needed to hurt him and hurt you and hurt myself." Now she had my attention. "Really, just tell me, It will be all right." How wrong could a man be?

"Honesty is so important in our relationship. I wasn't with friends in Milan. I met an old friend. I fucked him! It was awful..." Before she could say anything else I screamed. "Get out! Get out!" "Listen to me..." she didn't move. So I did. I walked out and walked the streets for hours. She sent me a text.

"I wanted to explain but you won't let me. Sometimes I really did want us, then again, I didn't. But I didn't want nothing either. Sometimes it was just me being what you wanted me to be. Trying to be everything you needed me to be, to be perfect for you. I needed you to think I was perfect. It was amazingly fabulous sometimes and it felt like love. But it was not real. The physical attraction is blinding. You take my breath away, I hate this, but I DON'T LOVE YOU! And I know you know that really. I don't think I've ever loved anyone — not in the way that you seem to love me. Not with that lightning bolt conviction and with that longevity. There were moments that I felt so very deeply in love — there still are and they are my way of being in love, but it's not the way that you want or need. (not many people do — I am destined to be alone in my self-destroyed world, I know that). I am so sorry for the hurt that I caused you. I couldn't end it. I needed you to hate me, that's why I did it. I hate that and I hate that we won't have a future. The sparky, sexy magical moments that have been my best moments ever. But they are not enough. Not going forward. Forgive me. Forget me. Goodbye."

I replied "Thanks. Good to know," then switched off my phone. I was in agony. I got back eventually and she wasn't there. I lay on the bed and didn't cry or curl into the clichéd foetal position. I just got into bed numb and strangely, I slept like a log. The next day I sat down and wrote Kitty a letter. Furious and trying not to be is hard. Heartbroken and trying to be reasonable is harder. But there was something inside me that made me want to be kind to her. Was it to win her back? I could forgive a fuck if she was really truly sorry. I don't know, I just wrote it out and put it in her mailbox.

Darlin', whatever this is, it's not good for you and it's not good for me. It had to end. Maybe because the highs are so high and we're so frightened of 'nothing', that we are clinging onto anything to keep us afloat. Well, I can't keep holding on. It's time to swim for the shore. You know all you have meant and will always mean to me. Now I need you to leave me alone to get on with my life and see if I can find what I thought I'd found with you. You know you broke my heart, but I'm not doing this to 'win' or hurt you or make a point. It's because even though it hurts — and your timing was appalling and your tactics fucking disgraceful — it ends up in the same place. There's no hope for us any more. Maybe there never was. We both know it if we're honest. Of course, I will be jealous as hell when if I hear you've found the "one". Yet I hope he's fantastic and perfect for you in ways I will never be. For us both to get what we need, we both have to get on with our own lives separately, physically and emotionally. We have to resist the temptation to text, flirt, booty call, "Run into each other" accidentally... Distance is the only solution. It's too tempting to fall back into old ways. We have different hopes, dreams, needs and values. What draws us together isn't enough to make it work. When there's enough scar tissue to cover all the wounds, we will both know we are healed. Until then, we have to be

*strangers with shared memories of something magical
that ran its course and then ended so badly. Be well,
goodbye, my love.*

It was totally insincere. I was devastated and still longed
for her. Why did she have to tell me? Why couldn't she
have said nothing? Why couldn't she just have let me
down the traditional "It's not you, it's me…" route.
Why did I not hate her? Why did I still love her? I was
fucked up beyond all recognition. I took time off work
and wallowed. Days passed, I didn't work, I did loads
of coke, chain-smoked and drank like a fish. Most of the
time I was… actually… I have no idea, as the one thing
I do know is that my anaesthetic routine generally left
me 'out cold'. I had no idea how I'd got to bed, where
I'd been or who I'd said what to. I called her and
sometimes she would pick up. We talked, but it was
awful. I was off my head and either professed my love
or screamed at her for what she had done. All very
grown up and helpful.

She asked me to meet her. She wouldn't come to
the studio, "Because we will just end up in bed…"
Which was exactly why I chose the studio! Instead, we
met in a coffee bar. She handed me a letter and said,
"You wrote me one. Just read this…"

*Rob, when you're not off your head, you say it's over
and you're right. You say, we need to stop everything,
again you're right, but I need to be sure you know some*

things. So, here goes. I don't love you, not in the truly, madly, deeply way I thought I did. In the way I need to, if we could ever have had a chance. It was the rest of our lives we were betting on, for goodness' sake. There's a huge amount I adore about you. You are wonderful in many ways. Too many people love and cherish and admire you for that not be true. At the same time, you carry so much baggage, yet you think a smart mouth and a 'fuck you' mentality disguises it. You're wrong. Anyone who knows you knows you're deeply flawed, hugely vulnerable and so, so sensitive — It's part of the charm, for me at least, but it's too much to bear. Especially as I have too many flaws of my own to settle for someone, just because they love me and so will overlook them. I did it once already. Settling is a time bomb. It comes back to haunt you and fucks up the lives of people around you when it goes off. My life is now crashing down around me. As for us, I fucked up. Do you think I don't know? Do you think I don't cringe in horror and shame when I think about what I did to you? I thought that the only way to end "us" was to make you hate me so you would never see me again. Milan was the only thing I thought would do it. If you don't see that, if you can't forgive me, then you never really knew me at all, so fuck you!

I've told you I am sorry. I am really so incredibly sorry. Accept it or don't. Don't wallow in it. It makes you look small. And I like you when you're the bigger man. The one I fell for. I think I gave you a lot too. My love at times — I really thought it was true then, I wasn't playing games. We had heaps of fun and special moments. we had crazy times in London, Paris and even just playing in town was great. And if I'm to believe you — the best sex of my life was the best in yours too. That was never our problem. And yes, even though I tease, it was more than just sex for me too. Entwining ourselves, naked in my bed was such an easy, Zen-like, calm. Hearing you say you loved me and would never let me go boosted my ego and even made me believe we had something. When we were open and honest and laid ourselves bare it was special — sometimes almost spiritual in its intensity. Yet in the cold light of day, faced with the reality of being with you for real, forever, I realized I would end up hating you, and even worse, you would end up hating me. I couldn't bear that. Never hate me, Rob, I absolutely forbid it. I know, it's ironic after what I did to make you hate me. I am so fucked-up. A huge part of me still wants us to be lovers. But if ever I weaken, please don't. It has to stop. Oh, why am I bothering, I know you too well and I know me too. This will never be really over, will it? We will see. And to quote you, back to yourself. I hope you find someone perfect for you. Then my vanity kicks in and I hope she falls short somehow compared to me, so I will always own some part of you. And I won't be just someone you had an affair with. I know that's not loving, it's selfish, but it's true and it's something, I just don't know what. Goodbye, my lovely wonderful addiction. You deserve more than I have to give. This may read all jolly and big-girl-pants-on, but I am now weeping like truly, madly, deeply all over this page. I can't bear this! I know we have to, but it hurts. I was so close to not losing it until this bit, but I am going to give it to you anyway. Sorry. Be happy. Please let me go, for both our sakes, Goodbye.

I looked up and, as if she were reading my mind and her letter to herself, she was crying. She kissed me and walked away. I had nothing to say. But I loved her then as much as any other moment. Weird, huh!

Chapter 41
When love breaks down

Most of the time it's staring you in the face. It's so obvious in hindsight that you can't believe that you missed it. All the signs, subtle and not so subtle. You make a list in your head and repeat the age-old cliché, "How could I have been so stupid?" or its less popular, more pompous variant "How could I have been so blind?" I hate to be a cliché so as I look back my inner dialogue is more "You stupid, fucking wanker!" Not so elegant but really much more on the nose.

I tried and tried to make sense of it. Was I really that tone deaf when she said, "I can't walk out of one relationship and commit to you…"? I wracked my brains and the best I could come up with was that she chickened out because she got scared:

of losing her kids because to them, I am the devil.

of Gordon turning really nasty about the settlement if I was still in the picture. She does love money.

of me being driven by lust and then finding her "mmmmmeeehhhh!" after a few years when the fire and her looks fade.

of missing out on other opportunities.

of other people's judgment.

of me cheating on her.

of not being good enough. (Yes, you think I'm insecure, but I know my self-worth and so did she.)

of not having the opportunity to fuck around and see what's out there.

of whatever?

Or maybe she saw my weaknesses and they matched hers. She needs someone who is strong were she is weak and weak where she can be his strength. Or maybe she is just a truly horrible, mad, mixed-up psycho, sociopath.

The day-to-day painful reality was the feeling of depression. That feeling that the pain was going to last forever. The hopelessness! The darkness! It engulfed everything: I felt so bad and I felt like I was going to feel bad forever. My brain simply could not fathom that that it is not the case. It's like fear of flying. If you feel it, then it's terrifying. People can explain the physics, they can show you the statistics, they can tell you that it's more likely you will be killed on your way to the airport than in flight… but none of it helps the feeling as you sit there when the plane takes off. No matter what anyone told me, no matter what I read, each day was just a dark empty mess.

So, I did what seemed the best thing for it. I called an old girlfriend. Ornella is Italian, a school-teacher and another one of my meaningless affairs. Kitty wasn't the only one who had taken advantage of the school's extracurricular options. Ornella was very lovely and very low-maintenance. We stayed friends and as she put it,

"I like how we fuck, but I couldn't ever be with you. So if we both want, we meet and fuck. Why not? If I meet someone and want to stop, we stop. Same for you."

When Kitty came into my life, Ornella went out. As good as her word, she never asked why.

I took her to lunch and played nice. It was clear where this was going and we both knew it. It was an obvious booty call. She knew it and I knew it and she didn't seem to mind. But here's the kicker. As we got back to her place, a bit drunk, but not very, she said, "I'm sorry I have my period, ahhh, the look on your face." I guess I did look a bit disappointed. "Don't worry, I'm a very generous girl and you look so pathetic."

So, we kissed for a bit then kissed passionately and then she escalated things and pushed me onto the bed saying, "This is a sixty-eight. So remember, you owe me one..." and I was the grateful recipient of a sympathy blowjob. Now, there's an old joke. Describe the worst blowjob you've ever received. Answer: fantastic. It's an old and not very funny joke. It's also based on a myth. The reality is that some girls are gifted, others keen and others just plain awful at it. Describe the worst blowjob you've ever received. My answer: a fucking nightmare of teeth scraping down my cock as the woman tried to pull the head off my cock, to the point that I had to physically restrain her before serious damage was done. This also taught me that diplomacy is essential in these situations as no woman wants to hear she gives terrible head. This was not the case with Ornella, she rather prided herself on her skills and she had every reason to be proud. Do you really want details? Really? Tough!

The long and short of it was it was all going swimmingly when the thought of my old-friend D.O. invaded the present very physical sensations. They got worse as I realized that there's no faking it with a 'beej'. That then led to a really unhelpful downward spiral as I could feel myself deflating slightly. It was then I thought about times and chances missed with Kitty. I pictured her in my head and in a flood of pent-up anger, reminiscence, nostalgia, and lust, I flooded Ornella. It was delightful and horrible at the same time. I'd just been unfaithful to three women simultaneously — a new record. That I could deal with. The truly horrific realization though was that no matter what anyone says, a beej isn't just a beej, a fuck isn't just a fuck. The simple awful truth struck home. The only one I wanted was Kitty. The only one I couldn't have. It wasn't a physical thing. It really was all in my head. All the good work with 'The Cat' had worked some wonders, but desire was not his territory. Talk about unresolved conflicts.

Chapter 42
Don't you remember you told me you love me, baby?

Months before, when the future was so bright, and everything was looking rosy, I saw Christmas looming and wanted to get Kitty something truly special. I spent a huge amount of time and effort and figured out the perfect gift. It was a Cartier American Tank watch. It's classy but not showy, yet still a little bit bling. Just like Kitty. They were on back-order, but I had time. Now it was all over I was sat holding a stupidly expensive woman's watch with no woman to give it to. I wanted to be the 'bigger man', I wanted to end things on the up. Now we were done, I still wanted her to have it. It would be something that celebrated the good times and somehow take away all the bad.

That's not how it went though. I asked her to meet me. Eventually, reluctantly, she agreed. As long as it was in Starbucks. It's not easy to make a big magnanimous gesture in a shitty coffee-shop. But I was determined. She didn't seem happy to see me. In fact, she was downright shirty. I realise now that it was because she had been given her marching orders by Milan boy. No woman enjoys the realisation she was a

'Pump and Dump'. At the time I just figured she was in a shitty mood. I soldiered on. "Hi, I want to give you something. It's was going to be for our first Christmas together… but anyway, I want you to have something that will last and hopefully remind you of all the good times."

I'd taken time with the card. It just said 'Because' on the front and inside I wrote:

Because I really like you, but you've never really believed that.

Because you taught me kissing in supermarkets is fun

Because a 'never to be repeated' one-time thing was so wonderfully repeated

Because it was never about what you thought it was about

Because I could find you immediately in a darkened room full of thousands

Because you got me to hide in a wardrobe

Because we cried together in an empty hotel bar

Because you were the best night in Paris ever

Because your giggle will always make me smile

Because kissing will never be the same with anyone else

Because you've never been on time and it's never bothered me

Because tragically, you are 'the one'

Because 'atelier' is now a sexy word

*Because waking up and seeing you is the best way
to start a day*
Because we entwine so well
Because you can always make me smile
*Because when my dick didn't work you wouldn't let
me feel ashamed*
*Because Le Jardin de Monsieur Li only works on
you.*
*Because I loved sitting on the bed watching you
dress*
*Because you showed me your heart and made me
brave enough to show you mine*
*Because a nine-letter acronym can tell our whole
story*
*Because over a hundred million seconds have
passed since that August night three years ago*
Because every one of those seconds was special.
Because this is the last time.

She opened the box and I could see she liked it. She really tried to cheer up and be nice and grateful. She put it on, and I saw that in this respect at least, I had really smashed it. It was perfect for her. It was all too little, too late. It was at that moment that I realized it really was all over. Whatever there had been, was gone and it was never coming back. I think she saw it as me making a last gasp effort to win her back with a big gesture. It wasn't, but then why does it still fuck me off that I think she still thinks that? What pissed me off, even more, was that when she left the Starbucks, she was still wearing the watch. She walked to the taxi rank and she thought I didn't see her throw the card in the bin. I did though, and that was the cruellest cut. Still, 'It's the thought that counts,' my old mum told me. Clearly, the thought was "Nice watch, shit card! Keep the watch, ditch the wanker" I always said she had excellent taste.

The truth was that even though I saw Kitty for all she was, I was stuck like Walter Fane in the *The Painted Veil*. "Kitty, I know that you're selfish, selfish beyond words, and I know that you haven't the nerve of a rabbit, I know you're a liar and a humbug, I know that you're utterly contemptible. And the tragic part is" — her face was on a sudden distraught with pain — "the tragic part is, notwithstanding that, I love you with all my heart."

And yes, that's why I call her Kitty.

Chapter 43
One last shot 'fore we quit it

After a couple more weeks of wallowing in a shitty studio, I was home. No tail between my legs. For all my faults, my wife loves me. God alone knows why. And the truth is that I also love her, too. The problem has been for too long that it wasn't that rush of blood, reckless, devil may care love. It never really was. Yet it has always been warm and caring and cherishing. On the upside, a woman scorned may have more fury than hell, but when they get you back, they want very clear physical proof of affection. Thankfully I was able to deliver that as the Cat and his magic had really started to work wonders. Totally reliable erections, and with the right pelvic tilting and lemon squeezing, I could deliver the goods again virtually at will. Even so, I was a bit sad (Actually, totally devastated). Yet big boys don't cry and all that, and as I'd been thrown a lifeline, it seemed only fair to grab on to it for all I was worth and at least act happy.

That was how it felt. Kitty and I had no contact. I heard through a mutual friend who knew nothing of our affair that Kitty had a new boyfriend. That hurt, but it was hardly unexpected. Does he know that the clock is ticking, I wonder? Talking of clocks, I used to reward myself when I'd beaten my record for not thinking about her. I was close to getting beyond forty minutes some days if I buried myself in work. How long will it take to really get past it? The answer is never. I'm still not over her. The wound is still raw, it will scar over but it will never truly heal. Time? It isn't a great healer. It's just that over time you don't forget, you just stop remembering so much. I discovered years ago that nostalgia literally means 'the pain from an old wound' that twinge in your heart is far more powerful than memory alone. I told myself to forget the last few months and cherish the thirty-six-odd previous ones, because, in the end, they're the ones worth remembering. But nostalgia was all I was left with.

Months passed. Home life was calm. Albeit an *All Quiet on the Western Front* calm. I was ready to dive for cover at any moment. What broke my resolve was a series of weird coincidences and a complete lack of resolve. I'd already given Kitty her big gift and it served well as a reminder of the good times I hoped. But her fiftieth birthday was today. I knew what day it was and I was sat at home with just our youngest. His mum volunteers at a night shelter — Yes, I know, how can such a self-obsessed arse have bagged a beautiful, kind, caring woman in constant need of reassuring sex, and still not be happy? Anyway, yes, I was sad, but big-boy pants needed to be put on. However, by ten-thirty that night, my resolve crumbled and I prepared a birthday message. A text — how romantic. "Darlin', in spite of everything, or maybe because of everything, I want you to know I wish you a fabulous birthday and hope it's the start of a truly happy time for you. As another poet put it, 'Ah, but I was so much older then. I'm younger than that now.' Don't count the years, just keep getting younger. With love. Pat."

I got my cup of tea and went to bed with a book. Trying my hardest to not imagine her with her friends and boyfriend having a marvellous time. I failed, but I did try.

I was woken at eleven-thirty by a ping. "Your note was lovely, my friends are leaving, I don't want to go home. Come and buy me a drink for my birthday."

I sat and pondered — but not for long. "Won't your boyfriend be surprised to see me?"

"He's not here. Come on!"

"OK, see you ASAP." I couldn't believe what I was doing. What a clown. Yet as the Uber dropped me off, I was just excited. The timing couldn't have been worse. She was in the lobby with the last of her friends. Thankfully, ones I didn't know. She was a bit drunk and looked like she was having fun. She told the girls I was an old friend and she'd be fine, and she'd leave ASAP after we had a drink. Off they went and as soon as they had gone, she kissed me. It felt great.

"You're drunk so I'd better get drinking." I ordered mojitos and we talked and kissed and danced and it was great.

"I'm so glad you came. I wanted to see you on my birthday."

I inhaled drink after drink to catch up with her and soon did. I couldn't leave it alone though. "Your boyf' can get to Milan but not here?"

A pained look crossed her face. "That wanker dumped me! I've got a new one." Then in retaliation, she asked, "How're things at home?" I didn't know if I was happy or sad. Yet I was glad to see her and wanted it to be a happy night, so, for once, I just let it go.

We got drunk and were happy and having fun. Two people, our age shouldn't be snogging in a posh bar, or dancing badly and snogging, or even worse — both. We didn't care. After an hour or so I said, "Let's get out of here." She looked surprised, "Where can we go?" I told her I still had the studio until the lease ran out and that there was still champagne in the fridge. She kissed me really hard and felt my cock against her thigh. She looked me in the eye, smiled and said "Okay."

We staggered into the studio and she said the strangest thing. "Can I have a mint tea?" I put the kettle on and opened the champagne. I handed her the tea and poured myself a drink. Were we just going to talk? I lay beside her on the bed and sipped champagne. She put her tea on the nightstand and said, "This is such a bad idea." Then she laughed and kissed me again.

You know the form with me and Kitty by now. I will spare you the details. Except one, as she was sat astride me grinding onto me, she came, then I did.

Instead of us cuddling up, she stayed on top of me and started hitting me on the chest, tears in her eyes she kept saying, "Why can't it be you? It can't be you," over and over. She was drunk and when she stopped, she fell on me and just sobbed — but not much. I was lost.

We drunk-slept for a while and I woke to see her checking her phone. "New boyfriend checking upon you?"

"Whatever!" was all she would say. She looked good, still half-drunk and dishevelled and that's how I liked her best. Clearly, I didn't give a bollocks about her beau. She rolled over to me and we were kissing again.

"You know I still love you…" It was out of my mouth before I could stop myself.

"I know," she replied with a smug look on her face. Things heated up and she said, "It's a shame we don't have a mirror."

"Oh, but we do."

I got the free-standing mirror moved it to the end of the bed and found the lube. I was still an advocate of the Cat's advice re-lube and wanking, so it was always to hand — as it were. This time, though, it had another use. The last time I ever fucked Kitty may not be your idea of the Hollywood soft-focus love scene. No, it was an action replay of Paris. Having followed all my treatment, it was all systems go. It was hot and wonderful and while many may think it was cheap, raw and raunchy, it was real lovemaking too.

Exhausted, we fell asleep, but with an alarm set for six. We both had to be home before the kids woke up. I called an Uber while she showered. I dropped her at her house, she kissed me, I could see she was exhausted, embarrassed, and about ten other things too that I couldn't decipher.

"Thanks, Rob, for making my birthday special." And she was off.

I sneaked in and showered and thought, *Blimey! What the fuck was that all about?* I also thought very selfishly, *I wonder if she will tell her boyfriend about this. After all, "Honesty is so important in a relationship."* I wasn't sure if I wanted her to or not. Making him feel how I did after Milan wouldn't make me feel any better. Would it?

Chapter 44
I know it's over

On Sunday, I sent a WhatsApp: "Last night was lovely. We need to talk."

I eventually got a reply. "Yes, it was. Thank you for a lovely time. Maybe sometime next week?" Okay! Not the reaction I was expecting, but okay. A few days later, I hassled her to meet me for a coffee and she agreed. I was cool. Somehow, the final night had put me back into some sort of control. I was ready to restart or just finish it. I told her so. This is verbatim her reply. "Saturday was lovely. But we can't go back to an affair and this (gesturing at her and me as a couple) is not what I want. I wish it was. But it isn't." I had so had enough of this nonsense. I just shrugged and said, "Okay."

Then, I said, "This is how I see it. I know you think I never listen, to you, or anyone — but I do." That made her smile. "I was jealous, thinking about you having a legit boyfriend and dinner with friends and weekends away and all that stuff. Then I remembered what you told me you had said to your youngest. Enjoy what you've had, not what you've missed'." Now with a big grin on my face, I carried on.

"I remembered all the snogging in taxis, stupid clandestine meetings in shitty hotels, the excitement of creeping around town, the simple joy of kissing in supermarkets. And while there were many languid afternoons of sex there were also fast, tanning-booth encounters, BJs in carparks, sex in toilets and more kissing in supermarkets, furtive fumblings in all manner of ridiculous places, hiding in wardrobes and so many more, silly, yet beautiful, memorable moments. Not just the sex but the excitement that went with it."

She was laughing now and said, "Yes. Yes, it was bizarrely wonderful."

"Now, I'd love to have had all the relationship stuff and to have missed out on the heartbreak and anger and pain. And I know you and your boyfriend can always do all of those things if you want: but it won't happen for you and anyone new. Why? Because you can always go home, or to the hotel and have a stress-free moment at will. You won't shag in the resto toilets and if you ever hit the tanning booth again it will be deliberate, to prove a point, not driven by a quickening we both felt and needed."

She looked truly interested. Not shocked or hurt or anything beyond really interested to know where this is going.

"So, my point? I was very lucky, I had something amazing with a splendid girl that no one else ever will. It was a crazy and wonderful and silly and senseless at the same time. Our friends may see it as tawdry, but it wasn't — it was our story and in its own way, so passionate and joyful. It made me happy then and it does now in hindsight. I hope you can look back on that unique way of being, with the same happy reflection, and like me, miss it — wistfully."

She had a big smile on her face and a definite hint of a tear in her eye. She just nodded. Then we had our coffee and we left. And that was that. Weird, huh?

Of course my little speech was just a bunch of baloney. It still hurts. I'm still full of longing. I'm still mad, mad at her and still madly in love. I just didn't understand, and she would never explain. I went through all the options. When the affair was running hot, we were blinded to the inevitability that it was always doomed. I at least, imagined that we were the exception. My best bet was that Kitty started feeling that her sacrifice was so much greater than mine. Only after her marriage was really over did the divorce become so brutally real that she saw that it was all a horrible mistake. She was so caught up in the infatuation that she never got around to figuring out if what we were doing was what she wanted, or just some 'amour fou' — a crazy distraction from her 'gilded cage' marriage.

Gordon was so angry and full of hate he told her he'd crucify her financially if she stayed with me. He weaponised the kids so I was the devil. They said if she didn't cut me off, they would go and live with their dad and never talk to her again. In all that, she joined them in believing I had inflicted so much pain on innocent people that I was the villain. She is also an incurable romantic: yes, really. When the crazy stuff fades, romantics like her, don't understand that this is part of the growth of any relationship, not its diminishing — me, too, probably. She doesn't know how to nurture it. Instead, it was easier to believe she had just fallen out of love with me. She would never admit it, but this led to resentment and disillusionment then anger and a need for revenge — hello, Milan. Paradoxically, I held up my sacrifice as some sort of burning flame that made me want it more and more and more until there was nothing left to feed the fire. Ironically, when the flame went out, the lights came on.

I read years ago about emotional anorexia. I suddenly realized we both suffer from it. Starving ourselves of love, then gorging on it, only to feel guilty about it later because of a sense of not deserving or having shamefully indulged. There's a state of mind that drives this — needing, but not having; having, but not wanting; hating having fed the need, then needing to feed it again.

Or to paraphrase Don Quixote:

"I have your test results. You have a severely broken heart, Mr Delaney," said the doctor

"Thank you, Doctor, but I'd like a second opinion."

"Okay. You're a cunt too!"

Chapter 45
If you don't know me by now

It's a small world, suburban England, so inevitably, I saw Kitty with her new boyfriend. Can one have a boyfriend as a middle-aged woman? Anyway, she looked great and I was pleased to see her — especially as the new bloke looked a bit of a tit. Yes, I am that shallow. He had his shirt out over jeans with a tweed jacket over that. He looked like the sort of trendy supply teacher who says to the kids, "Don't call me Sir, call me Jeff." Then a couple of weeks later at drinks at mutual friends, I ran into her again, I learned he was a banker.

"They're famously interesting, aren't they?" I suggested.

She said he was, "Really intellectually stimulating…"

Oh, Kitty, is the sex really that bad? I thought. She said he was Italian, and I offered with a laugh, "I thought they dressed like stylish poufs, not trendy supply teachers"

"Oh, he's so not gay!" Her response had the absolute opposite effect than she had hoped. In trying to tell me he was smarter than me and a better shag than me, she said so much more. I said nothing, but I knew.

Think about it if it's not already clear. If you were dating 007 and someone suggested he might be effeminate you would 'Shake it off' like Taylor Swift. You certainly wouldn't feel the need to say how very heterosexual and virile and exciting, life with James Bond is. On my way home, I was halfway between belly laughs and euphoria. I was right. She'd found herself a rich, nice, boring, Gordon replacement. Like I said, I really am that shallow.

We texted occasionally and saw each other from a distance. Months passed. Then I was pleased and surprised, but not that surprised, when I got a message. "Is this what I wrote last time? Come and see me at my house on Wednesday at eleven. This is a one-time, never to be repeated thing. If you are coming no need to leave a note in my mailbox. This time, you may reply to this message."

What should I do? Fuck her, or tell her to go fuck herself? It's another dilemma. Both are very attractive. Learn from experience, or do old dogs never learn new tricks? Or simply ask what matter wounds?